Vanessa Jared's Got a Man

Vanessa Jared's Got a Man

LaQuette

ST. MARTIN'S
GRIFFIN
NEW YORK

First published in the United States by St. Martin's Griffin, an imprint of St. Martin's Publishing Group

VANESSA JARED'S GOT A MAN. Copyright © 2022 by Laquette R. Holmes. All rights reserved. Printed in the United States of America. For information, address St. Martin's Publishing Group, 120 Broadway, New York, NY 10271.

Designed by Jen Edwards

www.stmartins.com

The Library of Congress Cataloging-in-Publication Data is available upon request.

ISBN 978-1-250-77339-5 (trade paperback)
ISBN 978-1-250-77340-1 (ebook)

Our books may be purchased in bulk for promotional, educational, or business use. Please contact your local bookseller or the Macmillan Corporate and Premium Sales Department at 1-800-221-7945, extension 5442, or by email at MacmillanSpecialMarkets@macmillan.com.

First Edition: 2022

10 9 8 7 6 5 4 3 2 1

To Kenya, Christi, and Naima
for being the best accountability partners ever.
I couldn't have finished this book without you.

Vanessa Jared's Got a Man

Prologue

Two Years Ago . . .

"THE WORST PART IS, I NEVER SAW IT COMING." VANESSA forced herself to focus, realizing she'd somehow missed a good portion of this meeting while attempting to sort things out in her own head. When she found the Mended Hearts Divorce Support Group, she'd hoped coming to this meeting, listening to people who had learned how to properly move on, would shine a light on ways to get past all this ugliness that seemed to dog her every waking moment of the day.

An older man with a full head of wavy white hair spoke. He wore stylish glasses and was dressed in a casual polo shirt and jeans. He looked like someone's wise old uncle as he walked toward the makeshift aisle and turned to face the group seated in the audience.

His watery gaze landed on Vanessa, as if he imagined there was some sort of commiserating bond between them. It made her uncomfortable. Sitting in a community center divorce support group was the last place she wanted her presence acknowledged or to make an emotional connection to the people around her. The few friends she had left after parting ways with Karl would shun her if they saw her here, huddled in the back row of what looked like a gymnasium that doubled as an auditorium.

Needing to distance herself, she took in the layout of the room. There was a small stage at the front, closed bleachers pushed against the wall in the back, and basketball hoops facing each other on each side wall.

Folding chairs were set up in theater style in the middle of the room, a fact she was grateful for. She'd assumed she'd be walking into a dreaded kumbaya circle with them all holding hands as they shared what she assumed would be one bitter divorce story after another.

The heavens were smiling on her, apparently. They had spared her that embarrassment. At least this way, she could sit in the back row and keep her distance and her secrets. Back here, no one ever had to know the specifics of her circumstances. No one ever had to know what Karl had forced her to become: his victim.

She settled into that thought, recognizing its significance. After nearly a year in therapy, she was finally able to understand and believe she hadn't done anything to deserve Karl's mistreatment of her. Everything she had experienced and was currently experiencing was his fault.

Giving up on her battle to focus, she took a glance over to her immediate right. The coveted seat closest to the door was occupied. A deep-toned brown beauty with full, round cheeks high on her oval face sat there, smiling at Vanessa. She wiggled her fingers in Vanessa's direction as she purposely scooted around in the seat Vanessa wanted.

Vanessa crossed her legs and straightened her back, refusing to let the woman see her need. She was Vanessa Scott; she'd spent a lifetime pretending to be unbothered, hiding her needs and her pain.

She closed her eyes to her therapist's voice reminding her that covering up her pain might not be such a great idea. Pretending was a survival instinct at this point. For good or ill, it was one of the only tools she had to keep the outside world from trampling her to death.

She tightened her body to prevent the shiver she felt circling the bottom of her spine waiting to vibrate through the rest of her body. If she started shaking, the ruse would be up and everyone would know she was only pretending to be Vanessa Scott.

As of two weeks ago, her divorce was finalized, and she was officially Vanessa Jared again. But who the hell was Vanessa Jared?

She'd spent so much time pretending to be Karl's perfect mate. He'd spent years molding her into what he wanted—an empty husk that only lived to provide and consider his pleasure—that she'd lost touch with her former self. Now, the only thing she seemed able to connect with was the anger over her divorce. The ugly bitterness that made her want to tie her lying, cheating ex's lips in a knot to stop him from spewing his crap.

It wasn't just the cheating, Vanessa, and you know that.

If only it were. The cheating she could've gotten past as soon as the documents were signed. The fear and pain that caused her to question every aspect of her life—every decision she made— regretfully had nothing to do with Karl's cheating and everything to do with the emotional abuse he'd heaped on her for more than two decades.

"A lady never scowls, Vanessa. It will give you wrinkles. Black might not crack, but it will sho fade if you don't take care of it, so fix yo' face." Another of her ma'dea's pearls of Black girl magic wisdom. How she missed that old spitfire and all the times she'd poured love into Vanessa's life. If she were alive, Vanessa wouldn't be here trying to find help with strangers. She'd be sitting at her grandmother's table with a slice of sweet potato pie topped with whole cranberry sauce instead.

Vanessa ached for the certainty of those days spent with her grandmother. Back then, she knew exactly who Vanessa Jared was: a bright, curious child who loved numbers just as much as she did pretty clothes. A happy girl who loved to play in her grandmother's shoe closet and jewelry box and wanted to take care of the finances of her friends and family the way her ma'dea and pop-pop did. A girl who knew her own strength and didn't cower at the thought of stepping out into the world and making her own decisions.

After Karl spent years taking an emotional ax to her confidence, Vanessa truly missed that little girl.

Unfortunately, her head couldn't shake the years she'd endured Karl's control over every aspect of her life. The fear of her abuser, the fear of losing herself again, even though she hadn't quite found the person she wanted to be, it all kept her trapped in her own head reliving the emotional torture her ex doled out with abandon. It was paralyzing her. Keeping her from moving beyond her fear and pain.

That's why she was here. Immediately after filing for divorce and seeing how fragile Vanessa was, her attorney had recommended she get into therapy. She'd balked at the idea initially. Black folks didn't go to therapy. They prayed, they threw themselves into things to distract themselves, or worse, they took on unhealthy, harmful habits that slowly ate away at their insides.

But when she'd found herself questioning whether her filing for divorce was an overreaction, she recognized that her thinking wasn't healthy. She quickly found a qualified therapist who was luckily a good fit for her.

Vanessa shut down those thoughts and tried again to focus on the man standing at the front of the room, wiping his face while trying to compose himself enough to speak his next sentence. "It's been twelve years since she left me"—he sniffed loudly, wiping his nose on his plaid sleeve—"and I still can't figure out where it all went wrong."

"Did he just say twelve years?" she whispered, except the concealed-in-a-cough giggle coming from her row mate in the coveted seat closest to the door revealed she hadn't been quiet enough.

Trying hard to school her features, she swept the room with her gaze, praying no one else had heard her. When her row mate came into view again, the smiling woman pointed a finger at the doorway to a woman who was gesturing for them to come to her.

Vanessa paused for a beat, looking around at Mr. Snotty Nose in the front of the room, and decided whatever this woman at the doorway wanted had to be better than witnessing this.

She and her row mate stood up at the same time and quietly padded out of the room one after the other. They followed the stranger into the building's entryway, where the three of them stood facing each other, like the points on a triangle.

"I don't know about the two of you"—she rolled her dark brown eyes before sharing a bright, wide smile with Vanessa and her row mate—"but if I have to listen to Fred tell his twelve years of loneliness tale again, I will scream. The expressions you two had on your faces tell me you're probably feeling the same. Could I interest the two of you in a drink at the bar across the street instead? First round's on me."

The stranger's skin was a warm amber color; her hair, cropped close in a dark Caesar haircut, accented her sharp cheekbones. She was tall, with full curves, the sweater dress and knee-high boots accentuating every one of them in the best way possible. With her hand on her hip and a spark of mischief in her eyes, the stranger exuded everything Vanessa had never been and wished she could be: happy, confident, and free.

The air of self-assurance around the woman was intoxicating. That fact both enticed and alarmed her. That bright flame of self-confidence was what had attracted her to Karl. He was so self-assured that she couldn't help questioning her own mind. And if she were to tell the truth, in all this time, she hadn't really stopped questioning her decisions. She was supposedly free now. Physically and legally, she was. But there was still a lot of work left to do before she could remotely entertain the idea that the worst parts of her trauma were behind her.

Before she could think herself out of her automatic decision, her head was nodding, and she fell in line behind the stranger and her row mate, exiting the community center and heading for the small pub across the street. Whatever waited in there had to be better than the despair she'd just witnessed or the rage and fear that clawed at her insides.

"And when I confronted him about his mistress, he smiled at me and said, 'Good, since my secret is out, I don't have to hide or lie about her anymore.' He'd simply tell me in advance when he had plans with his girlfriend the next time."

Vanessa took the final swig of her margarita as she spilled the embarrassing tale of how her marriage went from conventional to open without her consent and gestured to the bartender for another round at their table.

She needed another drink.

She needed to drown out the missing parts of that story, the part where her husband emotionally abused her for more than two decades, the part where she'd ignored all the alarms going off in her head and by the time she'd recognized his manipulations for what they were, it was too late to break away. More alcohol would dull that pain or make her forget it entirely. Either way, she'd be happy to push those memories away if only for a few hours in a small bar in the middle of a sleepy little town in Pennsylvania.

"Girl!" Janae Sanders, the woman formerly known as Vanessa's row mate, shook her head. "I'm assuming since you're sitting here with us and not in a jail cell, you didn't kill him. A fact I applaud you for, because honey-chile, if it had been me, I would have called the cops first, took him out, then sat down on my couch sipping wine while I waited for them to come get me."

Maybe it was because they were on their third round of drinks, but Janae's response to Vanessa's story seemed perfectly rational. Unfortunately, Vanessa hadn't thought of it at the time. Her mind was so twisted, and her sense of self-preservation had been so badly brutalized, that his cheating hadn't stoked her anger or need for vengeance. It had only made her question how she'd managed to lose his favor and who she was if she wasn't the object of his perverse obsession, cloaked as attention. It was the typical "He only treats me this way because he loves me" toxic thinking that many survivors of abuse had been trained to initiate anytime they angered their assailant. The only problem was, back then, she hadn't recognized it as manipulation. She'd thought, as warped as it sounded, that toxic thinking was love.

Since she hadn't seen the abuse for what it really was, Karl's announcement had paralyzed her. And not just in the moment—it had taken her three months before she found the nerve to file for divorce. "No, I didn't kill him. My lawyer suggested I do something worse: take him for everything he was worth and live out the rest of my life happily on his dime."

Vanessa had been so detached and uncertain, she couldn't possibly have made any sort of calculated decision such as that on her own. Her lawyer was a shark, and had done what she'd seen was best for Vanessa, including encouraging her to get into therapy to work on herself. She knew that particular detail was the only reason she'd found a path ahead at all.

"Oh, I like the way your lawyer thinks. All mine got me was child support and half his pension," Janae responded. "What about you, Cree?

Cree Brenan, the feisty stranger who had lured them here with a smile and the promise of drinks, shrugged her shoulders. "My ex and me had an amicable divorce. We kept our businesses separate, split the personal assets down the middle, and moved on with our lives. It was a mutual decision, and the execution was pretty straightforward. I'm guessing you two didn't have that situation."

Vanessa shook her head because she sure as hell hadn't had an amicable divorce. Karl fought her tooth and nail for every red cent.

The only problem was that as his accountant, she knew where all his money was hidden. He couldn't hide it from her the way he had anyone else who'd tried to get at his cash.

"No," Janae whispered. The liveliest and boldest one of the three, she seemed unafraid to say exactly what she was thinking. Except for now. A server brought over their next pitcher of margaritas and refreshed each of their glasses before leaving them. Janae sipped her drink, then took a deep breath before she continued. "We had a nasty custody battle that dragged on for a long time. My husband didn't necessarily care for my supportive parenting style over his authoritative one and fought me for full custody. It took a while, but I won."

Cree raised her glass and Janae and Vanessa followed. "Congrats on that. Mama bear don't play when it comes to the kids."

"No, I do not," Janae answered while cool resignation settled her features. "Even though I wanted to kill him during the divorce, I know if I'm gonna do what's best for my boy, I gotta find some common ground with him. That's why I came to the meeting tonight. I needed to try to figure out how to move on with my life, get past my anger, so I can do what's best for my kid. Why did y'all come?"

Cree sipped her drink before placing it back on the table. "I came to figure out what's next. I've always had a plan for everything in my life. Getting divorced wasn't part of that. Other than my business, I don't really know what's on the horizon for me. What about you, Vanessa?"

Vanessa shifted in her seat as the weight of their combined stares settled over her. She hardly knew these women. A few rounds of margaritas didn't make them friends by any stretch of the imagination. Nevertheless, sitting there with them, she somehow sensed these two strangers might be the best place to leave her burdens. Or at least she hoped it was the best place. Given her track record of terribly misjudging character, she really couldn't tell.

"I spent so long being his wife and now I don't know how to be me. He betrayed me, then traded me in for a newer model, and moved on with his life like I was an afterthought. Sure, I took his money, but I never touched *him*. Me, on the other hand, I'm still a mess. I have no idea where I go from here or who I am without him."

That was all true, even if she hid some of the darker reasons for this self-realization. Vanessa attributed the startling amount of self-pity spilling from her lips to the amount of alcohol she'd consumed. Too ashamed, she pulled her gaze from theirs and focused on her hand shaking nervously on the table. The warmth of amber-brown skin covering her hand stopped the shaking. Soon, Janae added her palm to the mix, and the fear and anger Vanessa carried around like luggage seemed lighter.

"You don't need to be ashamed." Janae's voice was soothing, quieting the embarrassment Vanessa experienced. "It's why we're all here. None of us got what we needed in that meeting where we'd have to put our business out in the streets to a crowd. Here, though"—Janae glanced around the dim bar—"at a secluded table with just the three of us, we can speak our truths and not worry about judgment."

Vanessa was eternally grateful for the no-judgment part. She'd suffered enough of that during her time with Karl.

"It appears we all have some very important things to do after turning in our MRS degrees," Janae continued. "How about we make a pact to help each other move on to our better selves?"

"Yeah, like accountability partners," Cree added.

Janae chuckled. "Yeah, that, and friends, too. We check on each other, help each other when we get low, and a year from today, we come back, reevaluate our goals, and possibly do it again. How does that sound?"

Vanessa smiled. A genuine smile, one that tugged at her muscles and made them ache slightly. This didn't make a lick of sense. Teaming up with two strangers to figure out her own crazy life wasn't anywhere in her plans. Despite how out of character this was for her, as the two women matched Vanessa's big smile with ones of their own, she knew this was exactly what she needed.

"We are savvy," Cree began.

"And sexy," Janae continued. "let's not forget the sexy part."

Vanessa laughed. She didn't know if she considered herself all that sexy. The resolute expression on Janae's face indicated she'd brook no argument on the matter, so Vanessa merely nodded. "And single," Vanessa added.

Cree squealed, grabbing her drink, holding it in the air, and motioning for Janae and Vanessa to do the same. When they did, she said, "That's exactly what we are. The Savvy, Sexy, and Single Club. Three women who are embracing life after divorce."

"Now, I like that." Janae raised her glass next to Cree's. "What about you, Vanessa? Are you gonna join our club, let Cree and I help you get better, and do the same for us?"

Without hesitation, she raised her glass and clinked it to theirs. Vanessa might not know these ladies well, but she couldn't ignore that she felt more alive in their presence than she had in the last few years of her marriage. And *that* was more than good enough.

"Absolutely."

Chapter 1

"YOU CAN'T LIE HERE FOREVER, VANESSA. EVENTUALLY, you'll have to get out of this bed."

Vanessa Jared groaned at her inability to cope with her new normal. Well, it wasn't exactly new, because two years had passed since her divorce was final. She took a deep breath, trying to force herself to believe the words she'd just spoken aloud.

Vanessa raised her head from the pillow and braced herself on one elbow to try to pull herself into a sitting position. "If I can get up, everything will be fine." She managed to get her other elbow into position but couldn't find the strength to lock it. Before she knew it, she was falling back against her pillow, looking up at the ceiling again.

She took a few moments to center herself. She had to do this. The big day was here, and she had a million things to do. Lying on her ass wasn't going to get a single one of those tasks completed. Regardless of how much she was panicking inside, she had to get it together and plan this divas' night.

She was just about to give this sitting up thing another try when her phone rang. She reached in the direction of her nightstand and patted the surface until her fingers connected with the phone. "Hello."

"Hey, diva!" Vanessa pulled the phone away from her ear as the loud duet of voices blared in unison across the line.

"It is"—Vanessa glanced at her bedside table to note the time—"seven in the damn morning. Why are y'all heifers so damn happy this doggone early?"

Cree's bubbly giggle filled the line. "Janae, I told you she wouldn't be up yet. You owe me five dollars."

"Dammit, Vanessa." Janae's sharp tone made Vanessa smile. "You know I hate it when Cree is right."

Vanessa laughed, her body shaking as each warm wave of amusement spread from the inside out. She pressed the speaker icon on the screen of her phone and laid it on her nightstand while she rearranged her pillows and finally made it into a sitting position against the headboard.

"It serves you right for calling me so early. Can't a girl get her beauty sleep without you two interrupting her?"

Janae clucked her tongue. "Chile, you ain't ever lied about that. Looking as good as we do over forty takes work, water, and rest. Lots of it."

"Usually I'd agree," Cree added. "But since we're supposed to be painting the town red tonight, I thought we should call you and make sure you didn't need help getting things together. You sure you're okay?"

If Cree had asked that question five minutes before, the answer would've been an unequivocal no. She wouldn't have admitted it. No, she would've swallowed her unhappiness and smiled, because telling her friends she still had no clue what to do with her life two years after her divorce wasn't really something Vanessa wanted to even imagine.

She'd spent the first six months after the divorce trapped in a prison of her own making with no real connection to the outside world except Cree, Janae, and her therapist. Six months after that, she'd gotten the hair in her head that she might want to start her own accounting firm, so she'd taken on a few continuing education courses to refresh her skills. But when it came time to actually set up the firm, she'd backed away and retreated into her empty home. Her therapist had assured her this was normal, but back then, it had just felt like failure.

This last year, wanderlust had set in, and she'd traveled to as many exotic locations as her travel agent could book for her. That had worked for a while, keeping the heavy sadness that threatened to swallow her at bay. This sadness wasn't to do with Karl and his abuse. Nearly three years in therapy had shown her Karl was to blame, not her. But her inability to figure out what she wanted out of life beyond being a rich divorcée plagued her day in and day out.

Afraid she'd unintentionally flag her friends' concern, she cleared her throat before speaking again. "All the plans for the Savvy, Sexy, and Single Club's second anniversary are underway. All you two have to do is show up. Your car should arrive by six thirty this evening. You should be in New York by eight."

"All right, Ms. Thang," Janae hollered. "Since it seems like you've got everything for tonight handled, how are you gonna spend your day?"

Vanessa chuckled to herself, swinging her legs to the side of the bed as she thought about a response. Before she'd heard the excitement in her girlfriends' voices, she'd planned to mope. Today was one of those days when curling up in a ball under the covers felt like bliss when the alternative was to see your friends living their best lives being blessed and unbothered with purpose.

This was especially true because she still couldn't seem to find her direction. However, after a few minutes in the presence of these women, even if it was over the phone, she was reminded that there was life still out there for her to live. She just had to keep looking for it until she found what worked for her.

That morsel of advice had come from her therapist. She'd commended Vanessa on doing the work of healing and being so dedicated to her recovery since she'd filed for divorce three years ago. Now, she kept reminding Vanessa to give herself grace as she entered a new phase of possibility in her life.

"I'm gonna do what any diva does when she's going to be in the presence of remarkable beauty. Spend my day getting pampered and airbrushed to perfection."

"Heeeeyyyy!"

"Get it, girl!"

They all laughed a few moments longer before ending the call. Standing on her own two feet now, Vanessa stretched and allowed the contagious charm and general good moods of her friends to infuse her with the energy she needed to pull her spirit out of the dismal valley it had wallowed in for way too long.

No sense in holding on to despair when food, fun, and shenanigans with her girls awaited her. And as far as she was concerned, misery wasn't on the itinerary tonight. It was time for her to stop living in the past. If only for the few hours she'd spend with her friends, she would focus on the present. "I declare today a divorce-free day. The only thing you get to entertain is the good time that awaits you and your ladies."

Showered and dressed, ready to tackle the world, Vanessa slid her arm through the straps of her purse, grabbed her travel mug and her keys, and stepped through the front door. She was in the process of locking it when she heard a voice call from her front yard. "Mrs. Scott?"

Life seemed determined to have a joke at her expense. It didn't go unnoticed that the very moment she'd found the fortitude to think about her present instead of her past, someone had to remind her of who she used to be.

She looked to see who was calling her by her married name and found an Asian man walking toward her. He was muscular. Not spend-all-day-in-the-gym muscular, just built enough that the fitted T-shirt he wore hugged every bump and ridge of his torso and put his pecs on display. When he stepped up onto her porch, the black denim tightened around his toned thighs and she had to remember that this stranger climbing her stairs had called her name and should therefore make her uneasy. Once he stopped in front of her, pulling his shades off and revealing deep dark eyes that demanded her full attention, uneasy was the last thing she felt. Well, she was unnerved, but not because she was afraid.

"Mrs. Scott?"

She cleared her throat and blinked through the haze this man's presence seemed to surround her with. "Jared. It's Ms. Jared. I haven't been Mrs. Scott in two years. How can I help you?"

"My name is Michael Park. I'm the sheriff in Monroe Hills, Pennsylvania." Her stomach cramped a little. Both Janae and Cree were from Monroe Hills. Was he here to bring her bad news about one of them? She'd just gotten off the phone less than an hour ago. What could've happened? Before she could find the courage to ask, he pulled a wallet from his back pocket and handed it to her. She opened it to see his badge resting against the leather of one side, and his identification card on the other. "I'm here to speak with you about your ex-husband, Karl."

God, the universe has a piss-poor sense of humor.

"Whatever he did, I don't want to be involved. Karl stopped being my problem two years ago."

She handed him his badge and watched him take a deep breath as he slid it back inside his pocket. "Honestly, I don't know how to say this any other way than to just to come right out and say it. He's somehow scammed my twenty-five-year-old sister into agreeing to marry him. I need your help to prevent that."

Vanessa raised an eyebrow as she tried to process what the stranger had said to her. "Obviously I haven't had enough coffee. Did you just ask me to help you stop my ex-husband from marrying your sister?"

"I did. She's young and this is the first serious relationship she's had. She can't see that Scott is bad news."

Vanessa shook her head and stepped around him. She was right; she definitely hadn't had enough coffee for this mess. "I'm sorry. I can't help you."

"Please, Ms. Jared."

She had one foot on the first step when the desperation in his voice called out to her. Against her better judgment, she stopped and looked at him, twisting her foot into an awkward angle that caused her to lose her balance. Before she could feel herself fall, his strong arms were around her, pulling her to him while simultaneously setting her to rights on the leveled walkway.

"Are you okay?"

"Okay" wasn't a word she'd use to describe what it felt like to be pressed against the wall of this man's chest. And damn if that wasn't exactly what it felt like—a wall. Hard to the touch, and strong enough to hold her up while his heat made her want to spread herself like warm butter against his skin, Vanessa was far from okay. Too young to be experiencing menopause, and with the early signs of fall keeping the sunny days cool, this sudden hot flash searing her from the inside out had to directly result from how good it felt to be held by this sexy man.

"Ms. Jared?"

"Vanessa," she mouthed, then cleared her throat, trying to make her mouth work to form intelligible words. "Please, call me Vanessa."

"Vanessa," he whispered, his mouth close enough that all it would take was a tilt of her head and she'd know what that full bottom lip tasted like.

She swallowed, trying not to look as desperate as her fluttering heart told her she was. Vowing that if she ever regained her composure, she'd put enough distance between the two of them that she wouldn't behave like such a sex-starved cliché. He stared at her for a long moment, and then he peeled his hands away and stepped back. "Please, Vanessa. Just hear me out. If you decide not to help me after we talk, I won't bother you anymore."

The way his dark eyes searched hers was enough for her to grant his request. When he added a sweet smile that curved that sexy mouth into the perfect bow and those deep dimples of his to the mix, Vanessa knew she was screwed—in the theoretical sense, anyway.

She threw up her hands and tapped one of the pointed toes of her designer shoes against the ground. "I'm gonna need more caffeine to deal with this." When his smile broadened, her heart missed a beat again. If she were smart, she'd recognize that for the internal warning it was and walk away. Yet watching relief mixed with a spark of anticipation flash across his eyes, she couldn't bring herself to say no.

These last two years, she'd honed her manipulation sensors. She wasn't picking up exploitation from him, only concern.

Still, even though he seemed on the up and up, she let caution lead. No matter how attractive he was or how concerned he was for his sister, Vanessa had to protect herself. Determined never to be vulnerable again, the new Vanessa had to at least put up a "strong woman" front. "You've got as long as it takes for me to finish my cup of coffee at my local coffee shop, and then I'm out."

Chapter 2

MICHAEL SAT IN A BOOTH IN A NEARBY COFFEE SHOP drumming his fingers against the tabletop while he waited for Vanessa. She'd insisted on meeting him there in her own car. He couldn't blame her. Badge or no, he was a total stranger. He could definitely see how unsavory getting in a car with him might've been. He liked her instincts and wished his sister Cindy had enough cynicism not to be so trusting.

It was a sin and a shame that one had to be so guarded in today's world. Unfortunately, life had taught him that people like Karl Scott preyed upon kind and open people like his baby sister, Cindy, and he wasn't having that. So before he ended up in chains for wrapping his hands around Scott's neck and squeezing as tightly as he could, Michael thought about how he would convince Vanessa to help him.

He'd collected enough information about her in his investigation of her ex-husband to know that she was an accountant by trade. She'd worked for Scott Pharmaceutical exclusively until her divorce two years ago. She spent most of her time here in Bergen County, and outside of a few public charity events, she didn't seem to have much use for high society.

He glimpsed her as she walked into the coffee shop, stopping to look around briefly until she laid eyes on him. She removed her large designer sunglasses, the type people wore when they were trying to keep the rest of the world out. She gave him a small, brief smile, and it was enough to make excitement zip through his chest. He nodded in return, afraid any other gesture would reveal too much. She held up a finger asking him to wait while she stepped toward the counter to place her order. When she was done, she stepped clear of the counter and he could get a better look at her.

It was like watching the heroine enter the scene in a movie; everyone in the room turned to look at her. The few steps seemed to drag out in slow motion, so everyone could take in her beauty.

Vanessa's dark hair was cut into a sharp shoulder-length bob that moved with each elegant step she took. The deep, rich brown skin of her face reminded him of spun silk: shiny, making you want to feel its smoothness against your own flesh. Her full lips were covered in a vampy matte burgundy color that highlighted her reddish undertones and made him wonder how long it had been since she'd allowed a man to worship them with kisses.

If he was honest, it wasn't the lipstick alone that had him wondering that. The way she'd been pressed against him when she lost her balance on her porch step did enough to put that tantalizing question in his head. He'd been this close to leaning in and attempting to find out when he thought about how his actions might affect his sister.

Cindy was young and too trusting for her own good. She had no idea what being an adult was about, and if Michael didn't take care of this situation immediately, she'd come to irrevocable harm.

Their family had suffered enough to last a lifetime. If he'd been there to take matters into his own hands ten years ago, they might never have known the ache of loss particular to tragically losing parents.

Determined to push that pain back into its designated box, he forced himself to focus on Vanessa and those luscious lips of hers again. He'd wanted to know what they tasted like, and her near-tumble had provided him the opportunity. That wasn't in the cards, though. Like always, his duty to his sister won out and he did the honorable thing instead, setting Vanessa on her feet before things could go too far.

Being honorable really blew chunks, because watching her in her fitted sweater dress that hugged her high-sitting, full bosom, and rounded hips that led into the thickest set of thighs he'd ever seen on a woman, made him wish he didn't have as much integrity as he did.

He continued to watch her. She was probably of average height. He'd put her at about five foot eight. But wearing those tall boots—the kind that put those curvy legs on display and would tempt a man beyond his limits—she was maybe an inch shorter than his just-over-six-foot frame.

Get it together, Michael. This is about Cindy, not your lackluster libido.

She sat her cup on the table and slid into the seat opposite him, and he was suddenly bothered that he'd chosen a booth for privacy instead of a table near the center of the seating area where chairs were pushed close together.

"So, I'm here. How am I supposed to help save your sister?"

He took another sip of his coffee so he wouldn't seem like a weirdo when he didn't respond. He knew the answer to her question. He just didn't answer immediately because he was still trying to get his head in the right space, where he wasn't thinking about how good she smelled, or how much he wanted to touch her. "The only thing I really want is for you to agree to meet her, talk to her about life with your ex."

"You're assuming my life with Karl was bad."

"I'm not assuming. I read the transcript for your divorce. Even on paper I can tell what a slimeball he was, how he treated you poorly. Am I wrong?"

She raised an eyebrow and shook her head. "No. He was pretty much a scammer from the day I encountered him. We met in college. I was a freshman; he was a junior. He trained me from then to always worry about his needs and support his dreams no matter what. It wasn't until twenty years later that I realized my wants and desires didn't factor into the equation. Once I did, Karl lost interest in me and in our marriage. He'd probably always been a cheater. When I refused to play by his rules, though, he didn't care to hide his dalliances any longer."

Michael felt himself physically flinch as he listened to Vanessa break down her marriage to Scott. No one should be treated that way, least of all the person you vowed to love and cherish for the rest of your life. He reached across the table and rested a tentative hand over hers when sadness seemed to cloud her dark brown eyes. "You deserved better than what he gave you. My sister does too."

She snatched her hand away, and the softness Michael had seen in her while she described her marriage to Scott was gone. With her shoulders pulled back in a stiff line, she narrowed her eyes. "I don't know your sister. She could be the person he was cheating on me with for the last few years of our marriage. Why should I help her?"

Her accusation could be the truth. He didn't know because his sister had been so secretive about their relationship; she had given no details about the when, where, and why of how they became involved. There was one thing he was crystal clear on. Even if Cindy was involved with that liar, she wasn't a home-wrecker. Not a willing one, anyway.

"I don't know when she started seeing him. She introduced him and announced their engagement a month ago. I may be short on the details, but I can tell you for certain my sister didn't know Scott had a wife."

Her neatly arched eyebrow seemed to lift even higher as a disbelieving smirk hitched the corner of her sexy mouth up. She folded her arms over her ample chest and cocked her head to the side. "Let me guess, you believe she didn't know about me because she's just not that type of person?"

He knew how silly it sounded. The impracticality of it didn't make it any less true, though. Cindy was too sweet to knowingly destroy someone else's marriage. She'd grown up sheltered, never stepping foot outside their small town to know how the big world worked. Determined to set the record straight, he pulled a newspaper clipping from inside the billfold of his wallet. He opened it up and slid it across the table to her. "She didn't, and I can prove it."

Vanessa looked down at the picture and her insides churned. It was a full-color display in the *Monroe Hills Herald*. Karl's piercing blue eyes, even in print, made her feel scrutinized. He was impeccable as always. Blond and gray hair mixing perfectly together in a tapered style, making him look a little too much like the actor John Snyder. Next to him was the woman she assumed was Michael's sister, Cindy.

She was thin, with her dark sable hair pulled back into a bun. The style looked so severe on her. Vanessa wondered if Karl had insisted on Cindy wearing it the way he had when they were married. "Subtle elegance" was what Karl called it, and she could see its influence all over Cindy. She looked like a little girl playing dress-up. Not because she was young—well, that wasn't the only reason, anyway. It was because this dowdy look was what Karl required of all the women he brought into the daylight.

She slid her gaze down the photo until she saw the caption below the handsome couple in the picture and nearly choked on the air that went down the wrong pipe as a result. "Widower Karl Scott to wed local beauty, Cindy Park."

"Widower?"

Michael nodded his head as she pulled her focus from the newspaper clipping. "He's telling people I'm dead?"

Michael shrugged. "I don't know what he's telling people, only what he's telling Cindy. Cindy placed that announcement in the paper. It's something we locals do. It's a small town, news like this makes everyone happy. That's how I found out about him. She wouldn't give me very many details other than they'd met when he came to town to meet with the medical boards at our two hospitals. He'd hired a local florist to create floral arrangements for his event."

Vanessa shook her head. "Just when I thought he couldn't get any sleazier. I don't get why he'd lie about that. Why not just tell her he's divorced?"

"My guess is being divorced doesn't get you the same amount of sympathy as having a dead wife."

"What does he gain from worming his way into your sister's life like this? Karl is a wealthy, attractive man who can get anyone he wants. Why does he have to lie to get your sister?"

Michael shook his head. "He's not as wealthy as he used to be. You took half his personal assets in the divorce. His business has taken some serious hits after a regulation scandal. He's barely breaking even right now. At least that's how it appears from the public records I could find."

She shrugged her shoulders. "That still doesn't make this make sense. No offense, but your sister is a florist. Unless she's got some secret millions stashed somewhere, I don't see why he'd attach himself to her."

"Because she does have secret millions," Michael said. "My sister and I were awarded large settlements when our parents were killed. The driver of an eighteen-wheeler fell asleep on the road. I sued the company and put most of the money in a trust. The rest of it I used to raise her and put her through college. On her next birthday she'll have control of it."

Vanessa let out a long breath as she put all the puzzle pieces together in her mind. When she was done, she shook her head and raised her hands in surrender. This situation was getting crazier by the minute. Karl was a cheater, yes. *Don't forget an abuser, too.* She closed her eyes trying to shut that thought out. Not that she was trying to protect him. No, that wasn't it. She still couldn't bear to acknowledge his mercilessness because somewhere deep down, no matter how much she pretended otherwise, she blamed herself for the way he'd treated her.

Shaking herself free from her musings, she was able to focus a little more on the situation at hand. Had Karl really sunk this low?

"Listen, I don't know what kind of long con Karl is working and I don't want to. I just know I want no part in it. Whenever I get mixed up with him, I come out worse off for it. I'm sorry your sister's in his sights, I just can't get involved. I cannot help you."

She slid out of the booth and stood up to leave when Michael stood up too, grabbing the picture and forcing her to look at it again. "I know you don't owe me or my sister anything, Vanessa, just please, I'm begging you to come talk to her. If I show her documentation that he's a liar, she won't believe me. But if I have the living proof in front of her, there's no way she can ignore what I'm saying. Please, help me protect her the way someone should've protected you."

Vanessa's heart ached with the memory of the one person who shielded her from the pain of the world. Her ma'dea, Doris MacKenzie Jared. She was a smart, fierce woman who had loved Vanessa with her whole heart. And when Vanessa's father was too busy with work to pay attention to his only daughter, Doris swooped in and loved on Vanessa so hard, all her cares slipped away. That woman had been the only source of light in Vanessa's life for a long time. And if Vanessa was honest, her death the year before Vanessa married Karl had worn just as heavily on her as Karl's mistreatment of her did.

She looked into Michael's pleading eyes, her empathy pushing her to give in to his request. Unfortunately, the thought of becoming involved with Karl again after barely surviving the first time, no matter how sorry she felt for this man's sister, she couldn't do what he was asking.

She was about to say just that, planning to let him down as easy as possible, when something in the picture caught her eye. She stepped closer, pulling the picture to her face to inspect the shiny ring on Cindy's left ring finger, and fire burned through her veins. "That son of a bitch."

"What's wrong, Vanessa?"

"The ring your sister's wearing is mine. It was my grandmother's engagement ring. My father gave it to Karl to propose with when he claimed he was too broke to buy me a ring while we were in school."

"Shit, that's low. Are you trying to tell me he proposed to my sister with your engagement ring?"

Low didn't even begin to describe it. Criminal was actually what it was. "I won this ring in the divorce decree. The last time I remember seeing it was when Karl came by the house to get the last of his belongings after the divorce was finalized. That bastard took my ring."

And the last direct connection she had with her beloved grandmother.

"And gave it to my sister."

She slid back into the booth feeling slightly unbalanced underneath the cloud of rage and sadness hanging over her. "I promised my grandmother before she died that I would keep that ring in our family. Karl knew that. He was in the hospital with me when I made that promise."

"That is a real dick move, and you should be mad as hell about it."

She raised her eyebrow at him again, a gesture she hoped he was interpreting as the civilized "Fuck you" that it was. Instead of cursing him out, however, she painted a fake smile on her face and said, "Thank you for your permission to be angry."

He laughed a bit. The situation wasn't funny at all. None of it. Especially knowing Karl had stolen something so precious to

Vanessa. It wasn't about the piece of jewelry itself. Although stunning, it wasn't the most extravagant or expensive piece she owned.

To her mind, part of her grandmother's spirit was imbued into that ring. And even though she hadn't worn it in two years, the knowledge that it was tucked away in a safe space near Vanessa gave her comfort she desperately needed when loneliness and pain tried to consume her.

"Look, you can be mad," he began as he held up his hands palmside up. "And no one would blame you, least of all me." He looked around the room in a conspiratorial way, as if he were about to share the deepest, most guarded secret in the world, then leaned in. "Or, you can be better than mad?"

She narrowed her eyes and leaned in slightly too. "What's better than mad?"

"Getting even," he offered as his tongue darted out and swiped against his full bottom lip. "Come back to Monroe Hills with me and blow whatever game he's playing with my sister to hell. You save my sister and get revenge on him all at the same time. It's a win for you all around."

She sat up, contemplating his request again. She didn't want to get involved. She was supposed to be getting her life back on track. She'd promised herself she'd use all her time and energy on herself so she could figure out her purpose without an all-consuming narcissist for a husband to focus on.

Her resolve growing, she couldn't let Karl steal another thing from her. Especially not something the person Vanessa loved most in the world had wanted her to have. If she was honest, leaving Michael's sister vulnerable to Karl didn't sit right with her either. She was a stranger to Vanessa, but even still, no one deserved the pain Karl would undoubtedly inflict on the unsuspecting young woman.

When she looked over her cup of coffee to see the devilish glimmer in Michael's eyes, her common sense lost the battle.

"Fine, I'll help you." She closed her eyes to settle that part of her that wanted to curl up and ignore anything that had to do with Karl. She shook it off, though, reminding herself of the promise she'd made to herself in front of her therapist. Vanessa would never again let anyone or anything control her. Not even the fear buried deep beneath the surface of her mind, where the mental and emotional scars she bore were hidden, would keep her from taking back what was hers.

When her gaze met Michael's, she watched a tentative smile bloom on his face. She lifted a finger to stop him from saying whatever it was he felt compelled to share in response. "But there's one condition. If I go to your little town and talk to your sister, you have to get me my grandmother's ring. I was very close to her and getting that small piece of her back means everything to me. I'm sure your sister is attached to it, and it's not her fault Karl's made her his latest target. That being said, that ring belongs to my family. Karl stole it, and she's flaunting stolen property."

She could sense his reluctance to agree by the way he sat back, pulling his shoulders into a straight line. It was probably for the best; she honestly didn't need to get involved in this mess, anyway. Agreement or no, she would get her ring back. And if he didn't agree to her terms, she'd be filling out a police report as soon as she left him here.

She thought he was about to walk away from the entire deal when he nodded. "Fine, I'll get you your ring. When should I expect you?"

She pulled her phone from her purse, opened a new contact on the screen, and handed it to him. "Plug in your info and I'll call you when I'm on my way."

Chapter 3

~

"DIVA!" JANAE AND CREE COLLECTIVELY SCREAMED THE word when she walked into the private dining room. Each year one of them would host the celebration. This year was Vanessa's turn. Yeah, she'd thought about bailing earlier, but whether she showed or not, her plans had been set in motion months ago. A private dining room in one of the fanciest restaurants in New York reserved just for the three of them. They'd spend the night enjoying each other's company while being catered to by the restaurant's staff.

It was the perfect way to celebrate her friends. They both worked so hard and had so much going on, Vanessa decided to give them a night where they didn't have to worry about anything. A private car picked them up from their respective homes in Pennsylvania and transported them on the hour-and-a-half drive to New York City in style while sipping on champagne.

If the loud giggles and their nearly overwhelming delight at seeing Vanessa enter the room was any sign, they'd enjoyed the champagne while they cruised along I-80. Even though she hadn't taken a sip of anything yet, she was equally thrilled to see them. Janae wore a metallic gold body-con one-shoulder dress that hugged every luscious curve of her plus-size body. The shiny gold color looked majestic against the deep brown of her complexion. Her long wavy hair spilled over one shoulder while the other, bare and beautiful, sparkled with a shimmer of body glitter. She was sexy, stunning, and Janae knew it, and Vanessa was pretty much certain anyone with eyes knew it too.

Cree was a statuesque beauty, six feet tall in her bare feet with curves that made an hourglass jealous. Her honey-brown skin looked sun-kissed even as the summer was quickly fading into the chill of fall, and with the black high-low number hugging her rounded hips, it was a wonder Vanessa hadn't seen a path of people struck unconscious by her sheer beauty. Her hair was cut into a dark Caesar, making her striking and easily recognizable as a queen who understood her own power.

Both her girls were powerful queens. She often wished the strength recognizable in these two women lived somewhere inside her too. They'd both built better lives for themselves after their respective divorces. They understood their purpose, a purpose that blazed brightly in both of them and had nothing to do with their relationship status.

Vanessa had been Mrs. Karl Scott. Even her skills as an accountant had been used solely to fulfill her purpose as Karl's wife. And when he was gone, Vanessa had nothing more to center her life. Now, she'd been floating listlessly for the last two years in search of what it was she was meant to do. She needed something that was just for her.

As her girlfriends fawned over her fitted black strapless jumpsuit, the long sheer gold duster she wore over it, and her sleek bob haircut, Vanessa realized that focusing on her impostor syndrome right now wasn't what she needed. No, instead she would let these women celebrate her, even if she knew it was all a lie.

"Would you look at us?" Cree spread her arms wide, wrapping them around Vanessa's and Janae's shoulders. "We are glorious!"

Janae snapped her fingers and hollered, "Yasssss, queen! We're out'chea stuntin' on 'em. They ain't ready for us."

Vanessa closed the circle, forming a group hug. Being with her girls like this strengthened her, making her feel more empowered than she ever did in her everyday life. "I'm so glad to see you two. How was your ride in? Did everything go okay with the driver?"

"Girl, you didn't have to go through the expense of sending a car for us. Janae could've driven us here."

Vanessa waved her hand dismissing Cree. "I wanted to do it. You two work so hard; you deserve to be pampered tonight. Just consider it me putting Karl's money to good use."

Janae shook her head and interrupted. "Nope, that is your money. You earned every bit of it. Every time you put your life on hold to support his dreams, every time you stood strong in the face of his cheating and humiliation, nah, that money is yours."

"You know Janae is always right. Don't argue with her. You earned that."

Vanessa felt the warmth of acceptance flowing through her, creating a buzz that no sparkling wine could compare to. "Thank you. I needed that."

Janae reached out and tucked Vanessa's hair behind her ear before cupping a gentle hand over her cheek. "Chile, please. Queens don't tear each other down. We fix each other's crowns. We got you, queen."

"Yeah, always," Cree said.

Vanessa beamed. Her affection for these two women filled her with positive energy, like she was tapping into the best version of herself. How she could ever have thought of ditching this event, she didn't know. Because more than anything, this was what she needed. A reminder that she was strong too, maybe even strong enough to finally tell them the full truth about her relationship with Karl.

The serving staff entered the room with covered platters, signaling that their evening was underway. While Janae and Cree went to settle in their seats, Vanessa grabbed her phone from her clutch and scrolled through her contacts until she found Michael Park's number. She tapped out a text telling him she'd make her way down to Monroe Hills sometime soon. She'd call him when she arrived. It was vague, unfortunately; she couldn't do better than that. Not until she got herself together to do this.

And she would do this. If only to prove to herself that she was no longer the same woman Karl victimized. Her girls reminded her that she was strong enough to stop Karl, to help another young queen, and to take back what was hers at once. Her grandmother's ring, her dignity, and her future were all within reach. All she had to do was spend a few more hours in the presence of the handsome man who'd held her in his solid arms and made her wonder what it would feel like to do that under a different set of circumstances.

Yeah, she could do this. She was a queen. Queens didn't turn and run, they stood and fought. And with a handsome knight like Michael Park by her side, it might actually be fun doing so. What could go wrong?

Michael rolled over on the couch when he heard the text message notification on his phone. There weren't many people who texted him. His sister, his best friends Adam and Derrick, and occasionally one of his deputies would message him to inform him of minor things at the office. Most of those people didn't reach out at nine at night, however.

He picked up the phone and saw Vanessa Jared's name, and instantly his concern slipped away and was replaced by curiosity. "What could she want at this time of night?"

> Gotta figure out my schedule first
> But I've decided to help you
> Call when I'm on my way
> Hope you're ready for me

Although his head was pretty sure she was referring to the uproar her presence would cause in his sister's life, his body took that comment an entirely different way, and he had to remind his lecherous cock that this was no time to be selfish. Cindy was the one who mattered. Not his undersexed, overworked self who spent way too many hours keeping the people of this town safe and not nearly enough taking care of his own needs.

He replied with an even *See you soon* and placed the phone back on his coffee table. His response might have been calm; his pulse, on the other hand . . . Just the thought of her, the way she moved, the way she spoke, hell, even the way she smelled of something light and floral when he held her in his arms, kept him preoccupied most of his day at work, and now again at home. If Michael wasn't careful, he might find himself in a terrible situation of wanting what he couldn't possibly have, and that wouldn't do for anyone involved, least of all his sister.

Vanessa Jared might appeal to his senses. Actually, there was no "might" about it. Everything about her turned him on. He was big brother first. Consequently, his first priority had to be protecting his sister. And even if his cock was still attempting to come to life as he thought about the dark-skinned beauty, Michael refused to secede control.

No, lust wouldn't win out. He would do what was right. He always did. Well, except for when he'd woken from a nap after dreaming about Vanessa, so hard he was almost in pain. Relieving himself in the shower with a necessary handjob that led him to such an explosive orgasm he was shaking—that shouldn't count against him, right? He couldn't be expected to control his dreams, after all. Once she arrived, however, things would be different. Even if the mere thought of this woman heated his blood, Vanessa was off-limits. Now that he'd put his foot down, he was certain things would be all right.

He crossed his ankles and placed his laced fingers under his head. Yeah, he had it handled. "I've got this."

Chapter 4

∽

"SO, I NEED A BIT OF ADVICE FROM THE TWO OF YOU." Janae was the first to lift her gaze from the plate in front of her. With a perfectly arched eyebrow, she gave Vanessa her undivided attention. Cree set her glass of champagne on the table and clasped her hands together as she stared directly at Vanessa.

One of the most significant things Vanessa valued about their three-way friendship was that no matter what it was, when one of them needed the others, they were always there. Fully engaged and ready to hang on her every word, the weight of their attention made her insides tremble.

She chided herself for hesitating to speak the truth to her friends. They wouldn't judge her. Or at least not much, anyway.

"I had an unexpected visitor today. Someone from that little hick town in the mountains the two of you call home."

Her friends looked at one another and then back to her. "Who?" Janae questioned, and by the breath she was about to take, Vanessa figured she'd better answer her or fall under siege of the long list of questions she knew Janae would ask.

"He said his name was Michael Park?"

"The sheriff?" Cree asked.

Vanessa huffed and lifted her eyes to the ceiling. "God, is that town really that small that all I have to do is mention his name and you know who I'm talking about?"

They both chuckled and nodded. "Pretty much," Cree replied.

"Was this an official matter?"

"Since I don't live in Mayberry with you, I doubt he'd have any official reason to seek me out."

Janae rolled her eyes and pointed her finger at Vanessa, showing her disapproval of Vanessa's likening of Monroe Hills to the idyllic fictional town of Mayberry on *The Andy Griffith Show*. "That's the last dig you take at our beloved town. What did Michael want?"

Vanessa reached for her glass of champagne and sipped until the bubbles rushing against her tongue made her relax a little.

"Apparently, Karl is up to his old tricks of making a young girl into his perfect Stepford wife. Your sheriff's sister, Cindy, in fact."

The two women stared at each other with dropped jaws and wide eyes before focusing on Vanessa again.

"I guess what they say about small towns and everyone knowing each other's business isn't true, then."

Janae shook her head. "Nah, it's true. I worked a double at the hospital, and when I got home, after we called you, I crashed until it was time to get ready for tonight."

"And I spent all day in meetings with Derrick and our staff," Cree said. "We're trying to clear our caseload before I leave for Tanner's wedding during the holidays."

Vanessa grabbed her phone from her purse and pulled up the link to the wedding announcement Michael had shown her. "According to the *Monroe Hills Herald*, the two plan to marry very soon."

She handed her friends the phone and watched as shock stretched their smooth skin into tight lines.

"I can't believe this!" Janae screeched.

"I can," Vanessa replied. "Karl has always been a jerk. This doesn't surprise me at all."

"Hold up." Janae lifted her head from the screen. "This says 'Widower Karl Scott.' Is that a typo?"

Vanessa shook her head slowly before grabbing her drink and taking more than the dainty sip her pedigree demanded.

"Your sorry-ass ex told the newspaper you were dead?" Janae's description of Karl made Vanessa chuckle. Even if she'd never met the man in person, she was spot-on with her impression of him.

"Not just the paper," Vanessa responded. "Apparently, he's told that to young Cindy, too. Karl's slimy demeanor must have tipped your sheriff off, so he did a background check on him and found it terribly interesting when he discovered I am in fact alive."

Janae propped her elbow on the table, using her fork to punctuate every word she spoke. "So, what exactly did Michael want? Karl is obviously an asshole, but that's not your business anymore."

"He wants me to come down and talk to his sister. To warn her off of Karl."

"And your response?" Janae stabbed one of the oversized shrimp on her plate a little harder than was necessary to get it on her fork and slid it into her mouth. "Please tell me you agreed."

Vanessa tilted her head to the side, slightly surprised by Janae's response. "I could've sworn you were gonna tell me to leave the pettiness alone and move on with my life. Why aren't you telling me that?"

Cree cackled loudly enough that if anyone else had been in the private dining room with them, they surely would've turned around to see what all the fuss was about.

"You do realize you're talking to the queen of petty here, right? This is the same person who, when someone kept stealing her lunch out of the staff break room, she put a laxative in a homemade slice of chocolate pie to teach them a lesson." Vanessa nodded as she recalled Janae recounting this particular tale. "Of course she's telling you to stick it to your ex any chance you get."

Cree's assessment of their friend resonated with Vanessa. If you pissed Janae off, she would not stop until she got you back.

"I bet you Dr. Glenn never opened a container with my name on it again after that. Never mind that, though. What did you say?"

"I agreed to come down."

Cree narrowed her eyes as she shook her head. "You're leaving out something. Like I said, Janae is the queen of petty. She would drive the almost one hundred miles between you and us to do this. That's not your style. What aren't you telling us?"

Damn Cree and her perceptive nature. It was why she was one of the best advertising executives in the business. She knew how to read between the lines and get to the nitty-gritty of the important, unspoken things people often left out.

"The ring Cindy's wearing." She took a breath, trying to fight the embarrassment attempting to climb up out of the pit of her gut to silence her. "It's mine. Or rather, it was my grandmother's. My father gave it to Karl to propose to me with. The judge awarded it to me in the divorce."

Janae dropped her fork onto her plate and sat tall against the back of her chair. "How did he get it if you won it in the divorce?"

"He stole it. Because the last I remember, it was in a drawer in my walk-in closet."

Janae's left eye twitched, making Vanessa slightly afraid she'd do something rash like stalk out of there to find Karl herself.

"Get that motherfucker."

Vanessa shrugged. "The only thing I plan to get is my grandmother's ring. I'm gonna go talk to Cindy, and once I do, Michael will give me my ring. Whatever happens to Karl after that isn't my business. Although I can't lie and say I'd be disappointed if me coming down to expose him for the liar he is blows up whatever little scam he's got going."

Janae placed a warm hand on Vanessa's, sensing her need for comfort. "You sure you're all right with this? Just because I'm petty enough to do something like this doesn't mean you have to be. Granted, after the way that jerk cheated on you, I can understand why you'd want to steer clear of him."

The truth hung heavy on Vanessa's tongue. She'd led her friends to believe the demise of her marriage was caused by Karl's cheating. Sitting here, however, feeling the comfort they granted her once again, she knew she couldn't tell them half-truths anymore.

"Karl's cheating would be more than a good enough reason for me to stick it to him." She swallowed hard, trying to push down the fear and embarrassment that threatened to overwhelm her. "But I'm doing this because after suffering from Karl's emotional abuse, I can't sit by and watch it happen to another unwitting victim without doing something to intervene."

The room was quiet for a moment. The silence was so profound she longed to fidget under its weight until she felt Janae's hand squeeze hers.

"I suspected as much," Janae whispered. She must have sensed Vanessa's rising discomfort. When people knew about something like this, they treated you differently. And more than anything, Vanessa didn't want to be treated like a victim or pitied by the two women sitting with her. "It wasn't noticeable to the untrained eye. I was a floor nurse for a couple of years. Domestic violence is something they train you to recognize. I didn't know what kind of abuse, I simply suspected it was more than just Karl's cheating."

Before she could turn her eyes to Cree, she heard her voice. "Janae shared her concerns with me and we both agreed that it was your story to tell in your own time, if at all. It never mattered to us, Vanessa. The only thing we cared about was that you were safe and healing."

"Good, because I'm not allowing my past to define me, and it would kill me if you suddenly started treating me as if I'm delicate or breakable."

The warm glow of their smiles covered her like a favorite blanket, reinforcing the trust and security she experienced. There was comfort in knowing she could open herself up completely to these two and she would always be safe.

"Thank you for not judging me."

"Judging you?" Janae's voice was tender yet strong. "Why would we judge you for surviving? You did what you needed to do to *survive* and worked your behind off to rebuild your life afterward. The only person we're judging is that slimy ex of yours."

Janae patted her hand. "Despite what I said before about getting Karl, if you don't feel comfortable with seeing him again, if being around him makes you feel threatened, you don't have to do this."

Vanessa shook her head, squeezing Janae's hand.

"I'm not afraid of Karl, not anymore. The last time I saw him was right after our last court date when he came to the house for the rest of his belongings. By the time our divorce was finalized, I'd been in intensive therapy for almost a year. It truly saved my life and helped me remap my thinking.

"Karl tried his old tactics when he showed up to the house. I was nervous at first, but then I realized I'd done the hardest part in walking away. His visit was like that scene at the end of *What's Love Got to Do with It* when Ike sneaks into Tina's dressing room and she ends up reading him to filth and dismissing him. Karl looked just as pitiful once he realized he couldn't control me anymore. That's when I knew for certain I was beyond his control and I wasn't afraid anymore."

She nodded, the same resolve stiffening her spine now as it did then. "Don't get me wrong, I still had a long way to go in my healing journey. But I knew no matter what, I would never again mistake manipulation and fear as love. And as long as that was true, I could keep myself safe."

Discovering she'd finally broken free of him mentally—that had been the moment she had truly reclaimed her power.

Cree's face blossomed with a full-on smile. "Exactly," she agreed. "Now, just like Janae said, get that motherfucker."

Janae and Cree both nodded with a flash of sinister glee in their eyes that empowered Vanessa, washing away any remnants of the fear she'd had that her friends wouldn't understand.

"You know you've got to stay with me," Cree offered. "I want front-row seats to this drama."

"She can't," Janae answered for Vanessa. "She can't stay with either of us. She's allergic to fur babies."

Never before had she been so grateful for her allergy to pet dander. As much as she wanted her friends' support, this was something she wanted to handle quickly and efficiently.

"It's not an issue. It's gonna be a quick overnight visit. I'll stay at a hotel, it'll be fine."

Both women shared a knowing look that put Vanessa slightly on edge.

"Monroe Hills isn't Manhattan or any of the fancy places in New Jersey," Janae said. "It's a small town. You won't find the Ritz-Carlton there. The Main Street Inn has nice cottages, but they fill up quick on the weekends, though. You'd better make a reservation immediately."

"It's the Poconos," Vanessa responded. "I thought it was a tourist attraction with lots of places to stay."

"In Shawnee or Marshall's Creek, maybe," Cree answered. "Not so much in Monroe Hills. It's a tiny speck right off of I-80. When those major hotels in the touristy spots fill up, the Main Street Inn gets the overflow. Janae's right. You better make that reservation as soon as you can. Otherwise, you'll be sleeping in the forest with Bambi and Yogi."

Vanessa tried to picture herself sleeping under the stars and almost burst into laughter. A fully loaded RV still wouldn't be enough for her to step her designer shoes into the woods. She was a city mouse deep down to the bottom of her urbane heart.

"I'll make a note to handle it first thing in the morning."

"Morning, Sheriff."

Michael looked up from his phone to see who was calling his name and huffed when he saw his best friends, Adam and Derrick, waiting in front of the sheriff's department.

He caught a glint of mischief sparking in Adam's hazel eyes, and he knew instantly these two were up to no good.

He tilted his head and squinted as hard as he could before he said, "What do you want?"

Michael took in the sight of his two oldest friends leaning against the railings in front of the entryway and shook his head at the sight the three of them must make together. Michael was Korean American, while Adam Henderson and Derrick Lattimore were both Black. The three of them couldn't have looked more different if they'd tried, but together, their friendship had always carried all three of them through some of the roughest struggles in their lives.

They all stood six feet or taller, and all three kept in good shape through weekly meetups at the gym and on the basketball court. Adam's skin was a honeyed sandstone; Derrick's was a deep spiced rum. Where Adam's hair was twisted artfully in long, sandy-brown locs, Derrick's dark curls were short and tight, with a naked fade tapered on the sides and back. Each man finished off his polished looks with a neat goatee.

Michael rounded out their crew with his fair complexion, a clean-shaven face, and ink-black wavy hair cut into a tapered style to keep in line with regulations for his job as sheriff. Unlike the two men standing in front of him, individuality in appearance wasn't allowed where he worked. Sure, he was the boss, and no one would say anything to him if he bent the rules. Yet to him, that meant he needed to follow the rules more than anyone under his command.

Adam pushed off the railing he was leaning against to slap a friendly hand on Derrick's shoulder.

"What I tell you, D? We come all the way over here to meet our boy on a Sunday morning and take him to breakfast, and he can't even muster up a pleasant 'good morning' to greet us. Just ungrateful."

Derrick's smile was wide, and he was barely containing the laughter Michael could see tugging at the corners of his mouth.

"I can tell by your smile he's up to something, D." Michael looked directly at Derrick to get to the bottom of things. "You know you want to tell me. Spill it."

Derrick's smile widened to show off his perfect orthodontic work. "He wants to take you to breakfast so he can find out how your meeting went with the not so-dead wife of your soon-to-be brother-in-law."

He shook his head before pointing a finger at Derrick. "Don't even play like that. That man will marry my sister over my dead body."

Adam stepped off the stairs and walked until he was in front of Michael. "Well, according to Ms. Judy at the catering hall, Cindy's already called about availability." Adam threw a brief glance over his shoulder to glimpse Derrick. "D, I don't know about you, but to me, that sounds like Cindy's pretty serious about her pending nuptials. What do you think?"

Derrick stepped off the stairs as well and completed the triangle they always made when they were talking to each other. "I think you'd better have had good luck with the ex-wife or we're all gonna end up being fitted for tuxedos."

Michael half groaned, half growled. His friends were right, and no one was more aware of what he was up against than him.

Adam slung an arm around Michael's neck and pulled him close.

"Come on, man, your shift doesn't start for more than an hour. Let's go across the street to the diner and get some food. The coffee will make you feel better, and the food will keep us from ragging on you while you tell us what happened."

Michael playfully elbowed Adam in the ribs and turned toward the diner. "Fine. Y'all are paying, though."

They were seated pretty quickly. Even though the morning rush was in full swing, Kelly, the owner, always kept a table free for Michael in the back to keep everyone in town from interrupting his meals.

Monroe Hills was a tiny town by anyone's imagination, and being the head of its equally small sheriff's department meant everyone in town made it their business to stop and talk to him. It used to annoy him when he'd first returned home from working as a detective in Philly. There, if someone had stopped to start up a random conversation, he would've thought they were either up to no good or unbalanced.

Coming back to Monroe Hills ten years ago when he lost his parents had been a culture shock. Even though he'd grown up here, the open friendliness took some getting used to.

Since Derrick was the only one of the three of them who had stayed in Monroe Hills after high school, he'd helped him reacclimate to small-town culture. Although Adam lived in New York at the time, it was both of them who'd held Michael together while he tried to take care of his then-teenage sister. Derrick was his rock, coming over almost daily to check in, and Adam kept Michael sane with reassuring phone calls while he handled Cindy's grief and his own.

These two men would always have his back and he theirs. So as much as they were giving him shit about his situation, Michael knew they were just as concerned about Cindy's engagement as he was.

After the server left with their orders, Adam sat back with his arms folded and his brow lifted. "So, what happened?" he asked bluntly and waited for a response.

"She agreed to come talk to Cindy," Michael replied.

"But?" Derrick asked, dragging out the word slowly.

"She didn't give me a date," Michael huffed. "Said she'd text when she was on her way. That could be tomorrow or next year."

The server returned with their coffee, bringing the beginnings of their conversation to a halt until she walked away to serve another table.

"And your type A personality is twitching because you can't plug the date and time into a calendar."

Michael could feel his brows knit together as he looked at his friend. "Dude, you were a high school principal for a lot of years in Brooklyn and you're the new district superintendent here. How can you not see the benefit of keeping to a schedule?"

Adam sipped his coffee and smiled at Michael as if Michael's ignorance baffled him. "My work life is very regimented, which is why I prefer my personal life to be a lot more relaxed. You are an uptight asshole every minute of your day, whether the uniform is on or off. Maybe this woman—"

"Vanessa," Michael interrupted. "Her name is Vanessa." Both his friends looked at each other, something silent passing between the two of them before they each returned their gaze to Michael.

"Vanessa," Adam continued. "Maybe Vanessa can't be managed on your timetable like everyone else in your life. Maybe she has to take some time to get herself together. I'm sure having to handle a situation involving her ex, especially since you said it's only been a couple of years since her divorce, isn't easy."

As much as Michael hated it, he had to admit Adam was right. Maybe this was a difficult thing for Vanessa to deal with.

"How long did it take you to get over your divorce, Adam?"

He shook his head and blew out a long whistle. "I'm not even ashamed to admit it: five years." Adam took another sip of his coffee before he continued. "And Jackie and I were only married a few years. When you looked into her, you said Vanessa was married to this dirtbag for a while, right?"

"Twenty years," Michael replied.

"Damn," Derrick responded. "That's a long-ass time to be married to a jerk."

"Exactly," Adam continued. "Ending a marriage, even under amicable circumstances, can change a person. I had to learn to be single again. And I'm not talking about seeing anyone. Just thinking of myself in the singular and not part of a unit, it took a long time to deprogram. After twenty years, I don't even want to imagine what all she's had to unpack."

Adam was the only one of the three of them who'd walked down the aisle. With no experience in the matter, Michael hadn't even thought about it in those terms until his friend had mentioned it.

"She was reluctant to get involved," Michael said. "Her first response was actually no. Considering she filed for divorce and won most of the marital assets, I would've thought moving on would be easier."

Adam shook his head. "Just from everything you've told us about this Karl person, walking away from someone like him can't be easy. Doesn't matter how many zeros were in her settlement."

Thoughts filtered across his mind of the dark-haired beauty who, even during a moment of her clumsiness, felt way too good in his arms. Except for her heel getting caught on a paving stone, she was the epitome of poise, grace, and control. After talking to Adam, Michael wondered if there was more to her than the gorgeous veneer she'd allowed him to witness for the few moments they'd shared talking in front of her house and in that coffee shop.

"Since you're the one with all the divorce wisdom, how should I proceed where Vanessa's concerned?"

"Slowly," Adam advised. "Take your cues from her."

Michael blew a breath until his cheeks expanded. "I'm up against a deadline, Adam. I can't let this go on too long."

"Give her until next weekend," Adam responded. "Just don't be so uptight about it. You know how to play it cool. Otherwise, D and I would've gotten rid of you a long time ago."

"Truer words, my G." Derrick lifted his cup to Adam's, and they clinked them in solidarity.

"Why the fuck have I remained friends with you two all this time?"

Derrick chuckled. "Because your life would be boring as hell without us."

"True," Adam joined in. "And you wouldn't've gotten laid half as much as you did in college if we hadn't spent all our teenage years teaching your pitiful ass the ropes so you'd have a clue how to act on campus. Until we took you under our wing, you had no game whatsoever."

Michael shook his head. He couldn't argue, so he didn't even try. Fortunately, their server had perfect timing as she arrived with their platters.

All right, Vanessa. I'll fall back until next weekend, but if I don't hear from you then, it's on.

Chapter 5

"HAVE YOU TOLD THAT MAN WHEN YOU'RE COMING down yet?"

Vanessa shook her head as she listened to Janae's very direct question.

"Good morning to you too, Janae."

Her friend sucked her teeth, too eager for an answer to care about good manners. "Stop stalling. What's going on?"

"If you must know, I plan to come down this weekend. The Monroe Hills Inn apparently doesn't have any vacancy until then."

"I'm still mad you'd insult me by coming to my town and booking a hotel."

"Ahh, as far as I know, don't you still have that cute cat you're always sending me pictures of? I'm still allergic to pet dander, which means both your place and Cree's are out of the question. We discussed this already."

"We did. But we might be able to work around that." Janae's voice perked up. "Just how allergic are we talking?"

"Janae," Vanessa reprimanded.

"What? Allergy symptoms can run from mild itchy eyes to anaphylaxis. Depending on how severe your symptoms are, you could pop a Zyrtec or Benadryl and you'd be fine."

"I can't believe they let you actually treat people in that hospital of yours," Vanessa responded. "You need your nursing license revoked."

Janae laughed, the sound so infectious it sparked laughter in Vanessa too. That's what she loved about her friends. No matter her mood, they always gave her good reasons to laugh.

"Fine," Janae began once she caught her breath from laughing. "Be that way and stay at the inn. It's only about fifteen minutes from my development and about twenty from Cree's house in the countryside. We can be there if you need us to be your backup."

Vanessa smiled, basking in the warmth of her friend's statement. This wasn't just about Janae and Cree being nosy. Of course she knew they wanted the details of everything that would transpire once she arrived in Monroe Hills. More than that, however, these two wanted to make sure she was all right. You couldn't buy that kind of support, in Vanessa's experience.

"I'm sure I'll be fine." She took a moment to reassure Janae and herself. This situation had the potential to blow up in her face in more ways than one. Facing your abuser was never an easy thing. Yet she knew if she ever wanted true freedom from his tyranny, and not just survival, this was the next step in taking back her life.

"I'm glad you and Cree will be close if I need to reach out, though. So, tell me about your sheriff. You called him by his first name when I mentioned him. Do you know him personally?"

"Chile," Janae began. "This is Monroe Hills. Everyone knows everyone. Michael, Cree, and I all grew up together in Monroe Hills. He left for college and became a police detective in Philadelphia. He was out there for a while and came back to stay when his parents died ten years ago. His sister was still a teenager, and he didn't want to uproot her after suffering such a loss. He transferred to the sheriff's department as a deputy and then was appointed sheriff when his predecessor went into early retirement."

Michael had given Vanessa a generic rundown of the same events when they'd met.

At least he was being truthful. *That's a good sign, right?*

"You know way too much about that man's business. I most definitely won't be in town long enough for the townsfolk to get to know me so intimately."

Janae chuckled. "Privacy can be a fleeting thing out here. Even still, knowing your neighbors and building community is a huge part of living in Monroe Hills. We're all here for each other."

Vanessa couldn't imagine what it would be like to live like that. Living in New Jersey, she knew her neighbors. Well, she knew the names of the people who lived in closest proximity to her large estate. She was unaware of anything regarding their personal lives beyond the orchestrated glimpses they'd allowed her, however.

That kind of structured social distance was great for keeping things hidden, like the abject misery you lived in when your husband's emotional torture was at its height and his cheating was an open secret in your marriage. What it wasn't great for were the moments when you desperately needed someone to comfort you.

"Well, I'll be there for a night, no more than two. I'm gonna text Michael as soon as I get off with you. He needs to set up this little meeting so I can be in and out with my grandmother's ring."

"Humph." Janae's discontent was clear in the rough tone of her voice. "I'm glad you're getting your grandma's ring back. Still, I'd be lying if I said it didn't disappoint me you weren't staying long enough for Cree and me to enjoy your company. I get it, though. You gotta handle your business."

If she'd handled her business a long time ago, her marriage would've lasted at least fifteen years less than it had. She was a slow starter, apparently.

"I just want this over. Karl needs to be a memory after this. It's my time."

"And like Auntie Maxine, you're reclaiming it. Girl, I would pay money to see Karl's face when you bust his con wide open."

Vanessa chuckled because she wasn't above the pettiness. Aside from getting her grandmother's ring back, that moment was the most tempting part of all of this.

"All right, girl, let me go. Gotta call a sheriff about a meeting."

Michael peered down at his phone again. It had been days since he'd heard from Vanessa. He was getting frustrated, to say the least. Yet every time he picked up the phone with the thought to text or call her, he remembered what Adam had said about his divorce. Maybe this was taking more of a toll on her than he'd accounted for when he'd hatched this plan. With the weekend fast approaching, however, he was hard-pressed to allow any more time to pass by.

He tossed the phone on the coffee table and flopped down on his couch. He could pretend all he wanted that his angst where Vanessa was concerned was all about his sister, yet deep down he knew that was bullshit. Yeah, Cindy's situation was definitely at the forefront of his thoughts. There was more to it, though.

He wasn't quite sure what that "more" was; he merely understood that there was something about Vanessa that made him think about things he hadn't given significant thought to in a long while. Things like dating, having a partner, having sex.

He huffed as he stretched out on his couch and tried to remember the last time he'd taken a trip to Philly to hook up. In a town as small as Monroe Hills, there was no way he could have a casual situation with anyone. It would be all over town, and before he knew it, the locals would have him married off.

He wasn't looking for any of that. His sister still needed him and being available to her was still his priority. Yet even he needed a little release that didn't come from his own hand.

And Vanessa is reminding you of that because?

"Because she's gorgeous and sexy as fuck."

There was no denying it, so he wouldn't even try. Full, dark, kissable lips and a body that felt so good pressed against him, he had to force himself to step away from her. Thick thighs and plump backside, pretty much his walking wet dream. Except she was the ex-wife of his sister's fiancé. And ultimately coming to town to presumably break his sister's heart. There was no way they could be anything after her conversation with Cindy.

He knew that, only his treacherous body didn't seem to give a damn, if the hard-on he'd woken up with after dreaming about stripping Vanessa naked and sexing her all night long was any indication.

He hadn't been that excited the last time he'd had sex with an actual woman instead of the figment of his imagination in his head. In spite of that, the vivid sensory details had set his blood and body on fire, even in sleep. When he awoke, before he could even open his eyes, his fist circled around his cock and he stroked himself to a quick and explosive release.

It wasn't until after the bliss of orgasm had dissipated and he was cleaning himself up that he realized the only image dancing around in his mind this time, or the previous time in the shower, was Vanessa Jared in all her glorious flesh on replay.

"Fuck me."

You wish.

He certainly did. His desire for her notwithstanding, he knew none of his imaginings would ever be more than just a dream. He was responsible for saving his sister. And getting involved with Vanessa would only complicate this situation.

He was about to repeat the same edict to himself again when the sound of his phone ringing made him sit up. Vanessa's name flashed across the screen, making his mouth go dry. He wasn't shy and rarely found talking to people difficult. Yet suddenly he felt like sixteen-year-old Michael trying to ask Janet MacGregor to junior prom. His palms sweating, his throat dry, and his heart pounding.

He shook his head, trying to snap himself out of it, and accepted the call before it could go to voice mail.

"Hello." He swallowed after managing to get his voice to sound normal over the phone.

"Hi, Michael. This is Vanessa Jared."

"I know who you are, Vanessa." How could he not? Especially when he'd been lusting after her for the better part of the day. "How can I help you?"

"I'm planning to arrive in Monroe Hills Saturday evening."

"That's perfect. My sister left today on a quick business trip. She'll be back on Friday. So, depending on what time you get here, we can either have the talk Saturday night or Sunday morning."

She was quiet for a moment, and he worried their call had disconnected. "Vanessa, you still there?"

"Yes," she responded quickly. "That's fine. I'm booked at the inn on Main Street, so if you text me the location of where and when you'd like to meet, I'll be there, ready to tell your sister everything I can about Karl."

She took in an audible breath before she continued. "Michael?"

The inquisitive sound of his name colored by the richness of her voice was doing little to keep his overactive imagination in check.

You really need to get laid if the sound of a woman speaking your name turns you on.

"Hmm" was the only reply he could come up with, since he was still trying to keep the lust out of his voice.

"Are you certain you really want me to do this? I know in theory this may seem like the path you want to take. On the other hand, you have to know me showing up proving Karl is a liar will be hurtful to your sister."

Michael shook his head, then closed his eyes and pinched the bridge of his nose. How was it that this stranger was focused more on his sister's well-being than he was? Determined to get control of his thoughts, he cleared his mind and focused.

"What choice do I have, Vanessa? I know this is gonna hurt her. I can't simply sit back and just let her ruin her life without telling her the truth, though. She may still decide to marry this man. But if she does, at least she has all the info to make an informed decision."

"Have you considered what happens if she hears what I have to say and still goes ahead with the marriage? Do you really want to put yourself in a position where she sees you as an antagonist? Are you certain she'll choose you over Karl if we do this?"

This woman's questions were rubbing his nerves raw. It wasn't so much that she was annoying him as she was shining a light on his fears. He'd asked himself these questions and came back with the same answers time and time again. Karl had to be stopped.

"I know you're just trying to get me to weigh all the options. Trust me, ever since I discovered you were alive, I've considered all the angles. I know I could lose my sister over this. I know I'll be hurting her. Honestly, even knowing that, I'd still make the same decision. Otherwise, he'll destroy her if I stand back and do nothing."

She exhaled deeply, as if she'd just relieved a substantial burden from her shoulders. Too bad the boulder sitting on *his* shoulders hadn't budged even a centimeter.

"If you're certain," she continued, "then I'll be there Saturday evening as planned. I just hope you don't end up hating me after you've used me as a tool to slice your sister's heart open."

He flinched from the sting of that blow. He could try to deny it all he wanted to, except Vanessa was right. He was using her as a blunt instrument to knock some sense into Cindy. Regret sank into his consciousness for all of a moment before he successfully set up a wall to block it out. The greater good, that's all he could focus on. Otherwise, he'd never be able to drag either of these women through this ill-advised plan of his.

"I'll see you Saturday, Vanessa."

The decisive click of the call disconnecting sent a shiver of cold down his spine. Destroying one woman and opening up an old wound for another, that's where he was right now. It wasn't a place he'd have chosen to be. Except duty always came first. Even when that duty sucked huge donkey balls.

Chapter 6

VANESSA STOOD IN HER FOYER LOOKING AT THE DAUNT-
ing image of her packed weekender bag sitting in front of the door.
She was really doing this.

She'd agreed to do this. Yet somehow she kept thinking that life
would find a way to intervene and Michael would come across the
good sense to call this entire thing off. Except here she was, standing in front of her door, ready to get in her car and drive more than
an hour down I-80 West to get to Monroe Hills.

Instead of looking at the ominous bag, she turned around to
make sure she had everything she needed. She shook her keys in
one hand and shoved the other in her back pocket to make sure
her phone was there. She'd packed a charger, and even if it had
somehow crawled out of her bag, she kept an extra one in the car.

"You're only going to be there overnight, Vanessa. Stop stalling
and get in the car."

She'd spent all day at the salon getting her hair, nails, and
makeup done. She may be going to Mayberry, but damn if she was
going to let her ex see her looking anything other than spectacular.

She wanted nothing to do with Karl. But she would make sure
he'd take one look at her and know she'd survived his worst. When

they were together, she'd dressed in dowdy clothes that made her look older and did nothing to accentuate her natural curves. Fortunately, one of the perks of having more disposable cash than she'd ever need was the ability to hire a personal stylist. The thing Karl valued most was his money, and knowing she was spending it to look like this would drive him crazy.

I guess Karl isn't the only one who knows how to play mind games.

With body-con dresses, fitted slacks, V-neck tops, and too many pairs of slinky designer shoes to count, her stylist had made her look twenty years younger. With her sleek shoulder-length haircut and the bold color makeup palettes she'd learned to carefully apply, she presented the image of confidence she'd always wanted.

Today she wore dark-wash skinny jeans that showed all her hips and backside, a fitted crop-top turtleneck, and a camisole under it, since she wasn't quite bold enough to expose her soft, flat-ish stomach. On her feet were over-the-knee leather boots that made her thick thighs look amazing, and when she took one last glance in the hall mirror, she knew she looked more than good.

Satisfied that she had no more excuses not to get in her car, she grabbed her bag and made her way to the brand-new silver Jaguar sitting in her circular driveway.

She pressed her key fob to start the ignition, slid into the driver's seat, fastened her seatbelt, and gripped the steering wheel. "All right, Vanessa. It's showtime."

One deep breath in and out and she put her foot on the brake and shifted the car into gear. As the car began to slowly crawl forward, she still questioned her sanity for doing this. This wasn't her fight. She knew this. Yet if she could stop Karl from crushing someone else's spirit, as a survivor of his particular brand of mayhem, she had to do this.

Resolute in her decision, no matter how messy it seemed, she continued on her journey, using the soothing sounds of old-school

R&B to calm her nerves and empty her mind. She was four miles from the Delaware Water Gap Toll Bridge when the evening sky with its scant remnants of light turned to a murky gray-black. She'd only made it a few hundred feet more before the heavens poured.

"Dammit." She turned the music down and focused more on the dark road while visibility eluded her. "I don't know who thought it was a good idea to build curvy, mountainous roads with damn near no lights and guardrails. Who decided safety was a luxury feature?"

The rain poured down so hard, motorists turned on their hazard lights to help prevent collision. The more the rain fell, the slower traffic crawled until she was sitting in bumper-to-bumper traffic in the middle of the bridge during what looked like a monsoon.

She pressed the speaker button on her steering wheel and directed Siri to dial Michael Park. While she waited for the call to connect, she thought back to all her pre-trip prep. She'd looked at the forecast before she left, and it called for light rain close to midnight. Since she'd planned to arrive somewhere between eight and nine, she should've been fine. The joke was obviously on her because this definitely was not fine.

A glance at the dashboard monitor revealed an ominous spinning wheel that made the hair on the back of her neck stand and her heart pound with anticipation. She grabbed her phone from the cupholder and looked to see not a single bar on her cellphone.

"You've got to be kidding me. Have I been out of cell range since I got on I-80? This is like a horror film setup."

No cell service, stuck in the middle of a highway that looked to be slowly leaning toward flooding conditions, she was either the unluckiest person in the world or Fate was having a big laugh at her expense.

"Maybe this is a sign I'm not supposed to go to Mayberry. I know I'm only two exits away, but perhaps the universe is telling me to take my ass home and wash my hands of this whole matter."

She'd nearly resolved to do just that when she saw the cars in front of her inch ahead. She took her foot off the brake and waited for her car to roll forward, but her engine made coughing sounds and the car refused to move.

"No, no, no! As much as I paid for you, you'd better not stall on me on this damn bridge." Her reprimand earned her a loud wheezing sound that panicked more than angered her. "Okay baby, mama's sorry she yelled at you." She stroked the dashboard nicely. "Please, we're almost there, just two short exits and we'll be at the inn. Please, be a good girl and do it for me." She put the car in park and prayed as she turned the ignition off and tried to start it again. When she pushed the start/stop button again, the car gasped and wheezed, but thankfully the engine turned over and the car crawled forward.

Between the weather and the drag on her accelerator, what should've been a five-minute drive took twenty. By the time she pulled into a parking spot in the back of the inn, her nerves were shot, and she was desperately worried about what the rain was gonna do to her fresh silk press.

She opened her glove compartment to find a small handheld umbrella and a rain bonnet. "Thank goodness, at least one thing has gone right tonight."

She adjusted her rearview mirror to make sure the rain bonnet protected every strand of her freshly straightened hair. Satisfied that Mother Nature wouldn't be able to ruin her look, she grabbed the umbrella.

With her hair tied up and her thumb on the automatic release button of the umbrella, she stepped out of the car and made a mad dash for her trunk. With her weekender secured to her shoulder and her Jaguar's security system engaged, she walked as quickly as her cute stiletto boots would allow and made her way into the reception area of the Main Street Inn.

Vanessa stood in the open foyer shaking off the excess water sliding down her face, arms, and hands. Even though she'd had an umbrella, with the lack of tall buildings to block some of the water, the rain came hard and heavy from all directions, including up from the ground.

Satisfied that she'd gotten as dry as she could get without an absorbent towel, she took a moment to look around. Being an inn in the Pocono mountains, she'd expected something rustic. And to some degree, it was. The carpeting was a mosaic of dark reds, beige, and different shades of brown. An enormous fireplace off to the right was made of bloodred exposed brick and the lounge chairs arranged around it were upholstered with deep red and brown fabric.

That area is definitely made for relaxing in the mountains.

With a slight shift of her vision to the right, she saw a large reception counter painted in a soft eggshell with a beautiful dark wood trim at the top of the counter. And even though the two areas were so starkly different, they seemed to form a happy balance of the old and the new in one space.

She gave the room one last glance, looking for signs of life anywhere her eyes could reach. When she didn't see anyone else after a few more seconds passed, she headed toward the front desk.

"Well, this definitely isn't the Ritz-Carlton," she mumbled. "No way I'd make it an inch inside this place without waitstaff falling over themselves to accommodate me."

She waited a second more until her impatient nature rose and she looked around until she noticed a bell on the counter.

"How quaint," she huffed, before tapping the bell a few times in rapid succession. She raised her hand to tap it again, but fought the impulse to follow the action through. Vanessa was never that type of rich woman who thought the world should cater to her. Part of her rehabilitation after ending her marriage was simply to be more assertive. Lately, however, she was finding it hard to see the clear line between asserting control over her life and not being a jackass.

As she took a breath, an older woman with silver hair and deep ebony skin ambled to the counter and greeted her with a wide smile.

"Oh, look at you, dear." The woman's warm voice broke through the perma-chill attempting to settle into her bones. "You're soaked."

"Yes," Vanessa answered, her voice softer than she'd intended. "The weather is terrible out there. I just want to get upstairs into my room and get out of these wet clothes."

The woman nodded slowly with compassion and what looked like sympathy shading her brown eyes.

"I'm Hannah," the kind woman stated. "And I wish I could help, but we're full up. And since the storm hit out of nowhere, I'm sure every available room will be packed with travelers needing a place to rest for the night. When storms come like this, driving in these mountains is impossible."

"No worries." Vanessa smiled. "I made a reservation earlier in the week. I registered under the name V. Jared."

The innkeeper pulled out a long ledger book that gave Vanessa flashbacks to her grandmother's bookkeeping days for the family business. Vanessa was no spring chicken, but even in her accounting classes way back in the day, these types of books were obsolete.

The older woman turned a few pages until she'd finally found the one she was looking for and scanned each line with her pointer finger.

"Jared, Jared . . . ah, here you go. Reservation made on Monday of this week. Reservation canceled two hours ago today."

Vanessa held up her finger. "Did you say canceled? There has to be some mistake."

The innkeeper shook her head. "Oh, no, dear," she responded quickly. "We have a very firm cancellation policy. The booking service we use sends an automatic confirmation via email. If we don't receive a response, we call two hours before check-in to make sure you're still coming. If you don't answer, we have the right to cancel your booking. Usually this wouldn't be an issue. Unfortunately, when the weather got bad, we got a slew of unexpected check-ins and all our rooms filled up. Including yours, I'm afraid."

Vanessa leaned forward, her brows stitching together in confusion. "Come again?"

The warm smile on the woman's face didn't soften the blow the second time around. "I'm afraid your reservation has been canceled and we're booked full."

"You have to be able to make an exception," Vanessa implored, and she could see the spark of regret flickering in the woman's eyes. "I was trapped on the highway in the middle of a monsoon with no cellular service. How could I respond?"

"That sounds right terrible, dear. Still, I'm afraid there's nothing I can do."

Vanessa felt annoyance pecking at her temple. She pressed a finger there to stop the throbbing ache from growing into a splitting headache. She opened her mouth to allow her displeasure to spill out into the air, but when she met the remorseful smile of the aging caretaker, Vanessa couldn't bring herself to voice her frustration.

"Do you know if there are any other hotels or inns nearby? Maybe one of them has a room."

"No, dear." She shook her head as she closed her ledger. "We're the only hotel around for twenty miles. And between this storm and the Main Street festival starting in a couple of days, everyone in the area is booked solid."

Just my damn luck to end up in Mayberry when there's literally no room at the inn.

"Can I call anyone for you?"

Vanessa shook her head and pulled her phone out of her back pocket, watching cell service return one bar at a time. "No," Vanessa sighed. "I'll make a call and hopefully can figure something out."

"Okay." The innkeeper smiled. "There's a desk across the foyer that you can sit down at to make your call. There's a hot-water dispenser and some herbal tea bags there too. Make yourself a cup and warm up while you wait. I could bring you in some warm oatmeal raisin cookies I was taking out of the oven when you rang the bell. Would you like that?"

Did she want a cookie? Could that damn cookie get her a hot shower and a warm bed? Of course not. Yet when she met kind, remorseful eyes, the part of her that was raised to respect her elders tamped down her aggravation. She took a deep breath to let some of the tension bleed out of her body before she nodded.

"Yes, please. I'd like that, Hannah."

The woman's smile brightened, and she shuffled off the way she came. All Vanessa could do was shake her head as a pitiful bubble of laughter slipped through her lips. She'd known a handsome man in a tight sweater showing up on her doorstep was a bad omen.

She made her way across the foyer and settled at the small desk Hannah had directed her to. She pulled out her phone, thankful she had four bars but still drawing a blank on who she should call. Cree went out of town on an unexpected business trip for the weekend, and Janae was probably already at work.

Not that either of them would make a suitable candidate. They both had fur babies, and Vanessa's allergies wouldn't let her be great in a house where pets lived.

"What the hell am I gonna do?"

She threw up her hands, letting them drop immediately to her thighs. With no alternatives, she resigned herself to do the only thing she could do and dialed the sheriff's number.

She sat back in preparation to wait for the ring, except halfway through the first one, the call connected.

"Vanessa?"

His voice was deep and rich, and the way it wrapped around her name was sinful. She shook her head. This wasn't what she was here for. And considering her current predicament, she needed to keep her thoughts straight. No matter how attractive that man was, she needed to stay focused on the task and not him.

"Vanessa, you there?"

She cleared her throat, trying her best to make sure her serious voice was firmly in place.

"Hello, Michael. I just arrived at the Main Street Inn."

"Oh, that's great. I was afraid you got caught in all this weather."

"Well, about that," she continued. "I did. My car nearly flooded. Gratefully, I made it here anyway. Although, it's looking like I'm going to have to turn right back around and go home."

"Why's that?"

"Well, through some clerical error." Yeah, that's what she was going with. There was no way she'd admit she'd been so distracted she'd forgotten to confirm her stay before she got on the road. "My room was canceled and rebooked."

She heard what sounded like a quiet snicker come through the phone, and the annoyance she was already struggling with fought its way back to the surface.

"Are you laughing at me?"

"You ignored the confirmation email and call, didn't you?"

God, apparently that part about people in small towns knowing each other's business was true.

"The email went to spam, and the call came through when I was stuck on the highway with no bars. I knew nothing about either until I arrived."

"Well, in weather like this and with the festival happening, there won't be any openings."

"So I've been told," she grumbled. "Look, I just called to let you know I arrived safe. Regrettably, with nowhere to sleep tonight, I might as well go back home. Perhaps we can reschedule another weekend."

"No." His voice was sharp. "The weather won't let up until tomorrow morning. Driving tonight would be too dangerous."

Now it was her turn to laugh. The sincerity in his voice was so convincing, she almost bought into it.

"Don't worry, Michael." Her amusement tinged the edges of her voice. "You don't have to pretend to be so concerned with my safety. I'll come back. Just at a more convenient time."

He blew out a long breath before he spoke again. "Vanessa, I'm the sheriff of this town. I care about the welfare of every person, both residents and visitors. Besides, if something happened to you knowing I'm responsible for you coming all this way, I'd never be able to live with myself."

There was no pretense in his voice. It was deep and steady with a thread of concern weaving through it that slipped through the phone line and spread like warm butter through her body.

"I appreciate you saying that. Thanks for your concern. Unfortunately, it doesn't do much for my predicament."

"I think I might have a solution. Give me a few minutes to finish up at my office and I'll be right over."

Before she could respond, the line clicked, and the phone disconnected.

"What the hell happened to goodbye as a conversation ender?"

She didn't have a chance to answer her own question. Hannah arrived carrying a plate filled with what looked like the most tempting cookies she had ever seen. When Hannah set them down on the desk and the sweet and spicy smell of cinnamon, sugar, oats, and butter came together, any thought she had of refusing went away.

"These smell divine. I couldn't possibly eat all of them, though. One will do."

Hannah chuckled and the skin around her eyes crinkled as her smile spread full across her face.

"Darling, one is never enough. You'll see." The older woman walked away, leaving her with the cookies. Figuring something good should come out of this wasted trip, she shrugged and picked one up.

Warm and soft, just as she liked, the treat nearly melted in her mouth.

"Mmm," she moaned as her eyes closed. She lost herself in the taste as pleasure danced over her taste buds. Realizing Hannah's pronouncement was correct, Vanessa reached for another one before she could finish chewing the last bite of the first. She recklessly bit off half of the second cookie when she looked up to find Michael standing next to her with a wide grin on his face.

"I see Hannah treated you to her cookies. They're famous around these parts."

Her eyes widened, embarrassed by the bulging cheek full of cookie she was currently chewing on. There was no way to disguise her gluttonous behavior, so she simply closed her eyes and pretended Michael wasn't there until she swallowed the last bite.

"How did you get here so fast? I thought you had to finish up at your office?"

"My office is two doors down. That's the beauty of being in a small town in the mountains at night. Most of the residents are home and it's pretty quiet. I was actually on my way home just before you called."

She stood up, not liking how tempting his tall frame was from her current vantage point. Perhaps standing would give her the appearance that she wasn't completely rocked by how sexy this man looked.

He was in a beige and brown sheriff's uniform. The drab colors alone should've dulled some of his appeal. Somehow, even in boring neutrals he still made her want to run her hands across his muscles again, just like she had when she'd tripped and ended up in his arms.

"So, you said you had a solution to my problem. What is it?"

"It's simple. You can come stay with me."

Chapter 7

⌒

GOD, SHE WAS SEXY. EATING COOKIES HAD NEVER SEEMED erotic to him. The way her face went slack with pleasure and her deep moan filled the air, it was the purest form of erotic viewing material he'd come across. All he could think about was what other pleasures would make her moan that way for him.

And even now, with her mouth slightly opened as the apparent shock of his suggestion washed over her, all he wanted to do was run his thumb across that full bottom lip.

Not what you're here for, Michael.

"Absolutely not." The sharp tone of her voice snatched him out of his not-so-proper thoughts as he raised his eyes to meet hers.

"Why not?"

"Uh, I don't know you from a hole in the wall. Why the hell would I go to your house?"

"Because it's either my house with a spare room and a comfortable bed or the high-back chair behind you."

She narrowed her eyes into slits while the cutest pout settled on her lips. If he didn't stop looking at her like she was as tasty as he knew those cookies were, he'd probably never convince her to accept his offer.

"Listen, if you're worried about your safety, I'm the sheriff. There's no safer place than in my home. And you can ask Hannah if I'm mannerly enough to bring a respectable woman home as a guest."

"Ask Hannah?" She parroted his words with a sharp, raised eyebrow. "I don't know her either. For all I know, besides making excellent oatmeal raisin cookies, she could be part of your secret abduction ring here in Mayberry."

She squinted again. This time her lids were even tinier slits and her puckered lips tempted him to lean in even more. He was certain he could resist the urge, no matter how much it permeated his being.

Yet when she let her gaze slide down the length of his body and he could feel the resulting heat trail quickly after it, he groaned. He closed his eyes and gave himself a quick shake, hoping she'd attribute it to his frustration with the situation and not recognize the desire her simple gestures were stoking in him.

He steadied himself before opening his eyes again and meeting the fire burning in her stare. He couldn't tell if it was anger, but something about the way she looked at him made him think he might just see a flicker of appreciation there.

"Well, it's the only solution I have to help your situation. Other than letting you spend a night in one of my cells at the office."

She cut sharp eyes at him and folded her arms. "Not even funny."

He shrugged. Aside from her sleeping in her car, those were the only accommodations he had to offer her other than his home.

"It's all I got since I can't prove I'm not a kidnapper in any acceptable way."

She dropped her hands, pulling her phone from her back pocket. "No worries, I have my ways. Give me a sec."

"What?" he queried. "You have a contact in the FBI?"

She shook her head. "No, I've got something even better. A sista circle."

It was his turn to lift a brow. He had no idea what she meant, but if it would hurry this process along, he'd go along.

She tapped on the screen and put the call on speaker. It rang several times. Just before it went to voice mail, the call connected.

"Hey girl, what's up? You in Monroe Hills yet?"

"Janae, thank goodness I caught you."

"What's going on, Vanessa? Is everything okay?"

"Not really. I'm here. Regrettably, they canceled my reservation at the inn."

Michael heard a familiar snicker fill the air.

"You failed to confirm, didn't you?"

He couldn't help but smile. If the Janae she was talking to was the one who lived in his town, she would know, like any other resident, the folly of not responding to that confirmation email or call.

"Listen, that's not the point," Vanessa continued. "I'm out of a room, and I can't find anywhere else to stay. The only room available is at the sheriff's house."

"Lucky bitch."

"Janae!"

"What?" Janae continued. "As fine as that man is, you could do worse. Hopefully, the storm knocks the electricity out while you're there and the two of you have to snuggle together to generate body heat. As dry as your love life is, you could use all the help you can get."

"Janae! You're on speaker!"

Spurred on by the visible embarrassment sparking in her eyes, the smile on Michael's face spread wider. Not that he wanted Vanessa to feel bad, yet finding out her love life was just as sad as his fanned a special kind of glee in his soul.

"Well, you should've known better than to put me on speaker without telling me. You know my mouth."

He certainly did, and even though he couldn't understand why it would matter, he was more than a little grateful she'd spilled the beans.

"Hi, Janae." Michael leaned closer to the phone Vanessa was holding in the air. "How's it going over there at the hospital?"

"Heyyyyy, Sheriff," she sang in her usual spirited greeting she'd been giving him since they were kids in high school. Exchanging his given name for his title, it was still filled with friendship and a tad bit of mischief.

"You taking my girl in for the night?"

"I'm offering to, but she's afraid I'm some sort of ax murderer hiding behind a badge here in . . ." He paused purposefully as he titled his head toward Vanessa, "Mayberry. Isn't that right, Vanessa?"

"I done told you about disrespecting the name of my town, Vanessa."

"Janae," Vanessa moaned. Her voice was full of exasperation, and Michael was delightfully entertained by her predicament. "All I called to find out was if Michael could be trusted and if I should take the room. I can do without the rest of this."

"Whatever," Janae responded with a slight note of annoyance coloring her tone. "You couldn't be in better hands. And unless you want to do an allergen challenge by being exposed to pet dander at my house or Cree's, I'd suggest you take him up on his offer."

Michael's shoulders shook with silent laughter until he heard Janae call his name. "And Michael," she continued, "take care of my girl. Don't make me come for you. 'Cause you know I don't care nothing about that badge you wear. You mess with her and it's me and you."

He resumed his laughter. She absolutely didn't. From the mayor to the Sunday school teacher, little old Ms. Johnson, if Janae had a bone to pick with you, she didn't give a damn about your title or position in life.

"I gotcha, Janae. Scout's honor, I promise to keep her safe."

"All right," she responded. "That's good enough for me. Listen, my break is almost over. You two get home out of this rain. I don't want you ending up in my ER trying to navigate mountain roads in all this mess."

"Thanks, girl," Vanessa added before ending the call and returning her gaze to him.

"So, you believe me now?"

She huffed before nodding. "Fine, you're safe. If the offer still stands, I'd be grateful for the room at your place."

He smiled, then leaned down to grab the weekender bag sitting on the floor near the desk. "Follow me, m'lady. Your chariot awaits."

"I could've driven my own car." *Only if you want to end up careening off the side of the road.* Vanessa sat rigid as the thought sped through her mind. She was a good driver; however, as she peeked out of the windshield into the thick darkness, she questioned whether she could handle the dark, windy mountain roads. She summarily decided the sheriff didn't need to know all that. Instead, she kept up her "I can handle anything" facade to keep up appearances.

"These roads are treacherous in broad daylight. Risking them when you're unfamiliar with them at night in bad weather isn't a good idea."

Common sense said he wasn't wrong. Considering the fact she was pretty certain his high beams were on, even though they were hardly cutting through the pitch surrounding them, it was just as well she'd agreed to take his car.

"Does the town have something against guardrails and streetlights? The roads don't need to be this dark and ominous."

He didn't take his eyes off the road. She could still see the slight smile lifting the side of his mouth, though. "Yeah, light and noise pollution."

She shook her head. "You lost me. How do lights and guardrails on the roads lead to pollution?"

"Although we're just a hop, skip, and a jump from metropolises like New York and New Jersey," he began, "we still lead a pretty rural community life. So, having lights on all the time would draw more people out. Visitors and residents alike would spend more time traveling through the town instead of retiring at night so we can all get some rest and start the day bright and early. As for the guardrails. People tend to drive slower when they realize the only thing standing between them and a steep drop off the side of mountain is decreased speed and careful driving."

She had to admit there was something calming about the almost silent night around them. All the noises of a city were absent. There was no music blasting from cars, no one honking impatiently behind you. There was no traffic, and the only sounds to fill the car were their voices and the crunch of tires against the dirt on the steeply inclined road they were climbing.

They pulled into what appeared to be a gated community. Where Vanessa's was cold with wrought-iron gates to keep people out, here, there was a brick security station and a simple boom gate to act as a vehicular barrier instead.

He pulled a pass card from his console, waving it briefly in front of a sensor. A green light flashed from the sensor and the arm of the boom lifted, allowing them entrance.

She could hardly see anything because of the thick night that engulfed them, but there was definitely a sense of bliss in the oblivion they seemed to ride into.

A few more windy dark roads, and he was swinging the SUV into the driveway of a large two-story colonial. He maneuvered the car into his garage and used the remote on his visor to close it before they exited the car.

He stepped out of the SUV, making quick steps to her side to open the door for her. When she stepped out, he closed the door, then grabbed her bag from the trunk.

They walked a few feet before he opened the door into what appeared to be a mudroom.

The room was a decent size, with a sink and a washer and dryer against the far wall, a folding station against one side wall, and hanging bars and an ironing station directly across from it. It was neat, with all surfaces empty, as if it were sitting ready for him to use it.

He led her through a door on the side of the room that opened onto a large kitchen with lots of windows. She imagined this room lit with sunrays in the morning despite the view of the endless darkness waiting outside.

"The fridge is fully stocked," he said abruptly. "And the flat and drink ware are in these two cabinets here." He pointed to the right. "If you want something to eat, feel free to make yourself at home."

He turned, still carrying her bag as he moved to a swing door that led to his living room. Bathed in warm burgundies, oranges, and browns, the room made you feel instantly comfortable. Where the marble and brass in her living room seemed cold in comparison, the wood in his made her want to settle in for a comfortable night.

That is not what you're here for. Don't get distracted by his interior decorating.

"The remotes for the TV are in the end-table drawer. The fireplace is fueled by propane. If you flip the switch next to it, it comes on."

She tilted her head as she observed him. "You make it sound like I'm going to be here long enough to settle in."

"With weather this unpredictable"—he shrugged—"there's no telling how long it will be before it's safe to travel. If it keeps raining like it is, we're gonna get flooding and getting out of Monroe Hills will be next to impossible. You might be here for a couple of days at least."

The dull throb in her head from earlier was returning with a vengeance. She'd never been officially diagnosed with migraines, but whenever stress got the better of her, a lingering headache would put her on her ass in a minute. She didn't have time for that right now.

Resolved to get control of the aggravation tightening the muscles at the back of her neck, she took a slow breath in and out.

"You all right?"

"Yeah," she answered. "I'm just a little frustrated. None of this was in my plans. Not having to involve myself with my ex-husband's foolishness again, and not this freak storm that seems determined to keep me trapped here."

He moved closer to her, placing a gentle hand on her bicep as he peered down at her with eyes almost as dark as kohl. "I'm really sorry about disrupting your life like this. Don't think for a moment I don't recognize the sacrifice you're making to help my sister. Whatever you need to make this more bearable, just let me know and I'll make it happen."

His touch was friendly and comforting. Something she was certain he would do for anyone who seemed to be in distress. Knowing that, even as he touched her, heat bled through the layers of her clothing, through her skin, spreading so quickly, she was caught off guard by its power.

She cleared her throat, trying to get her body to obey her instead of disintegrating into ash in front of this man she hardly knew.

"I appreciate you saying that, Michael. It's difficult. Only, I made you a promise, and unlike Karl, I keep my promises. So, I'll deal."

He nodded and turned toward the stairs by the front door and led her upstairs to the second level. It was a long hallway with one door on the right, two on the left, and one directly in the center at the end of the hall.

He headed toward the first door on the left and opened it, flipping the light switch on before ushering her in. Once she'd crossed the threshold, he placed her bag in front of the wooden chest of drawers. A quick glance around the room and she found a queen-size bed covered in white bed linens with red and gold accents. As her gaze swept the room, she saw the repeated pattern of colors throughout the room.

"The door on the right is the bathroom. There's a linen closet inside filled with clean towels, sheets, and toiletries. The other door is the closet. It's not as grand as what I'm sure you're used to. I think there should be enough room for the one bag you brought, though."

Awkward silence followed, and they both stood there, staring at each other, trying to figure out what was next. Thankfully, Michael ended her torture by speaking. "Did you have a chance to eat dinner before you got on the road?"

"Unless we're counting Hannah's cookies, nope."

A soft smile illuminated his features, drawing her gaze to his face. By anyone's standards, Michael was an attractive man. Tall, built well enough to make his sheriff's uniform look like male lingerie, and when you added in the quiet confidence in his broad shoulders and stance, it would be hard for her to imagine any circumstance where he wasn't the center of attention in a room. And somehow she'd found herself staying in his home alone with him.

Too afraid to question why any of that mattered, she offered him a smile in return.

"Well, as much of a delight as Hannah's cookies are, they won't hold you through the night. I'm gonna put a pre-prepped lasagna in the oven. If you want to unpack and get settled in, it should be ready in about an hour."

"Sounds like a plan," she answered. "The shower is calling my name. A hot meal after that would be the perfect ending to this very hectic day."

There was a spark of something odd in his eyes. Something intense that she couldn't quite make out. There and then gone in a flash, its lingering effects heating up those earlier flames she'd experienced when he touched her.

He didn't speak right away. He simply nodded. Backing away slowly as if his survival depended on his strategic retreat.

"Sounds like we've got a plan, then. See you downstairs."

He closed the door behind him with a quiet click that somehow clanged against the walls, leaving her with nothing but her thoughts to consider. The universe was playing havoc with her life right now. That was the only explanation she had for how she'd ended up in this sexy man's house as a guest.

If Janae were here, she'd tell her to have a little pleasure with her work. Tempted by the idea, Vanessa knew she could never indulge in that fantasy. There was something too intense to describe about Michael. The more time she spent in his presence, the more apparent it became. That kind of power and confidence could ruin a woman. And since she'd spent too many years living the truth of that experience, she'd be damned if she'd willingly invite that kind of chaos into her world now.

Chapter 8

MICHAEL RUSHED INTO THE KITCHEN TO CHECK ON his lasagna. He'd taken as quick and functional a shower as he could for fear too much time with thoughts of Vanessa naked under the cascade of water would drive him to do something stupid like stroke off at the thought of her again.

Determined that his body would behave, he kept the water cold and his time short so he could dress in sweats and a T-shirt before his food burned to a crisp.

With ten minutes left before the food was ready, he pulled plates and glasses from the cabinets and cutlery and napkins from the drawer. He'd just completed the place setting when he heard a quick rap against the back door before a key turned the locks.

"Dammit, not now."

A second after he voiced his displeasure in the air, his best friend Adam stepped into the kitchen.

With his locs cascading freely down his shoulder and a broad smile on his face, Adam focused on the dual place settings at the table.

"Is all this for me?"

"Unlikely," Michael responded, "since I wasn't expecting you. What are you doing here, anyway?"

Adam folded his arms and gave Michael his usual smirk. "I came over to check on your place in all this rain, making sure nothing happened to your property while you were out protecting and serving. The least you could do is offer me some of whatever it is that smells so good."

Michael groaned. It was the blessing and curse of having your best friend live three houses down from you. Since Adam's return to Monroe Hills a few weeks ago, he often checked in on Michael's property when his schedule as sheriff became a little too hectic. Regrettably, it also meant Adam could pop up at an inconvenient time, like now.

"Not a chance. The house is fine. Thanks for checking. I'll catch up with you later."

"Why?" Adam asked, with an even bigger grin showing most of his teeth. "Am I interrupting something?"

The oven timer going off gave Michael an excuse not to answer his friend. With oven mitts on, he concentrated on carefully removing the piping-hot casserole from the oven and placing it safely on top of the cooling rack in the middle of the table.

"Adam, I'm serious, I need you to—"

"Michael, that smells divine."

Vanessa walked through the kitchen door. Her hair was pulled back into a low ponytail and her gleaming skin was free of the makeup she'd worn earlier. She wore an oversized sweatshirt that left one shoulder bare with a tempting swatch of deep brown skin on display. Her shapely legs were covered in black leggings that outlined all of their thickness.

Michael was suddenly ravenous, and it had nothing to do with the tasty meal he'd prepared for the two of them.

"Oh, I'm sorry," she said as she realized Michael wasn't alone. "I didn't know you had company." She walked over to where the two men stood, and Michael pulled his gaze from her gorgeous form to see his friend looking a little too intently at her.

Not that he had the slightest right to be possessive or even a little bit upset. Something rankled in his gut to know that Adam was appreciating her the same way Michael was.

She extended her hand toward Adam to greet him. "Hi, I'm V—"

"This is Vee," Michael interrupted. He slipped a hand around her waist and pulled her against his side. She was either too shocked or angry to say anything, because the confused look on her face told him she was definitely questioning what the hell he was up to. "She's my date."

Spending a decade as a Philadelphia police detective, adapting to the unexpected was second nature to Michael. Just like before, when she'd stumbled on her stone path and landed in his arms, he was knocked off his game. The feel of her pressed against him set off all sorts of bombs in his head and his body that were so damn inappropriate he probably should consider locking himself up.

"Oh, I'm sorry," Adam chimed in as his gaze passed between Michael and Vanessa. "Damn, man. If you'd told me that, I wouldn't have barged in like this." Fortunately, she was still looking up into Michael's face, so Adam wasn't privy to the bewilderment currently settled in her eyes.

"Do you tell me about every date you have?" When Adam opened his mouth to speak, Michael cut him off with, "Beforehand?"

Accepting his friend had him caught in the crosshairs of the truth, Adam nodded his head as a sly smile crept on his face. "A-ight, man. You got me there. I'll get out of your way. Vee, it was lovely meeting you, no matter how briefly." He stepped backward and headed toward the door before Vanessa could answer. He opened it and tossed out, "Do me a favor and save me some of that lasagna for lunch tomorrow."

"Get out, Adam, and don't forget to lock my door."

His friend gave him a pointed look before smiling and closing the door behind him. It wasn't until Michael heard the last lock tumbler click into place that he realized he was still holding Vanessa against him, as if she really belonged to him.

It was certainly a fantasy his overactive imagination wanted to feed into. Eventually, though, common sense won out and he uncurled his fingers from her hip slowly as he separated his body from hers.

"I'm sorry."

She regarded him carefully, and he couldn't decipher what she was thinking. Was she mad, intrigued? He couldn't tell.

"I don't want anyone to know about you."

She lifted a brow and tilted her head. "Come again?"

He held up his hands in surrender. "I didn't mean that to sound as salacious as it did. I meant I don't want to give Karl a chance to get a story together. It's best if no one knows your true identity and your relationship to Karl."

"What about Hannah? She knows who I am."

"How did you register?"

"Under V. Jared."

"And the name on the credit card you used to hold the reservation?"

"The same."

He shook his head. "It's really not safe to use just your first initial on your financial documents. Identity theft is real and you're making it easy for scammers."

She rolled her eyes and crossed her arms before huffing out a loud breath. "Thank you for the security tip, Officer. Now can we eat?"

He chuckled as he pulled a chair out for her and went to take his seat next to her at the small kitchenette set in his breakfast nook. Still smiling as he watched her carefully unfold her napkin and gracefully place it across her lap, he couldn't help but continue to be tickled by what seemed to be the opposing parts of her personality.

She was proper and came with a distinct whiff of the pedigree her background afforded her. The underlying realness that slipped beneath her well-crafted veneer stoked his interest, making him ache to claw at her perfect, unmarred surface until he unearthed the real her.

"So, will any more unexpected guests be dropping by? Did you have to explain my presence to anyone before I arrived?"

He served her a healthy square of the lasagna and did the same for himself before answering her.

"Is that your roundabout way of asking me if I have a girlfriend?"

She shrugged. "Girlfriend, boyfriend, friend with benefits." She waved the fork in her hand casually in the air. "I'm not here to judge. I just want to make sure I don't make unnecessary enemies while I'm trying to execute this unorthodox plan of yours."

She looked down at her plate and pretended to focus on her food.

Well, well. Maybe I'm not the only one thinking inappropriate thoughts.

"I haven't dated anyone seriously since I came back home to raise my sister a decade ago."

She still wouldn't bring her eyes to meet his, but he could see by the way the muscles in the side of her neck contracted that she was definitely paying attention to what he was saying.

"That's a long time to be alone."

"I didn't say I was alone all that time. I said I hadn't dated anyone seriously. My sister was, *is* my priority. There was no time to invest in a relationship. Not to mention, when you're a small-town sheriff, your time is never your own. It's just not fair to ask someone to make that kind of sacrifice."

She lifted her eyes to meet his, staring quietly as she studied his face. Again, her expressions were always so guarded and he couldn't really tell what she was thinking. Whatever it was, he could feel the intensity of it tethering him to her from across the table.

"I don't think I've ever met a man who thinks so much about others. You're a rarity, Michael Park."

The compliment had come from nowhere, landing a metaphorically unexpected slap upside his head. He sat there for a beat, wondering what other surprises she had hidden in the depths of those brown eyes. Whatever they were, he was eager to experience every one of them. He knew that was a problem. Yet as he watched her take her first forkful of food and relax into a wide, satisfied grin, for once, he wasn't concerned with courting trouble.

His landline rang, breaking the friendly spell. He moved to the far end of the counter to answer it.

"Hello."

"Michael, thank God."

Panic rose from his gut as his sister's alarmed voice traveled across the line.

"What's wrong, Cindy?"

"I've been trying to contact you with no success. Is everything okay?"

"Yeah. We've got terrible weather right now, so both landline and cell service have been iffy. What's happening, Cindy?"

"Both Philly and Lehigh Valley airports are closed. I can't get anywhere near Monroe Hills. They canceled all flights until this system passes."

Michael could hear the frustration in her voice. It pained him that there was nothing either of them could do about it.

"It is what it is, Cin. It's supposed to pass in time for the festival, so everything will be fine."

"Not exactly," she answered. "I'm supposed to make a stop in Boston tomorrow before we head home. I can't catch my connection now. I have to meet this contact, Michael, but he doesn't have another opening for a week."

Michael glanced quickly at Vanessa and panic started settling in.

"Cindy, you can't stay gone for another week. You're needed back here. What about the festival?"

Yeah, because the festival was really what you're worried about.

"I know Michael, I'm sorry. If I can just strike a deal with this exotic flower dealer, it will be a tremendous boost for the shop. I was hoping you would fill in for me to help me out, Oppa."

The muscles in the back of his neck tensed. Cindy was a master at using the Korean endearment for "big brother" to convey tone and emotion. When she was pissed with him, the word was sharp and biting. When she was happy, it was colored with excitement and joy. And when she wanted something from him, she knew how to say it ever so sweetly to get him to give in to her whims.

"Cindy, I can't take off a week from work to watch your shop."

"Of course you can, you're the boss."

"Being the boss means being dependable, and taking a week off without notice is not responsible."

As the firstborn and only son of second-generation Korean American parents, Michael had been groomed from the cradle to be an expert on responsibility. His parents' job was to provide for him. His job was to follow the rules and do what his parents and his elders expected of him, to honor those who had come before him. As a result, Michael didn't buck authority and responsibility. He embraced it, upheld it.

He supposed that was part of why he felt so at ease in law enforcement. Rank and file meant there was a defined chain of command, a right way and a wrong way to do things. Being fifteen years younger than him, Cindy hadn't learned those lessons so well.

She huffed and if he were standing in front of her, he'd bet his badge she had her arms crossed and was pouting.

"Cindy, I can't do this."

"Fine," she answered. "Can you at least handle the festival? I'll ask Sarah if she can pull the extra hours to cover for me after that."

He ran a frustrated hand through his dark strands, trying to keep his annoyance from bleeding into his voice.

"Fine, Cindy. I'll handle it for the festival. After that, if Sarah can't do it, the shop will be closed until you return."

"Thanks, Oppa. I'll see you next week."

He hung up the phone and turned to find Vanessa staring at him.

"Do you usually do that?"

"Do what?"

"Always give your little sister what she wants when she asks for something that inconveniences you? From your end of the conversation, it certainly feels like this isn't the first time Cindy's pulled a stunt like that."

Vanessa was right. Cindy did pull stunts like this regularly, and because he was her oppa, he swooped in to save her all the time. Somehow, hearing Vanessa point that out didn't sound all that good.

"She's my sister. She was fifteen when we lost our parents. Forgive me if I've overindulged her a bit over the years."

Vanessa shrugged. "Sounds more like spoiled instead of overindulged."

Michael was beginning to get defensive. It was his nature to always protect Cindy. He was all she had. If he could help, he would. Even when the mess she'd made was of her own doing, he couldn't just stand by and do nothing. Especially when he remembered the last time he'd failed to step in and do what needed to be done. If he'd done so then, maybe they wouldn't be orphans.

"Listen," Vanessa continued, "I understand how important it is to have love and rock-solid support from a loved one. At some point, however, you're going to have to let Cindy find her own strength. That was what my grandmother did for me. She poured everything she had into me in order to make me stronger, still she never failed to let me know when I was getting it wrong. It's one of the reasons I came here to help you. I could almost hear her telling me this was the right thing to do, and I needed to dig deep and find the strength to do this."

She had this far-off look in her eyes as she talked about her grandmother, as if she were remembering a specific memory with the woman.

"You sound like you miss her a lot."

"I do." She offered a wavering smile as she returned her gaze to him. "And I always will. She always believed in me and, like you, would help me any time she could. I want so desperately to be the woman she believed I could be."

She must've decided that was enough sharing, because she picked up her fork and pointed it at him.

"Anyway, let's get back to you. So, all your scheming and Cindy's not even gonna be here?"

He shook his head as he returned to his seat at the table. "It appears that way."

"Why did you have me come out here if you knew she was away?"

"Because she was supposed to return today before the rain came in. I figured tomorrow would be perfect for us to meet."

She picked up her fork and cut into her food before speaking again. "Well, you tried." Her voice was sincere and comforting. "The plan was to get me down here to talk to Cindy and then for you to get my ring back from her. That's obviously not going to happen now. So, we might as well enjoy our meal and get a good night's sleep so you can take me to my car in the morning and I can be on the road."

"I'm really sorry, Vanessa."

She twisted her mouth into a playful smile. "Don't be. You'll just mail me my grandmother's ring as soon as you retrieve it."

He opened his mouth to speak, and she held her finger in the air. "Nope, I held up my end of the bargain. Poor planning on your part doesn't invalidate my efforts. A deal is a deal, Sheriff."

He half groaned, half laughed. She was right. A deal was a deal, and she'd held up her end, trudging out to the middle of nowhere in the middle of a monsoon. His plan might have failed, but he couldn't break his promise.

"Fine. I'll make sure you get your grandmother's ring."

She smiled at him, full and genuine, and he ached a little in the presence of its splendor. He was going to miss that smile. And even though he wouldn't let himself admit it, he was going to miss Vanessa more.

Chapter 9

VANESSA SAT QUIETLY AS MICHAEL PULLED HIS SUV INTO the inn's parking lot with a growing sense of sadness mixed with regret twisting inside her. There was a rock sitting heavy in the pit of her stomach, and she couldn't quite understand why it was there.

This scenario couldn't have worked out better for her if she'd planned it. She'd come to Monroe Hills as promised, but the universe had somehow turned things around so she wouldn't have to deal with a situation that was sure to be messier than Vanessa wanted to admit. The cherry on the top: she'd avoided dealing with Karl and she'd still get her grandmother's ring back.

This was a win-win. So it shocked her when sorrow swelled inside of her. Even more surprising was Michael's kind face. It didn't mirror the disappointment slightly growing in her chest, and that fact troubled her.

"Well, we're here." His face was blank. She didn't know him well enough to determine if this was his usual, unbothered look or a facade he put on just for her sake.

"Yeah. We are."

The awkward silence grew until she took a breath and spoke.

"I'm sorry things didn't work out the way you wanted them to, Michael. I really wish your sister the best."

She placed gentle fingers on his exposed forearms. As soon as her skin connected with his, she knew the gesture was a mistake. The prickle of smooth hair underneath her fingertips was more tempting than a glass of ice water in hell.

Realizing her mistake, she regretfully peeled her fingers away until she'd completely separated herself from him. Only, it was too late. Her pulse was already jumping with the need to know what the rest of him felt like. Was the rest of his body covered with this soft, fine layer of hair, or was it thicker and coarser where she couldn't see and where her hands shouldn't touch?

"Vanessa?"

She cleared her throat at the sound of her name and linked her fingers together to prevent them from doing something stupid like reaching for him again.

"Thank you for trying to help my sister. I appreciate it. And even if it didn't work out the way we intended, I still owe you a debt. If you ever need anything, just call me."

Oh, she needed something all right. Asking for it was off the table, however. Besides, propositioning a law enforcement officer to strip naked in a car so she could run her hands and tongue all over his body was probably illegal in this tiny town.

"My grandmother's ring will be thanks enough, Michael."

Liar!

Yeah, that was an accurate description. She was sitting in this car, lying through her teeth. And as she sat, staring at him, aching for him to make a move she was too chickenshit to initiate herself, she called herself that and worse.

When he didn't move, Vanessa decided she had to end the torture somehow. Reluctantly, she grabbed the door handle and stepped out of the car. She heard Michael doing the same. Because the need to turn around and look at him was so strong, she had to concentrate just to put one foot in front of the other. She refused to look back for fear she wouldn't find the strength to keep walking toward her car.

She pressed her key fob and her trunk opened just in time for Michael to step in front of her and place her weekender inside. She closed it, smiled at him, and then took her place in the driver's seat. She refused to look his way as she prepared to start the ignition. Leaving, getting away from whatever this thing was that made her want to fall in his arms every time she saw him, was paramount. That was all she had enough energy to do.

She stepped on the brake and pressed the ignition button, desperately waiting for the hum of her engine coming to life. That sound meant freedom, and more than anything, she needed to escape this town and this man before she did something ill-advised like forget the handsome sheriff was off limits. To her surprise—and not the disappointment that should have flooded her—the engine made a wheezing sound instead. She tried it again, and it sputtered much like it had last night on the bridge.

"Come on, baby. What's going on?"

A tap at her window pulled her attention from her console and placed it directly in the path of dark, smiling eyes.

She tightened her hands at the bottom of her steering wheel before she pressed the button to lower the window.

"I'm assuming your car doesn't normally do that, right?"

"No," she groaned. "Not before I got stuck on the bridge last night in all that rain. It sputtered a bit and was slightly difficult to handle the rest of the way to the inn."

He leaned into the window, bringing his intoxicating smell of spice, and sexiness, and him, which had become her new favorite aroma, disrupting her peace.

"Fancy cars like these don't do well with water damage. As long as you were sitting idle on the road with all that flooding, you might have damaged something in the electrical system."

Determined he was wrong, she stepped on the brake again and attempted to get the engine started. Much to her dismay, the wheezing and sputtering grew louder and more daunting, and was followed by abrupt silence.

"Hmmm, that doesn't sound good."

She cut her eyes at him, embracing the anger sliding through her veins. It was better than the lust that was clouding her judgment earlier. At least this gave her clarity through the haze of desire that engulfed her whenever she was in his presence.

"You don't say?"

He dropped his head as he chuckled a bit, then stood up, reaching for the outside door handle.

"It's obvious you're not going anywhere right now. Let me call our mechanic and see if he can get you back on the road."

She stepped out of the car when he opened the door and leaned against the driver's door.

"Let me guess, there's only one mechanic in this one-pony town, so it could take forever for him to get over here and check my car out."

He nodded, a mix of sympathy and mischief settling in the half grin on his tempting lips.

"Usually," he responded casually. "But Jeb owes me a favor, so hopefully I can get him to come straightaway."

"Of course his name would be Jeb," she mumbled.

"Sorry, didn't catch that."

She pinched the bridge of her nose, hoping the slight discomfort would siphon off some of her annoyance. The anger didn't recede, however, until she felt his strong touch on her arm. At that point, all that was left was a rising need Vanessa knew she'd better get a handle on before she did something reckless like lean into his touch.

"Vanessa, this is just a minor inconvenience. Don't let it get to you."

Trust me, Sheriff. It's not the car trouble that's getting to me right now.

She gathered her strength and blinked, trying to clear her vision so she could at least act like a levelheaded adult, even if she was feeling far from that right now.

"Fine," she huffed. "Call Jeb and see if he can work a miracle."

"Sorry, Sheriff. It doesn't look good."

Michael could feel the displeasure coming from the tense ball of anger Vanessa had twisted herself into.

"What's wrong with it, Jeb?"

"Can't be exactly sure until I get her back to the shop and run a diagnostic. Off the top of my head, all signs point to electrical damage. If it turns out to be what I think it is, we'll have another problem."

Vanessa stepped in front of him to talk to Jeb directly. "What other problem could there be?"

"I think you've got a throttle-body issue. If my guess turns out to be right, you're gonna need a new part. We don't get many luxury vehicles like this 'round here. I'd have to order it from a supplier in Philly. It might take up to a week for me to get it, install it, and get you back on the road."

"What?"

Michael could see this was about to go sideways from the lines on her furrowed brow and the terse way her lips sat pressed together. Michael nodded toward Jeb. "Take it back to your shop and call me when you've got definitive information. Ms. Jared will be with me while she waits."

Jeb, a smart man with a wife and three daughters, caught on quickly to what Michael was doing. Incurring the wrath of a beautiful woman didn't appear to be on his agenda either, so he simply reciprocated Michael's nod and backed away. He quickly jumped in his flatbed and maneuvered it so he could hoist the Jaguar onto it.

"Michael, I can't stay here a week. I have a life to get back to."

"I understand your concern, Vanessa. Your worries notwith-standing, I can tell you, that man is never wrong when it comes to cars. If his assumption is right, there's not much else you can do about this situation."

She threw her hands up in frustration. And even though he felt sorry for her predicament, it was the cutest thing he'd ever wit-nessed. He wouldn't admit that out loud, though. He was smart and valued his life; therefore he kept his amusement to himself and tried to be supportive.

"Listen, I can't stay here."

"Okay, I can drive you home, then," Michael said. "When your car is ready, I'll make sure to get it back—"

"That might work," Vanessa interrupted, tapping her chin as she seemingly considered his words. "I'm less than two hours away. If we leave now, you could be back before noon."

He shook his head as he prepared to burst her bubble of hope.

"You didn't let me finish." He held up his hands palm-side up, trying to get her to slow down. "Vanessa, I can't leave for the next four days. We have a festival that kicks off tonight and lasts until Tuesday. Soon our streets are gonna be filled with more visitors than we see any other time of year. I have to be here to make sure everyone is safe."

She groaned loudly. "Don't you have deputies?"

"Yes. Unfortunately, this is an all-hands-on-deck sort of situation. If something happens and I'm not here, the mayor will have my ass and I'll be out of a job. I can't risk that. No matter how much I want to help you."

She slumped against his car and watched as Jeb drove away with hers. He could see defeat in the slouch of her shoulders and it made him want to hold her, be the strength she needed even to get over something as mundane as car trouble.

"Fine," she sighed. "I don't want you to get fired. I'll make some calls to see if I can get a car service to come pick me up. If that doesn't work, I guess I'm stuck here until Tuesday."

He nodded and gave her a cautious smile as he opened the passenger door on his car and closed it when she was comfortably seated inside. He knew the likelihood of her finding a car service to come all the way out here on such short notice was probably slim. After the day she'd had already, he wasn't keen on sharing that particular truth just yet.

"So," he said as he sat in the driver's seat. "After the morning you've had, I'd say I have the perfect thing to lift your spirits, Vanessa."

"Yeah?"

Her voice drained of any of the sass or fight he knew her for and that made him uneasy.

"What's that?"

"Strawberry pancakes from the local diner. They are heaven on earth."

She shook her head. "No thanks, I don't need the carbs."

"Nonsense," he answered. "You have to have them. They'll make you feel ten times better."

She looked like she was prepared to argue again and get herself all worked up. Desperately needing to avoid that, he gave her what his friends called his "officer look," eyes focused on his target, arms folded over his chest, and lips pulled into a straight line. As always, it worked like a charm. Vanessa dropped whatever she was going to say. Instead, she lifted her hands as she shrugged. "What the hell, might as well indulge in sugary goodness that's gonna end up on my hips if I have to be stuck here, right?"

He looked down at her full curves, unable to help the appreciation he knew must be all over his face.

She was gorgeous.

It was Michael's job to see the details, and hers were carved into his memory. Even seated, and obviously annoyed, there was no hiding her deep curves or the resulting thickness that made him want something he shouldn't. The idea of her losing any of her lushness to fit into some stereotypical, unobtainable, bullshit standard of beauty grated on him more than it should have.

He shouldn't care. She was practically a stranger to him. It was only a very unique set of circumstances that crossed their paths. He shouldn't be invested in her in the least.

Yet, sliding his gaze back up her seated form and caressing the dips and valleys of her body, the resulting struggle made him grip his steering wheel to keep his cock from hardening.

Convinced he had himself under control, he cleared his throat, hoping his voice wouldn't betray the lust bleeding through his entire being the way his eyes had.

"You don't need to lose weight."

His voice was gravel mixed with sand. Although the sound was foreign to him, he couldn't deny those were his words. And from the intense stare he met when he finally brought his eyes to her face, she'd picked up on the undercurrent of want lacing the edge of his voice too.

"I wasn't suggesting I did," she answered, her gaze steady, never wavering even once as she openly bathed in his appreciation. "Strawberry pancakes sound exceptionally decadent. I shudder to think what my body might do if I indulged in all that sweetness regularly."

She tilted her head, lifted her brow, and locked her eyes directly on his. She wasn't hiding from him. She wasn't playing coy. She was giving him as good as she got, and it sent a shiver of need through him that both surprised and delighted him.

Even from his limited knowledge of her, nothing he'd learned made him see her as anything other than a strong and capable person. The fire he saw flashing in the depths of those deep brown eyes, however, made him wish more than once that they'd met under different circumstances. Because if she'd been any other woman on the street and not the woman who would ultimately break his sister's heart at his insistence, he'd be all over the not-so-subtle innuendo in her reply.

Chapter 10

～

VANESSA STEPPED INTO THE DINER AS MICHAEL POLITELY held the door open for her. It was quaint but festive with its bright yellow walls and white trim. There was a quiet hum of conversation as people ate and talked that felt usual and welcoming in a way those Michelin-star eateries she'd patronized while married to Karl never could.

Michael placed his hand at the small of her back as he guided her toward the far end of the diner. The gesture was polite and couldn't be misconstrued as anything other than him being the gentleman he appeared to be. Nevertheless, that bit of truth didn't stop the resulting spark of something hot and dangerous inside her.

Get a grip, girl.

It wasn't as if she hadn't been around handsome men during or after her marriage. She definitely had, and none of them made her feel needy as Michael did.

Well, it has been a while.

"A while" being a euphemism for nearly three years. As soon as she'd discovered Karl's infidelity, she'd refused what little physical attention her ex-husband paid her. And these last two years since the divorce . . . Well, rebuilding your life from the ground up took too much energy to spare on physical dalliances.

Her libido had been a nonexistent thing in all this time. Why was this man ringing all her bells now?

They arrived to a booth in the rear. He waited for her to take her seat and slid into the other side of the booth, giving her an amiable smile as they settled in.

"I promise you're gonna love the strawberry pancakes."

The delight dripping from his face amused her enough that she was ready to forgive his pushiness in the car. After spending so many years with a man like Karl micromanaging every aspect of her life, she didn't care for anyone telling her what to do. Not even when it was something as simple as food recommendations.

After surviving Karl's abuse, his total control over her, she guarded her independence with a desperation that bordered on obsession. Sitting here watching Michael's eyes light up over these pancakes pushed away the negative tinge of discomfort that had tried to grab hold of her during their debate over the pancakes. It was as if the respectable sheriff had turned into a kid waiting for his favorite treat right before her eyes. How could she be mad at that?

"I take it you eat these often."

He spared her an eager nod and handed her a menu sitting on the side of their table.

"I do. Two of my friends and I have come here for the last three Saturdays after our game of basketball at the high school."

"You're on a team?"

"Nah. My friend that you met briefly last night—"

"Adam?" she interjected.

"Yes," he continued. "He just moved back from New York about three weeks ago to start a new job. It's been a while since Adam, Derrick—our other friend—and I have been able to hang out regularly like this."

"Having good friends so close is probably a relief."

He gave a simple shrug. "It has its difficulties. I love hanging with my boys more often. Having them underfoot all the time, though, gives them the opportunity to lecture me about the failings in my life."

She was about to ask him what he was talking about when their server came and took their orders and poured coffee in their waiting mugs sitting on the table. When they were alone again, she met his gaze.

"You were mentioning your friends getting on you about your failings. You're the sheriff. What could possibly be wrong with your life?"

He leaned back against the seat cushion and sighed. "I work a lot and I help my sister . . . a lot." There was a story behind that pause. Since they didn't know each other that well, and especially after he got slightly defensive when she pointed out the fact that he was spoiling his sister, she figured it would be rude to dig any deeper than she was by commenting just then. "It doesn't leave a lot of time for a personal life. They just want to see me happy, so they're always reminding me not to take myself so seriously and have a little fun."

Didn't that sound familiar. Sounds like his friends were just like hers. "You're in good company then," she responded. "My besties do the same."

"Work and family obligations keeping you busy too?"

She'd love to run with the out he'd provided her. She should just nod and go along with it. Yet there was something so refreshing about how open he'd been with her about his shortcomings. She felt compelled to do the same.

"I wish I could use that as an excuse." She took a careful sip of her coffee before she spoke, hoping the caffeine would calm the butterflies flapping their wings in her belly. "The only job I've ever had was as the head of the accounting department at Karl's company. After the divorce, it took me a while to figure out what I wanted to do with myself."

She also had a hard time processing the drastic way her life had changed seemingly overnight. Deciding he didn't need to know all that, she kept it to herself. Her divorce was public record, and he'd already read it in his quest to help his sister. No need for adding any more embellishment on the ugly details.

"Have you?" His question struck her as odd.

"Have I what?"

"Figured out what to do with yourself?"

She sighed, though not because she was ashamed of the answers. It was the restlessness that bothered her most. She hated feeling so listless.

"I know I love accounting and I want to get back to it. I don't think I necessarily want to return to corporate accounting. It's just . . ." She paused for a minute, almost afraid to speak her desire into the air for fear somehow it would disappear. "I've always dreamed of hanging a shingle somewhere and starting a business of my own."

She'd run Karl's accounting department. Its cold and distant nature was the complete opposite of everything her grandparents had built. Her grandmother had used numbers and finances to bring her family together in that small mom-and-pop accounting shop she and Vanessa's grandfather had run. Vanessa ached to have that kind of warmth and togetherness in her life again.

"What's stopping you?"

The frankness of his question made her reel back slightly, as if she were dodging a blow. Her silence must have tipped him off that he'd caught her off guard because he held up his hands and offered her a contrite smile.

"I'm sorry. It's none of my business. Sometimes my inner investigator gets the better of me."

She pulled her gaze away from his to fortify herself a bit. Did he see through her bullshit as well as her girlfriends had? Or was her listlessness tattooed across her forehead?

"It's all right," she replied. "It's a fair question." She ran a single finger around the rim of her coffee cup. The expected monotony of it giving her something else to focus on other than his dark, penetrating gaze.

"I was pretty much shell-shocked after discovering Karl was unfaithful."

And acknowledging his abuse, don't forget that part.

She shook her head. There was no way she could forget.

"Was he that good at covering his tracks?"

She shrugged. When you were with a powerful man like Karl, it became easy for him to cover his tracks. Only, she knew there was more to her situation than that.

"I'd always known somewhere in the back of my mind that there were others besides me even though he'd never been blatant about it. He'd never provided me with any concrete proof. So when he openly admitted his indiscretions to me, at first, I was just shocked that he would actually confess so easily."

She lifted her eyes to meet his and found an inscrutable expression plastered across his face that almost unnerved her. It was like he was looking right through her, reading between the lines and coming to a conclusion she didn't want him to reach.

"Is that why you divorced him so quickly? You were so surprised at his infidelity?"

"No," she answered quickly. "At the time, it didn't seem all that quick. It was three agonizing months to the day before I began proceedings, and another nine months before the divorce was actually finalized." Her therapist assured her that needing time to process it all was completely normal and healthy. Vanessa didn't actually believe that at the time, but through the course of her healing journey, she'd come to understand it was the truth. She needed that time to process what was happening and what was the best course of action for herself. In the grand scheme of things, the only thing that mattered was that she'd eventually found the strength to do what she needed to protect herself. She'd survived.

"It wasn't the shock of discovering his infidelity that forced me to file. Him not bothering to try to conceal it let me know our marriage was over. He was no longer concerned with whether or not he hurt me. I didn't matter in the least to him in that moment. I realized then the best thing for me to do was end the marriage. It was hard, and Karl fought me tooth and nail, dragging out the process for a full year just to spite me. But in the end, I knew where he kept all of his metaphorical dead bodies buried, so he gave me what I asked for and I took my freedom and ran."

She tried to drop her gaze again. The last thing she needed to see in his eyes was pity. She'd gone through a terrible ordeal at the hands of her ex. She didn't want that to define who she was for the rest of her life, though. She'd worked hard to shed the pain and scars Karl had inflicted. She'd survived. But every time she saw that pity in someone's eyes, it made her feel as if she were still stuck in that nightmare.

She knew she wasn't. She'd found her way to healing herself through therapy and doing the hard emotional work. Now she was ready to put it all behind her and finally embrace who she was meant to be. Her current lack of purpose was definitely a sore spot for her. Not because of her past. But because she was eager to live her future. This was her time now.

Warmth enveloped her hand. She glanced up and found Michael's palm gently covering hers. When she lifted her eyes, his gaze was heavy, filled with a sternness that made her chest fill with relief. As long as it wasn't pity she saw staring back at her, she could handle anything.

"The next time you tell someone that story," he said, in a quiet whisper that was powerful enough to send shivers through her system, "make sure you tell it with a bold smile. There is no shame in ending a toxic relationship before it destroys you. I only wish my sister could find the kind of strength you managed. Because if she had half your fortitude, I wouldn't have needed to barge into your life and bring you down here."

She blinked, trying to give herself a moment to process his words. By the time she'd found her tongue, the server returned with their food. Michael pulled his hand away and the sudden loss of its warmth left her bereft and slightly bemused. Then he grabbed his fork and a huge grin parted his lips.

His joy was contagious, and even without tasting them, she knew these would be the best pancakes she'd ever had because they gave her the chance to witness him in what she could only describe as bliss.

"Dig in," he encouraged her. "I promise, nothing will ever taste as sweet and decadent as these pancakes."

She seriously doubted that. Playing with the memory of him walking around the house in sweatpants and a T-shirt last night, she could think of quite a few things that she knew the confection in front of them paled in comparison to.

She reciprocated his smile while she cut into her food and let her thoughts flow. It wasn't smart to enjoy this man so much. Especially with the complicated nature of their connection.

Consequently, smart or not, Vanessa accepted this moment for what it was. A good time with a handsome man. She'd deal with the rest later.

They left the diner and walked up the block until they were standing in front of a closed storefront.

"Where are we?" she asked.

"My sister's floral shop. She's the local florist. Along with your everyday floral arrangements, she also deals in rare and out-of-season flowers. This means she draws in business from all over."

He pulled a set of keys from his back pocket and tapped in a security code on the keypad above the doorknob. The familiar scent of perfumed blooms filled the air and made him take a deep breath. He savored it, before quickly flipping the lights on so Vanessa could see her surroundings. He didn't need the light. He'd spent so much time in this place growing up, he knew every corner of it by heart.

He watched her stand in the center of the shop, taking in all the flowers in the refrigerated units against both parallel walls.

"How long has your sister been in business?"

"My parents started this business when they got married. Built it up from nothing and made it into a success. Both Cindy and I were pretty much raised in this place, considering all the hours they worked."

A pang of loss tugged at his heart as the memories of his family together, as an intact unit, ran across his mind.

"I considered selling it when they died. Ultimately, I just couldn't part with it. It was the last tangible piece of them I had. One of only three gifts they'd given me that still remained with me."

He saw compassion fill her eyes, soothing the dull ache that tried to emerge. "What were the other two gifts?"

He smiled. It was obvious she was trying to make him feel better by distracting him from his pain by making him talk about the joy his parents brought him instead.

"The Korean language and my sense of duty." He watched for her reaction. Would she mock him, or worse, suspect him of lying to her? He needn't have braced for the worst. Her soft smile warmed him from the inside out.

"My parents didn't demand strict adherence to Korean customs in our house. It's been nearly a century since my great-grandparents migrated to the United States just before the passing of the Oriental Exclusion Act of 1924. By the time we came along, the Parks had been very Americanized save for two things: the Korean language, and the hierarchal nature of Korean culture."

His parents had insisted he and Cindy be both fluent and literate in Korean, a fact he was grateful for now that they were gone. Back then, it was just the norm, the language he spoke at home or when visiting extended family and his parents' Korean friends, or when he spoke to Korean vendors in town. But now that they were gone, whenever he spoke the language, it was almost like receiving a hug from them, reminding him he was loved. "Although I don't get to speak our language as often since they've passed, it's still very important to me. Korean, their belief that duty came before everything else, and this store are all a big part of my life."

The soft smile on her lips called to him, pulling at something he wasn't quite ready to relinquish yet.

"In lieu of selling it, I hired two employees to handle the business during the week and Cindy and I worked here on the weekends. When she graduated college, she took it over."

She walked over to the case full of white roses, her fingers touching the glass as she gazed at them.

"I understand the need to hold on to things from our loved ones. That engagement ring was the thing my grandmother was most proud of. My grandad's family were jewelers. Even though he preferred numbers to carats, when he was ready to propose, he put down his accounting ledger for a bit and had his father help him make a ring he thought was a perfect representation of her. She absolutely loved it, and her love for him shone in her eyes every time she looked at it."

She turned around to face him with a sad smile tilting her lips. "You did a good thing by keeping this place running, keeping your parents' legacy alive."

Silence passed between them for a long pause. He watched her fidget from one foot to the other, as if the quiet was too much for her to handle. She cleared her throat and spoke. "So, what are we doing here today?"

"The shop is integral in the festival. We sell specialty arrangements. And with each purchase, customers earn a chance to bid at our civil service singles auction. It's a big-deal gala we hold every year."

Her eyes widened, and he could see a spark of amusement fill them. "A singles auction? That sounds fun."

He groaned. "Trust me, it's not. Well, not for those of us forced to participate."

She furrowed her brows and narrowed her gaze. "Forced? By whom?"

"The mayor," he huffed. "Every single civil service worker is encouraged to take part. It's a community fundraising effort for the town's college fund. With it, we're able to send a handful of local kids to Monroe Hills University on full scholarships."

The amusement left her and a softness he couldn't explain caressed her features. Still learning her, he could tell something he'd said intrigued her enough to make her move closer to him as they continued their conversation.

"That's admirable," she replied, and stepped farther into his personal space. Her nearness was doing strange things to him. His heart rate ticked up a beat, his skin prickled, and his fingers rubbed together on their own as he fought to keep from running them through her sleek bob.

"How does the mayor entice his workers to participate?"

Her voice was playful and sultry, and it made him wonder how much richer it would be in the throes of passion. Since he wasn't a total idiot, he swallowed down the impulse to find out instead.

"He offers comp time, which usually gets folks to volunteer. For those of us who report directly to the mayor, though, there's really no choice. We represent his office, so we have to show up."

"In other words, you absolutely hate it, but you have no choice because of your job?"

Her keen wit made him chuckle. Her assumption wasn't wrong. He'd much rather donate directly to the college fund, which he did in addition to participating in the auction. Standing on that stage every year parading around in a tux made him feel ridiculous. Fortunately, he loved his town and the kids in it. So he sucked it up and did what he needed to do for a good cause. No need to bitch and moan too badly about it.

"I'm really intrigued by this. How's it all work out?"

"The winners get a date with the single person they bid on," he answered.

A broad smile curved her lips, revealing mischief with a tad of wickedness mixed in.

"And let me guess, the town's favorite sheriff usually brings in the highest bids every year? I bet all the single folks in this town jump at a chance to spend a little time in your company."

She was laughing at him now, and he couldn't quite decide if he was offended or amused at this point. To give himself time to consider which, he moved away from her and stepped behind the counter to set up for the day.

"I do, all right. And the dates are pretty harmless except for when they're not."

She followed him, standing on the customer side of the counter as she leaned on it, placing her elbows on top of it and her chin in the palm of her hands.

"Oh, do tell, Sheriff."

He sighed deeply, wondering why he'd even brought any of this up. She chose that moment to smile at him again, batting those lush, dark lashes of hers, and Michael was lost. At that moment, he'd pretty much offer himself up on a silver platter if she'd wanted.

God, I'm so fucked.

"There's a resident who has a personal interest in me she hasn't been the least bit shy about voicing. She's won for the last couple of years. Every time, she uses the dates as an opportunity to make our association more than platonic."

She nodded. "So, she's pushing up and you're not interested. Why? She not your type?"

He searched his head for the right words. There wasn't anything wrong with Amanda Sayers. She was the epitome of the white American standard of beauty with a slim frame, long blond curls, and blue eyes. That standard often excluded anyone who didn't possess those features. That wasn't Amanda's fault per se. He didn't hold that against her. However, the fact that she'd proven over and over again that she thought those looks made her special, superior, that was all on her. Her being a social climber didn't help endear her to him either. Everyone who knew her understood her only goal was hooking up with one of the top officials in the town. With the mayor and fire chief married, that meant she firmly placed her target on Michael's back.

"Amanda's fine," he responded. "I don't make it a habit of dating locals. I'm the sheriff. Much of my life is very public in this town. I just feel whom I choose to keep time with shouldn't be up for public consumption."

"And yet you let your best friend believe I was your date last night. That doesn't seem like you cared all that much about folks knowing your business."

She had him there. But he wouldn't give in that easily. "Are you upset that I led him to believe we were dating?"

She lifted a brow, adding that cocky grin of hers that was fast becoming an addiction for him.

"Great job at deflection, but no." She pointed a finger at him. "I wasn't upset. Not after hearing about your Amanda troubles, anyway. I'm just wondering now if you didn't let that slip intentionally to allow you to use me as your beard to keep her off your back."

He cocked his head to the side as he thought about her assumption. "Actually, I hadn't thought about the possibility. If you're up for it, though, I wouldn't turn the offer down."

"How's that gonna work out?" she asked. "Aren't you supposed to be working during the festival?"

"Not technically," he replied. "As the sheriff, I can't leave the town with such a huge event going on. Anything could happen. Yet since I'm actually participating by helping my sister out with her booth, I'm there to keep watch, anyway."

"I thought you told your sister you couldn't watch the shop while she's away."

"I can't," he responded. "I'd already arranged my schedule so I'd be free to help her during the festival. I'm due back to work the day after the festival ends, though. I can't just disappear without notice. I won't do that to my chief deputies."

An appreciative smile graced her lips before she stood up from her perch on the counter. "You're really as good of a guy as Janae made you out to be, huh?"

"Don't know," he groaned, letting a slight bit of annoyed tension slip into the air. "I have no idea what Janae told you. Knowing her, I'm not sure I want to know either."

She laughed and her entire face lit up, making her almost too beautiful to look at. When he realized he was staring well past the time that was appropriate, he pulled his eyes away and focused on an invisible speck of dust on the counter.

"She sang your praises," she answered. "Gave me the impression you took your job seriously and were a decent guy."

He lifted his gaze to find her sliding an appreciate look down his torso. And more than ever, he wanted to puff his chest out and preen.

"I don't know, though." She stuck her tongue in her jaw as her appraisal continued. "I'm kinda wondering why such a good guy would try to sidestep the advances of a woman he admits is beautiful."

He didn't know what came over him, except the fact that his common sense exited and his ego stepped up front and center. He came from around the counter, meeting her on the other side, standing as close to her as he could.

To her credit, she wasn't the least bit put off by his proximity as she leaned into him.

"The thing that makes me good at my job is that I love putting puzzle pieces together to figure out what makes people tick. Once I put all the parts together, I can figure out what motivates folks to do some of the drastic things they do."

He lifted his hand, slowly pushing the sleek strands of her hair behind her ear, letting his thumb settle at the edge of her jaw.

"Call me old-fashioned." His voice was a low rumble he almost didn't recognize. "But I like to do the chasing when I'm interested in a woman."

She lifted a skeptical brow as they continued their stare-off. "So, you're not into strong, independent women who know their own minds? You need a docile woman to make yourself feel like a big man?"

"I want nothing less than a strong, independent woman who knows her own mind." He paused a moment to let his words settle in. "Only I want to put all the pieces together and figure out what she wants before I make a move. I want her to know her worth and make me chase her like the queen she knows she is. I want her to make me work for it. Where's the fun in having you if I didn't have to actually put in any work to get you?"

It didn't escape him that his pronouns for this imaginary woman had switched from third person to second in the span of a few words. He wasn't even sorry enough to explain he was speaking in generalities to try to cover it up. They both knew he wasn't, so what was the point? Fire flashed in her eyes, and as sure as he knew his own name, he recognized it for what it was: desire.

He leaned in, noting how bad an idea this was as he did. Then again, watching her lean in as well, he didn't give a good goddamn. Her plush mouth was slightly parted and he could feel the drum of her pulse beat faster and harder at her neck. Bad idea or not, there was no way in hell he was giving up the chance to know how that mouth would feel against his.

"Stop me now if this isn't what you want?" He was gone,

intoxicated by his growing need for her. Still, even at the height of this building lust, he wasn't so far gone that he would ever do this against her will.

"If it wasn't what I wanted, I'd tell you."

That sharp tongue was so sexy, and he'd bet all he had that that would be even more true once he tasted it. His thumb still at her jaw, he laced his fingers behind her neck and tugged her against him. The answering spark of fire in her eyes said she was all for this, and his inner caveman couldn't help but be excited.

The first press of his lips against hers was soft and seeking, the two of them trying to figure out how far and how fast to take this. He'd intended for this to be nothing more than a peck. An opportunity for him to get a taste of what he'd been craving for so long. Then he remembered what Ms. Sonia used to tell him at the bakery whenever he'd ask for a sample of whatever she'd made: "Chile, a taste will only make you mad."

She was right. Finally, his mouth was on hers and the need he'd tried so hard to press down since the day they'd met climbed to the surface and spilled into that kiss. He increased the pressure, and when she responded with the most delightful moan he'd ever heard, a low growl escaped him.

He walked her backward until she was leaning against the counter, deepening the kiss with each step they took. He nibbled at her bottom lip and then soothed it with a firm flick of his tongue. She released another moan, this time opening her mouth and giving him access to what he'd ached for.

Effortlessly, he slipped his tongue inside her mouth, nearly floored by the experience. She tasted like strawberry syrup from the pancakes they'd just eaten. Despite it being one of his favorite flavors, having her natural essence mixed in turned it into the most intoxicating substance ever.

His free hand wrapped around her waist, then slid to the deep curve of her hip. God, he was an asshole. They were standing in the middle of his sister's store and he was mauling her like she was a piece of meat. He'd like to say that realization was the reason he gentled this kiss and pulled away. It wasn't true, not even a little bit. The only reason he separated his mouth from hers was because his lungs burned, screaming for life-giving air.

When he looked into her eyes again, his chest heaving, his mind spinning, and his cock hard and heavy in his jeans, he realized he'd made a grave miscalculation. He'd thought it was worse not knowing what she tasted like. Now that he did, he didn't know how he'd go without experiencing it again.

Chapter 11

"GOD, I HOPE YOU DON'T REGRET THAT."

His words were choppy as he tried to catch his breath. She'd laugh at him if she wasn't trying her best to gulp down as much air as she could too. Shit, her marriage lasted twenty years and she'd dated through much of high school and college. How had she gone this long and never had a kiss that made her dizzy, her breath hard to catch, and her legs wobbly?

She braced her hands on the counter behind her, trying to find purchase so she wouldn't end up on the floor.

"Regret isn't the word I'd use."

His fair skin flushed bright and his pink lips were slightly swollen and bruised and she didn't think she'd ever seen anything more arousing.

He leaned down, placing his forehead against hers and his large hands at her hips. The feel of being surrounded by him set her blood aflame and stoked the fire growing at her core.

This man is a crisis waiting to happen.

He was. There was no denying that. At the moment, there was a bigger problem she had to contend with than just him being sexy as hell. She liked his sexiness. She liked him.

"I've wanted to do that since the day I saw you on your porch."

She dared to raise a hand to his face, letting her fingers glide against the smooth surface of his clean-shaven jaw. The feel of him pressed against her like this, where she could feel the thumping of his heart and the heaviness of his arousal against her belly. It felt too right.

"I might've had similar thoughts too." She chuckled, languishing in the easy banter that seemed to flow between them before placing her palm flat against his chest and putting a bit of distance between them. "As nice as it is, you have to admit this is probably the most inconvenient timing ever."

He took a step back, releasing her and placing his hands on his hips. He'd probably meant that as a means to deescalate the situation. But all it did was put his strong shoulders and broad chest on display underneath that damn muscle shirt.

Gosh, did he own any other kind of shirts? Because she didn't think she'd survive too many more.

"You're not wrong, Vanessa. This isn't convenient. Yet it also doesn't feel as wrong as it should either."

She couldn't argue with that. Because there wasn't a sliver of guilt anywhere inside her after locking lips with him that way.

"Michael, I'm leaving in a week," she huffed. "Less than that if your mechanic can get the part for my car sooner. What would be the point?"

"That would be exactly the point," he countered. "As far as I can tell, neither of us has made much of an attempt to have a social life. What would be so wrong with us enjoying each other's company while you're here?"

She let her gaze scan his face, looking for any signs that he was joking. He had to be joking. He couldn't possibly be considering what he seemed to be proposing.

"Michael," she sighed. "You brought me here to essentially break up your sister's engagement to my ex-husband. That has messy written all over it."

"If you lived in Monroe Hills and we ever had to see each other again, yeah, you'd be right. We don't, though. You'll go back to your mansion in New Jersey and I'll stay here with my sister, helping her rebuild her life after she kicks that manipulative bastard to the curb."

She scratched her temple. "I can't believe you're suggesting sex with the woman who is gonna hurt your sister."

"I'm not," he responded. "Don't get me wrong." He bit his lip as his gaze slid down the length of her body, heating her blood as he did. "You're gorgeous, and I would love nothing more than to spend a night or two in your bed, but I wasn't really suggesting that."

She lifted a skeptical brow and pursed her lips, calling bullshit on his statement.

He at least had the decency to dip his head and lifted his hand in surrender.

"Okay, I'm lying," he continued. "I'm totally hoping this leads to a whole lot of sex in the short amount of time we have together before you have to talk to my sister and leave." She took a breath to reply and he lifted a finger to silence her. "I'm also hoping that we can spend some time together over the next few days and enjoy each other's company too."

Everything about the way his eyes met hers said he was speaking the truth. And even though what he was suggesting was problematic as hell, there was relief in knowing he was guileless. He wasn't plotting anything. He just wanted her.

God, how fucked up has my experience with men been if a man speaking the truth is refreshing. What does that say about your choices in men?

He took her hands in his, rubbing his thumbs over her knuckles as he stared at her.

"Vanessa, this isn't ideal by any stretch of the imagination. Frankly, working at my sister's booth during the festival can be a pain in my ass. How about spending some time with me to keep me company?"

"So, you want me to be a distraction for you while you're bored?"

He nodded. "Pretty much."

"And what do I get out of this bargain?"

She didn't know exactly what he was going to come up with. With the intensity of his gaze heightened, she could feel his enticing heat emanating from him, as if it peeled back the layers of her clothing and caressed her bare flesh.

"You get all of my attention focused on you."

Her mouth was dry, and her heart raced in her chest, thudding against her rib cage. If his kisses had nearly melted her into a puddle on the floor, what would the full force of his focus do to her?

Was she brave enough to find out?

Vanessa walked into the back of the shop to get more of the special-order arrangements they were selling in exchange for tickets to the auction. Her phone vibrated in her pocket just as she was about to reach for the prepared tray of flowers.

A quick glance at the screen and she saw Janae's name flash across brightly.

"Hey, girl, what's up?"

"I'm good, just checking in on you. How did it go at Michael's place?"

"It went fine," she answered. "He was a perfect gentleman."

"Good," Janae countered. "I didn't want to have to hurt him."

Vanessa chuckled because even though Michael had the badge, she'd bet money if they ever came up against each other, Janae would definitely be the victor.

"So," Janae continued, "are you available for lunch today or are you still waiting to talk to Cindy?"

She huffed, letting a long sigh escape her lips. "Yeah, there have been some changes to the original plans. So, if you're up for it, I'm free for lunch. I'm actually at the floral shop now, setting up arrangements with Michael. I'm sure he wouldn't mind if I dipped out for a bite with you."

"Me and Cree," Janae corrected.

"She's back from her business trip?"

"Yeah, she arrived first thing this morning. She was in Philly, that's only about three hours from here. We'll pick you up in fifteen minutes. I'm craving a greasy burger and cheese fries. Is Johnny Rockets okay? It's at the Crossings outlet mall and it's far enough that we can dish about the sheriff and his sister where everyone and their mama can't overhear."

"Sure, I'm not picky."

Janae laughed. "Yeah, okay. I bet your bougie ass is wearing some sort of designer shoe right now, even though you're standing in the middle of a bunch of flower petals on the floor."

Vanessa looked down at her wedge booties. "They're Steve Madden booties. That's not really designer."

"For you, maybe," Janae teased. "When you're in my income bracket, paying two hundred dollars for ankle boots is considered designer."

Vanessa couldn't help but laugh. "All right, all right." She acquiesced. "I might be a slight bit bougie." She was, so there was no need denying it. "That still doesn't change the fact that even I can't resist cheese fries. Hurry up, now that you've got my mouth all fixed for some."

"Vanessa, you okay, back there?"

She looked over her shoulder to see Michael coming down the hall to the storage room.

"I'll see you when you get here, girl."

By the time Michael stepped into the storage room, she'd ended the call.

"Hey, everything okay?"

"Yeah," she answered. "Janae just called to invite me to lunch with her and Cree. Since I'm gonna be in town a little longer than expected, I thought it'd be fun."

He nodded. "Good, those two together are always fun. How do you know them?"

She pointed to the crates of flower arrangements she'd come to get. "Help me get these into the front display cases and I'll tell you all about it."

He easily picked up the trays. One in each large, carved arm. While watching him, she had to wonder if a man carrying flowers intended for someone else was ever as enticing. Refusing to let herself dwell on it too long, she shook herself free of her musings and followed him into the shop.

He placed the crates on the floor and they set about placing the large bouquets in the display cases where customers could see them.

"So, Janae and Cree." The intrigue etched into his face was almost comical. She wondered if he wanted to know because it was his natural inclination as a police officer to always want the details to piece the picture together, or if he was just plain old nosy.

"I met them two years ago, immediately after my divorce. I wasn't doing very well and needed to connect with someone who understood what I was going through. Confiding that I felt weak and discarded to my so-called friends in rarified circles, it would've been like committing social suicide. I'd already been ostracized enough for filing for divorce, I couldn't give them any more ammunition against me."

She picked up another arrangement and fiddled with it on the shelf until it sat perfectly with all its red, pink, and white blooms on display. Not that she knew anything about floral arrangement. She just needed something to do with her hands as she spoke her truth.

"So, I went online to look for divorce support groups. There were a few near me, but I couldn't risk it for fear someone I knew would see me. I found one in this tiny little town of Monroe Hills that was close enough for me to drive to, but far enough no one in my circle would ever see me."

She shook her head as she listened to how pathetic this all sounded. It was her truth, however, and she owned it. No matter how ridiculous it was, it was her story. No sense in denying it.

"It didn't take me long to realize the group wasn't really what I needed, and when Janae and Cree rescued me, we all decided to go to the bar across the street and commiserate over drinks instead. That night, we formed the Savvy, Sexy, and Single Club, and we've been inseparable ever since."

Finished telling her tale, she found the fortitude to look at him. Expecting to find ridicule, she found an inviting smile that made her even more eager to lean in and taste his lips again.

"Knowing the two of them, I can say you found yourself a good group. They're loyal as hell."

She tilted her head. "So, it's true that everyone really knows each other in small towns?"

"Yes and no," he answered. "I know most people in the town. I don't have a personal relationship with everyone, though. I went to school with Janae and Cree. We hung out in the same circles. Still do."

She turned to him, hoping he'd see the gesture as an invitation to keep talking. "So y'all were besties?"

He shook his head. "I wouldn't go that far. Cree and my other best friend Derrick have been inseparable since the cradle. While the rest of our little crew all left to go to school and live in other cities and states, Cree and Derrick stayed here and went to the local college. They never drifted far away from one another."

She nodded, encouraging him to continue. She'd heard Cree mention Derrick a million times, yet she'd never shared the bit about them being as inseparable as Michael stated.

"Janae and Adam were academic rivals throughout our entire education. The only time they've ever agreed on anything was when they had to tag-team tutor me in calculus and chemistry so I could graduate. God, they bickered like an old married couple." He lifted his eyes upward as if he were pulling those memories from the ceiling. "Fortunately for me, they had a singular focus when it came to taking pity on their clueless friend."

She chuckled, imagining Janae, in her drill-sergeant way, beating equations into Michael's head.

"That sounds like the Janae I know. She's pushy as hell." Pushy being a euphemism for bossy. Janae was always in charge. As long as everyone around her knew it, they got along just fine. Except her assertiveness was never about her needs and wants. "She always has the best interests of the people she cares about in mind. She and Cree pushed me to go through all the stages of grief regarding my marriage, never letting me wallow too long in my misery. I couldn't have made it to the other side with them."

He closed the display case when they finished putting away the rest of the flowers and turned to her. There was something unreadable dancing in his eyes. Whatever it was, she knew he was thinking carefully about what came out of his mouth next.

"So, are you over it?" When she didn't answer immediately, he continued, "Your divorce, are you over it? I was so caught up in my sister's situation that I didn't think to stop and ask you that before I brought you into this mess. I'm sorry about that."

His features were soft and sincere, a mix of concern and regret that she'd never seen grace her ex-husband's face.

"No need to apologize. I came here because it was the right thing to do. Am I over it? The regret and grief about losing a life I'd lived for twenty years? Yes, I'm over that." The relief washing down his face was visible. She could've left it at that. She probably should have. Yet something inside of her compelled her to continue. "In the place of all that grief and pain, there's a restlessness I wrestle with now. I'm ready for the next phase of my life. I just can't seem to figure out what that actually is."

He leaned carefully against the display case and smiled down at her. The inside of the shop was chilly from the refrigerated cases that lined the walls. The nip in the air notwithstanding, being positioned in the wake of his warm smile was like sunbathing in July on a Caribbean beach—hot, glorious, and utterly decadent.

"I have no doubt you'll figure it all out in your own time."

"Well," she hedged, trying to get herself together. "It's been two years and nothing yet. I'm starting to go a little stir-crazy, to be honest."

He shrugged in a carefree, nonchalant way that had the audacity to make him look sexier than he had any business being.

"The idea that we have to have everything figured out at any given point in our lives is a lie. You know that, don't you?"

She didn't know that. That was the problem. She'd spent every day of her life since she'd married Karl knowing exactly what would happen in her life, until she didn't. And since that moment, everything in her world had seemed out of focus and balance.

"Hopefully, I'll remember that the next time I'm feeling like I should know what to do with my life."

He placed a gentle hand under her chin and lifted her gaze to his. The moment was intimate in a way that ran much deeper than any physical connection. It was as if he was seeing inside her, the real her. And even more surprising was the fact that he seemed to enjoy what he saw.

"Don't worry," he said. "I'll make sure to remind you if you forget."

And just like that she stepped off the cliff into something inexplicable—something too amorphous to label while intense enough its presence was undeniable.

Welp, you done gone and fucked up now.

What the fuck are you doing?

If Michael knew, he'd certainly answer his own question. He'd crossed the line, kissing her, and now he was digging into the private parts of her life that he had no business asking for access to.

Getting close to her was a bad idea.

You said that already.

Apparently, it still bore repeating. When the question about her being over her divorce had slipped out of his reckless mouth, he'd thought it was morbid curiosity. As he held his breath waiting for her to answer, hoping with all he was worth that she said yes, he realized this wasn't about his naturally inquisitive nature. He wanted her to be over her ex for his own gain.

And you know why that is, don't you?

If he didn't, then he couldn't deny it now. It was so she'd have room for him.

See, this is why you should've never kissed her in the first place. It was supposed to be harmless flirtation, maybe a little fun in the sack. Your ass shouldn't be caring about taking up space in her world or her heart.

His conscience was so smart. Too bad he couldn't say the same about the rest of him right now.

"So." She stepped away from him, causing his finger to drop from her chin. She walked behind the counter, arranging and rearranging things. Since he guessed she hadn't a clue how to run a flower shop, he figured this was her way of breaking the tension he'd created. "Is there anything else we need to do?"

He shook his head. "No," he answered. "The booth is set up outside. The only thing it needs is us."

She stopped fiddling with the things on the counter long enough to look at him. The intensity of her gaze bore into him, burning through skin, blood, and bone to get to the core of him, the cellular building blocks of him. Whatever uncertainty he'd seen in her eyes a few moments ago, it was replaced with something decisive and powerful.

"That's fine. Give me a sec and I'll meet you outside."

Tempted to ask what she was thinking, he stopped himself. He figured he'd probably pried into her personal thoughts more than enough for one day. Although the way she stared at him with a mischievous grin, tilting her full lips, taunting him, daring him to push for more, he wondered if she wanted him to press a little further.

He took a breath, forcing his hands in his pockets to keep himself from doing something rash like walking behind the counter and putting his hands all over her. He should've just walked away. Instead, he continued to stand there, making himself a promise. Before Vanessa left Monroe Hills, he would know exactly what every one of her looks meant.

Chapter 12

"SURE, SEE YOU THERE."

Vanessa watched Michael as he backed up to the door and walked outside. Through the storefront glass, she could see him walk under the ten-by-ten tent they'd set up earlier.

He'd turned around to look at her, but a patron passing on the street stepped in front of him and pulled his attention away. She shook her head, trying to gather her composure. She might not look a mess on the outside; inside, though, everything was quivering.

Everything.

This man with his wicked smile and do-me body did things to her she couldn't quite explain. And even though she couldn't understand how he did them, she knew she liked it. Every single thing.

She. Liked. It.

She laughed quietly, slightly amused and a little bit scared by whatever was happening between them. She hadn't felt like this in . . . ever, if she was honest.

She'd been so young when she'd met Karl. Yes, she'd dated other young men. That detail didn't erase the fact that she was still trying to figure out what being an adult meant when she bound her life to her ex-husband's. Yet with this, this thing with Michael, there were no promises. This was just about fun. And since Michael seemed game to play a bit, she reckoned it was only right she did the same.

She found the nearby order pad and scribbled out a very personal order of the festival arrangements. When she finished with it, she put it in the to-be-delivered envelope Michael had shown her earlier, then removed her credit card from her wallet and made the purchase.

Whatever this was, it made her feel giddy and light. And as long as she was stuck in Mayberry, she was determined to enjoy whatever time she had with Michael to the fullest.

"Hold on there, Vanessa." She smiled at the happy reflection she saw in the glass doors of the refrigerated display case. "If you keep it up, you might just stumble onto a good time."

And she didn't feel the least bit bad about that.

"So, how was sleeping with the sheriff?"

Vanessa nearly dropped the strawberry milkshake in her hand. Good reflexes kept her drink upright before she looked up to find both Janae's and Cree's eyes locked on her.

"Come again?"

"I believe that's what we're trying to find out," Cree said with a squeal, amused by her own joke.

"I slept in Michael's guest room." Janae opened her mouth to say something else, but Vanessa raised a hand to silence her. "And he slept in his bedroom. I just met this man. Why would you think I'd sleep with him?"

"Because he's fine as hell," Cree answered, and she and Janae burst into a fit of giggles again.

"I swear I'm the only adult at this table."

Janae shrugged. "Stop it. Just because you like to pretend like you're above a little fun doesn't mean you don't recognize a good thing when you see it."

Janae was right. It didn't matter how much she loved rules and order, there was no way she could ignore the fact that Michael was definitely tempting.

"The two of you have known him all your lives. Why haven't either of you jumped on him if he's so irresistible?"

They both furrowed their brows as if Vanessa had just said something incomprehensible.

"Michael is like a brother to us," Cree said with just enough "eww" coloring her voice to indicate Vanessa's suggestion was ludicrous.

"Speak for yourself," Janae continued. "I don't see Michael as a brother. But he's always been a really good friend to me. Trying to hook up with him now would be weird."

"And you're suggesting it wouldn't for me, a total stranger, to sleep with him after meeting him twice?"

Janae shrugged as she dipped a fry in a dollop of ketchup. "Listen, after meeting us once, you bonded with us. And look how great that turned out. Maybe hooking up with Michael might work out even better."

Before that panty-melting kiss in the flower shop, Vanessa would've called bullshit on Janae's reasoning. Now, she wasn't so sure. Because if he'd pushed for more than that kiss, she didn't have a doubt in her head she'd have willingly gone along with it. Fortunately, her girlfriends didn't need to know that.

"He's attractive." She kept her eyes focused on the fries and bacon cheeseburger in the basket in front of her. "It's not like I've never seen attractive men before, though. And let's not forget why I'm here in the first place. I'm about to blow up his sister's life. That's not exactly a great way to flirt."

They both nodded in sync and relief washed over Vanessa. Whatever this thing was between her and Michael wasn't anywhere near the stage where she could discuss it openly with anyone yet. No need to let these two in. Not when that kiss might be the only thing that ever came of it.

"So," Cree began. "What's the plan there? When are you going to talk to Cindy about Karl?"

"Not anytime soon, if ever," Vanessa replied.

Janae jumped in before Vanessa had a chance to elaborate. "What's that supposed to mean?"

"Last night's bad weather screwed up her travel plans. She's on some sort of business trip that was supposed to include her stopping off in Boston for some important meeting yesterday. Well, her meeting got pushed back to next week. She's staying in Boston until then."

Janae's eyebrow popped up. "And you're waiting an entire week just to talk to her?"

"No," Vanessa replied as she slid down into her chair, groaning as she remembered her predicament. "My car decided now was the right time to have some electrical problems. Your town mechanic can't get the part until next week. So I'm stuck here."

Cree cleared her throat before taking a sip of her soda. "And you're staying with Michael until you get your car back?"

"Or until one of you graciously offers to take me home so I don't have to be stuck in Mayberry any longer."

Janae narrowed her eyes and pointed a fry at her. "I done told you about bagging on our town. It serves you right you have to stay here while your car is repaired. And even if I wanted to—and to be clear, I don't—I couldn't drive you home, anyway. I took off to hang at the festival with my kid and as a result, I'm working back-to-back shifts at the start of the week."

Vanessa tipped her chin in Cree's direction. "What about you? Take pity on me and drive me home."

Cree shook her head. "No can do. I don't do long-distance driving."

"It's less than a couple of hours away. It's not like I'm asking you to drive to New Mexico."

Cree's features softened, even though she continued to shake her head no. "I love you, Vanessa. But not even for you would I do it. Derrick drove all the way to Philly and back. Otherwise, I'd have hopped my happy hips on the Martz bus. Can't you just hire a service or a rental to get you home?"

Frustration bubbled up again. "I tried while we were at the flower shop this morning. They either don't travel out this far, they don't have any cars available because of this stupid festival, or they're booked. It's like the universe is working against me to keep me stranded here."

She took an unladylike bite out of her burger and sulked as she chewed. It was ridiculous that a person of her means couldn't find a way out of this place.

"Well," Janae spoke up. "Maybe the universe is trying to tell you to sit back, relax, and stay awhile. It would probably serve you better to listen than fight it." She smiled widely, sharing a conspiratorial smirk with Cree.

"Besides, you get to stay here and have some fun with us. That should be more than an incentive to get you to enjoy your stay. That"— she turned to Vanessa with just a bit of deviousness coloring her dark eyes—"and the pretty man you're shacked up with for the duration."

"Ladies, I've already told you—"

Janae reached across the table, laying her hand on top of Vanessa's. It was soft, yet firm. Meant to act as a source of comfort and a reprimand all at the same time.

"Vanessa, for the two years we've known you, you've worked hard to get beyond your past. For once, instead of everything being so heavy and serious, do something completely unexpected. Flirt, be open to whatever possibilities that present themselves. No one's saying you have to marry him. Still, I don't see why you can't have a whole lot of fun while you do some good here and blow up Karl's con."

"Janae's right, Vanessa. Both you and Michael are the most

responsible people I've ever known. The two of you deserve some fun. If the universe is presenting this opportunity, why not take it?"

Her mind began turning over their words. She'd been thinking hard about letting herself enjoy anything that happened between her and Michael. Maybe it was time she fully committed to it during her entire time in Monroe Hills.

Satisfied that she had enough information to make a decision, she raised her half-empty paper cup of strawberry milkshake and smiled at her friends. "To my unexpected vacation."

They each raised their cups in solidarity and made a show of clinklessly tapping them with hers. "To your unexpected vacation," they said in unison.

At least she wouldn't have to talk to Cindy or see Karl. Depending on what day next week the mechanic had her car ready, if luck was on her side, she might just make it out of Dodge before they returned.

"So, ladies"—she beamed at the two of them—"what kind of fun do you have in this town?"

Michael watched as three familiar faces walked toward him with shopping bags on their arms, laughing and smiling as they stepped in unison.

"Afternoon, ladies," he greeted all of them, but he couldn't seem to pull his attention away from the woman in the middle as he spoke. "Seems like lunch was very productive."

"It was," Vanessa answered. "Since I didn't bring enough clothes for my unintended extended stay, Janae suggested we hit the Commons to get me some festival-appropriate clothing, namely, some flat shoes."

Michael narrowed his gaze. "You mean the Crossings?" She nodded her head at his correction.

"Yeah, the Crossings. Forgive me, I'm still getting my bearings around here."

She took a moment to dig around in one of the shopping bags and removed a white bag dotted with grease all over it. "And because I'm not completely heartless, before we left, I stopped and got you lunch."

She held the bag out like it was a prize and he gladly accepted. He'd been so busy, he'd forgotten about lunch.

"Thank you, ma'am." She responded with a bashful smile that made his blood simmer. What the hell was happening to him? One kiss and he was acting like a besotted teenager.

Michael heard someone clearing their throat, and the mutual gazing he and Vanessa were doing was broken.

"Well," Janae interrupted. "It seems you two need some alone time, so Cree and I will leave you to it."

"Speak for yourself," Cree responded. "I wanna watch."

He laughed. Same old Janae and Cree he'd known all his life. They were fun and spontaneous, and he often envied their zeal for life.

"You two are welcome to stay and help us man the booth. Although many folks have stopped by early to buy auction arrangements, the real festivities don't kick off until this evening."

They both shook their heads. "Nah," Cree replied. "We didn't come here to work. We're going to be spectators like everyone else."

"Fair enough." He chuckled. "See you tonight, then."

The two of them both nodded and said their goodbyes to Vanessa, and then Michael and Vanessa were blissfully alone . . . on a public street standing in front of his sister's shop.

"I'm sorry about the two of them."

He waved his hand. He'd been dealing with them since they were kids, so he was used to them by now. They were fun and supportive, and he was glad Vanessa had found them during a rough patch in her life.

"Janae and Cree are who they are, and I wouldn't change them for the world. Small towns can get a little routine. They always bring a spark the rest of us cherish."

She smiled, sitting beside him, the delicate scent of something sweet wafting off her skin, making him want to lean closer. If they weren't sitting on the sidewalk and he wasn't the town's sheriff, he would've done so much more than lean in.

You didn't seem to mind who saw you when you were kissing her with nothing but large glass windows in the storefront between y'all and anyone happening by on the street.

No, he hadn't. Somehow, though, it seemed more scandalous touching her so intimately on the sidewalk.

The crowd was picking up and more than a few people headed to their booth, ostensibly to purchase flowers. But by the way each passerby seemed to stop and stare at Vanessa, he knew it had more to do with Monroe Hills trying to figure out who the new, pretty woman was in town sitting next to the sheriff.

"Is it usually this busy? If we keep up with this, your sister won't have to sell another long-stem rose for the rest of the year."

"We usually do pretty well," he answered, handing an arrangement to Mrs. Anderson from the butcher shop three doors down. "But we're at about half our usual number of orders and we haven't reached midway through the first day. Mind you, the official kickoff isn't until tonight."

"What do you attribute all the foot traffic to?"

He waved at Mrs. Anderson, who gave him an approving look as she left them alone. "You."

He could see the slight tint of mauve under her deep brown skin and wondered how the rest of her skin looked with such a tempting blush.

"How could I have anything to do with this? I only know three people in this town."

He held his hand flat against his stomach as he chuckled out loud. For all her sophistication, she was so out of her depth in the confines of a town that was probably smaller than the exclusive neighborhood she lived in.

"We had breakfast at the diner and you're sitting here with me selling my sister's flowers. That's enough to have us married and choosing names for our firstborn in this place."

Her jaw hung open, and he laughed even harder at her obvious surprise.

"How do you deal with everyone being in your business like this? I bet you miss the anonymity of living in a big city like Philly."

Philly was so long ago now, it almost seemed like another life for him.

"There are pros and cons to living in both places. You just gotta figure out what works best for you."

"Does it?" she hedged, her eyes scanning his face, gauging just how far she could take this line of questioning.

"When my parents died in that crash, the only thing I could think about was getting home." He rubbed his hands against his thighs, trying to give them something to do other than reaching for her. "To my sister . . . and to them."

He could see compassion softening the line of her jaw, tempting him to reach out and stroke it. "And once I came home, it just didn't feel right to leave. Cindy's fifteen years younger than me. If I'd dragged her back to Philly with me, I'd have uprooted her in the middle of high school. After experiencing such a loss, I didn't want her to lose anything else that was familiar to her. Me relocating was the only solution."

She moved closer to him, her arm rubbing slightly against his. The brief touch was innocent, from anyone else it would've barely registered. Still, his skin tingled where the light pressure of her bicep rubbed against his.

"Was it difficult to transition from being a big city detective to a small-town sheriff?"

"I didn't start out as the sheriff," he said, and boy, was he grateful for that. If he'd been thrown into that fire, he'd probably have run from the town screaming. "I was a lieutenant in Philly PD. Having that prior experience made me eligible to apply for a colonel's position. After five years, my supervisor promoted me to one of three deputy chief sheriff positions. I worked that for three years before the mayor appointed me sheriff two years ago after the previous sheriff fell ill and needed to go into early retirement."

"Appointed? I was wondering why you were forced to do this auction at the mayor's behest. Aren't sheriffs elected?"

"Yeah." He nodded. "I'll be running my first campaign next year. Until then, I'm the mayor's bitch."

"Stop it." She nudged his shoulder playfully, bringing a bright spot of levity to the moment. "Appointment or no, you're here for one reason alone."

Curiosity got the better of him and he leaned in. "Oh yeah? Well please, do enlighten me. Why am I here?"

"It's simple." She laid her hand on his forearm and let graceful fingers wrap around it. Even through his lightweight sweater, her touch burned through the intricately woven layers of yarn, through to his skin, spreading electric need across his body like a live wire to gasoline. "You're a good brother who'd do anything to help his sister. It's why you brought me here. It's why we're sitting under a tent on the sidewalk selling flowers."

He blinked, unsure how to respond. There was no denying her assumption. She was spot-on. From the moment he got the news about his parents, everything in his world became about his sister.

She squeezed his arm, bringing his attention back to the here and now, back to her. "I wish I'd had someone looking after me like that. She's a lucky woman."

There was a brief bit of sadness in her eyes that he wanted to root out and destroy. Everything he knew on paper and in person about this woman spoke to how genuine she was. And if Michael had anything to say about, she'd never be sad again.

That was the tricky part, however. He had nothing to say about it. She wasn't his in any way that gave him a right to meddle in her life. So instead of giving in to the possessive rumbling in his gut, he placed his hand gently on top of hers and squeezed.

"You deserve that too, Vanessa."

And strangely enough, in this moment, he'd give anything to be the one to give it to her.

"I'm exhausted!" Vanessa's proclamation rang throughout the foyer as they walked into his house. "After the day I've had, I have a newfound respect for florists. Who knew selling flowers could be so taxing?"

She bent down to take off her wedge boots at the bottom of his stairs, and his heart nearly stopped. All that ass in the air gave him thoughts he probably shouldn't be having about a guest in his home who was here to blow up his sister's life. Except the way the dark-wash denim of her designer jeans perfectly cupped each cheek had him halfway to hard in two-point-five seconds flat.

Stop being a perv, Michael.

Taking one last lingering look as she pulled off her last shoe, he turned around, making a display of closing and locking the front door.

He thought he had his body and mind under control and was ready to face her again when she said, "I'm gonna run up and take a shower." And there he was, fighting the image of her naked with her supple curves slick with water and whatever that delicious-smelling shower gel she used was. He closed his eyes, forcing himself to think of police reports and employee evaluations he had to get done, anything to make his mind stop picturing himself under that damn water with her.

He cleared his throat, turning around to find her staring at him with questioning eyes, scanning his face for an answer to whatever question she had yet to speak.

"Yeah." His voice was raw, too thick with need for his tastes, so he cleared it again. "I'm gonna do the same. I'm not really up for cooking tonight. He made a show of pulling his cell phone out of his pocket. "What kind of takeout would you like?"

"This town has a good Chinese takeout place?"

"Yup." He kept his eyes on the screen as he looked for the restaurant's number. "Know what you want?"

"General Tso's with vegetable lo mein."

"They make it pretty spicy; you want me to tell them to go easy on the peppers?"

He chose the wrong moment to pull his gaze up to hers. There was something electric in her eyes that filled the small space between them with heat.

"That's fine." Her devilish smile amping up the heat already licking at the edges of his being. "I like it hot."

He tightened his hand around his phone to temper his autonomic need to lay his hand on some part of her body. He battled the obvious attraction he had for her. And it didn't help matters that he was slightly pissed off that he couldn't tell if this was just an innocent slip of the tongue or an innuendo he wholeheartedly wanted to explore.

"I'll make sure the lady gets what she wants."

She nodded in thanks and turned to take the first step to the second floor. She looked over her shoulder, giving him one last smile that made him lose all focus on anything except the way those full lips spread and how much he'd like to see them wrapped around his cock.

She broke the connection, turning around and continuing her trek upstairs, and it wasn't until she was completely out of sight that he finally took a breath. He'd proposed fun between them.

Only, what he was feeling wasn't lighthearted fun. It was heavy, serious, and powerful, and if he didn't get control of it, this shit could go sideways quick.

He placed their delivery order and took the steps two at a time to get to the sanctity of his room. He pulled off his clothes one article at a time, leaving an untidy trail from the door to the bathroom. He wasn't a slob by nature, but right now, if he didn't get in that shower, he'd do something stupid like barge into her room so he could find out if the fantasy in his head matched the reality of her naked with water cascading down her soft brown skin.

He turned the water on in the shower stall, not waiting until the water warmed up to step in. He needed the shocking cold spray to douse some of the flames that seemed to consume him from the inside out.

He was supposed to be bathing, washing the remnants of the day away. Instead, he leaned into the spray that was slowly warming up, placed a flattened palm against the cool ceramic tiles, and gripped his heavy cock with the other.

This was going to be quick and dirty, so he didn't bother with his usual routine of shower play. For one, if he took too long, Vanessa might come looking for him, and if she did, there was no way he was going to withstand her siren's call like this. Second, their order would be here in about twenty minutes, and since he really had a taste for the sweet and sour chicken he'd ordered, he couldn't take forever to grab hold of the release he'd desperately needed all day.

That first rough stroke with a fast twist of his wrist was fucking bliss. He buried his teeth into his bottom lip to keep the raw need from spilling from his mouth into the air. This was an old house, and the walls were thin as shit. He had no doubt she'd know exactly what the fuck he was doing if he couldn't keep his voice down.

Another rough stroke, coupled with the image of Vanessa in her bathroom across the hall, wet and slick in all the right places. Downstairs, he'd had to fight to keep things respectful. However, in the confines of the glass walls of his shower and the billowing steam fogging up the enclosed space, he could let his imagination run wild.

In his mind, she'd slide down against the ceramic tile until she was in the stooped position with her legs wide open, her darkened folds held open by her exploring fingers as she directed the spray of the handheld showerhead right over her slit.

As imaginary Vanessa swirled elegant fingers over her swollen clit, his desire burned hotter and brighter, competing with the near-scalding water pelting against his skin.

And when she took the same fingers she'd been playing with in her beautiful pussy and brought them to that sexy mouth, sucking off her juices, juices he was desperate to taste himself, his arm gave out and his forearm was against the tiles, his head laid on top of it as fire swirled in his heavy sack, swirling up around his spine, causing his muscles to lock through no power of his own.

What was this woman doing to him? Just the thought of her had him—for the second time since he'd met her—with his hand around his swollen dick, tugging for fucking life.

His mirage continued, luring him closer and closer to the edge of completion. And when she placed first one, then two, and finally three fingers inside her channel, fucking herself until she cried out his name in release, he fell quickly off the mountain peak of pleasure until every last bit of need spilled from his cock onto the tiles and the glass walls.

Thank heaven the showerhead in his bathroom was detachable too, because he didn't have time to do a thorough scrub-down of the surfaces. When his legs felt strong enough, he pushed himself away from the wall, grabbed the showerhead, and did his best to get rid of the proof of his desire for Vanessa.

He left the bathroom, dressing quickly in an A-line T-shirt, sweatpants, and a thick pair of comfy socks. By the time his foot hit the last step, the bell rang. He grabbed his wallet from the foyer table, pulled out three bills that covered the cost, and left a generous tip for Johnny, a friendly teenager who lived a few doors down from Michael. When he opened the door, Johnny was standing on the other side with a smile on his face as he held up Michael's food.

"Here you go, Sheriff. It's hot-n-ready."

Vanessa chose that moment to come down the stairs in a turquoise satin pajama shorts set with the matching long robe trailing behind her in a regal display of grace and beauty.

Hot-n-ready was the perfect description. He felt his cock try to twitch, and he'd never been more grateful for jerking off in the shower. Otherwise, this would be a seriously awkward delivery.

"Thanks, Johnny. Don't work too late."

"I won't, Sheriff. Have a good night."

Johnny handed Michael the food and jogged down the porch steps quickly before reaching his car. Convinced he could be an adult and sit down and have dinner with Vanessa without mauling her, he took in a deep breath and exhaled slowly through pursed lips.

"Get it together, Park," he mumbled to himself, hoping that reprimand would be enough to keep his baser desires under control long enough to have a pleasant meal with his guest. But when she smiled at him as he stepped down into the living room, where she sat on the sofa looking comfortable, as if she belonged in that very spot, he could feel his resistance slipping.

By the time he sat down next to her, putting the bags on the coffee table, he gave up trying to fight whatever was building for her. Vanessa Jared was a beautiful woman whether she was in couture or pajamas. And he would not feel bad about noticing that either.

Accepting his newfound perspective, he pulled out her order and held it out to her. "Do you need a plate or are you okay eating out of the carton?"

"I'm good with it just the way it is."

And so was he.

Chapter 13

THE CREDITS OF THE MOVIE ON HIS BIG SCREEN ROLLED, signaling the end to a perfect day.

"You wanna watch something else or are you ready to go to sleep?" Michael stretched as he waited for Vanessa to reply.

When she didn't answer, Michael turned to find her tucked into the corner hugging one of his sofa pillows under her head, fast asleep.

He shut off the TV, then thought about what his next move was. He could grab a throw blanket from the secret compartment inside the nearby ottoman. Or, and this was a big or, he could carry her upstairs so she wouldn't wake up achy from sleeping on the couch. It was fine for sitting and watching a couple of movies on, even for a brief catnap. Getting a full night's sleep on that thing was terrible on your back, though.

He leaned down, brushing a lock of hair from her face, enamored by the intoxicating peace he saw there.

"Aleumdaun." He whispered the Korean endearment as he continued to stare at her. Relishing the unobstructed view of her beauty before scooping her up in his arms, he made sure he had a secure grip on her, then took a step. Vanessa stirred in her sleep, snuggling closer to him than their position already allowed. The feel of her pressed against him did little for the hard-on he'd been fighting all night.

He made it up the stairs and into her bedroom without her moving, grateful for that small favor, because if she pressed herself against him like that again, all bets were off.

He was about to place her on the bed when she stirred and tightened her arms around his neck, moaning his name in a soft, sexy way that almost broke his resolve.

"Vanessa." His voice was stern and the sound of her name across his lips hovered somewhere between anger and need. "Vanessa, I need to put you down."

He felt her tense in his arms, waking and lifting her head to look up at him. There was confusion at first. Then, shortly, something raw and fierce flashed across her gaze.

"If you keep moving against me like that, this might turn into something altogether different than me tucking you safely in bed."

She stared at him, her gaze intense and certain.

"And what if I want it to turn into the something more than you're referring to?"

He glanced down at her, noticing her protruding nipples through the thin satin material of her top. He forced his eyes back to her face, needing to make sure her mind wanted what her body was preparing for.

"All you have to do is speak the word." They both remained quiet, visibly considering his words, his body hot and every nerve he possessed sparking with this unexplained chemistry the two of them shared. "Do you want to have sex with me, Vanessa?"

She nodded, and he shook his head, closing his eyes. "I need your words. Do you want me to strip you of this material I've been dying to peel off you and take my time paying homage to every inch of your body with mine?"

"Yes . . . I do."

He couldn't remember what happened next. One minute he was standing at the side of the queen-size bed cradling her in his arms, the next she was underneath him in the bed, writhing against his clothed cock.

It lay hard and insistent inside his sweats, as if he hadn't already come all over his shower stall. That seemed an unimportant point. His body was primed for more. More of Vanessa, more of her luscious curves, and more of those delicious sounds he was working overtime to swallow.

His mouth against hers, waiting for an invitation to deepen the kiss, hitching their desire up a notch the moment his tongue made contact with hers. His hand covered her breast, cupping the soft and heavy flesh in his palm.

It was so good to be with her like this. To openly display the dogged need he'd carried since the moment he laid eyes on her. Still, it wasn't enough. The soft material of her pajamas was getting on his nerves. He needed more.

"I'm sure this probably cost more than one of my paychecks." He fingered the silky material, marveling at its beauty and texture. "Even still, if you don't take it off right now, I'm going to tear it to shreds so my skin can touch yours."

She tucked her full bottom lip between bright white teeth as a mixture of sass and hunger tugged at her features. She pushed at his shoulder, and he pulled himself away from her. Instantly regretting the loss of physical connection, he never took his eyes off her.

She shrugged out of her robe, then quickly pulled the camisole over her head, tossing it on the floor behind her. She was about to tuck her thumbs into the waistband of her shorts, but he was too quick for her. Before she had a chance to process what was going on, he was on his knees, pulling her shorts down, ready to worship at the altar safety tucked between her thick thighs.

He wrapped his arm around her waist as a preventative measure to keep her upright and rubbed his face against her mound. It was hot to the touch, bare, and the scent of her arousal sweet and spicy, just like her. He pushed a hand between her thighs, encouraging her to widen her stance to make room for him.

He started by placing gentle kisses there. Each one meant to tempt and tease, not satisfy. It didn't take long for her need to build for her hips to jerk forward seeking more.

If she wanted more, he'd give it to her until she begged him to stop. He licked two fingers, rubbing them up and down her slit, delighting in the deep shiver that vibrated through her body. He took that as a sign that she was enjoying things so far, so he leaned in, letting his tongue follow the path and movements of the fingers he had teased her with.

She moaned his name instantly, making his dick harder. Although he'd conjured it up in his head, the dream in no way compared to the reality. The way she called out to him as his tongue bathed her clit and licked between her wet folds made him feel more powerful than ever. Fuck a firearm. The sound of Vanessa riding his goddamn tongue was the deadliest weapon in the world.

Her juices were flowing, dripping all over his face and down her legs, and he was loving every minute of it. He could've stayed there forever, except he was too old to be on his knees this long on a hardwood floor, so he gentled the laps of his tongue, leaning back on his haunches before standing up.

He pulled her to him, needing her to know just how sweet she was. He licked inside her mouth as he let his fingers circle around her clit. The combination must've hit the spot, because he could feel her shaking against him, as if she couldn't keep her balance on her own. Taking pity on her predicament, he wrapped both arms around her waist and lifted her off the floor, still devouring her mouth as he gently laid her down on the bed.

"You don't know how much I want this." He wasn't sure if he was talking to her or himself. The way this woman was fucking with his head, talking to himself wasn't out of the realm of possibility.

Desperate to return to his feast, he slid down her body until he'd reached his destination.

He hooked one leg over his shoulder, spreading the other until he had enough room to work. And work he did, diligently even, as his tongue, his fingers, and his mouth caressed every inch of her sex.

She didn't know it, but eating pussy was probably more fun for him than it was for his partner. Sure, he made certain his partner climaxed, yet the joy he got from spreading a woman wide and having her ride his face as she came had brought him to his own climax more than once in his lifetime.

Tonight might add another instance. His cock was so hard, trapped between his thigh and the cotton linen, he was already on the verge of losing control. No matter how he tried to focus on her, every sound she made had him aching, throbbing, begging for a release of his own.

Her hips jerked in rhythmless motion, signaling just how close she was. He thumbed her clit, making his tongue stiff and sliding it inside her opening. The taste, the feel of her walls clamping down around him as she stiffened, her arousal raining down on him, brought him closer to the edge.

When she was done, he wiped his face, placing a brief kiss on her thighs before disappearing across the hall into the bathroom. He rooted around in the vanity drawer until he found what he was looking for.

Michael grabbed hold of the foil packet between his fingers and headed back into the bedroom where Vanessa was laying with one leg cocked up and her fingers disappearing in and out of her pussy. Without thinking, he opened the condom, sliding it carefully over the sensitive head and down his straining length.

"You obviously don't want this to last, because me watching you play in that pretty pussy of yours is a surefire way to make me come right where I stand."

She didn't stop, just smiled at him as she picked up speed, chasing what looked to be another blissful climax. Desperate to know what her coming on his cock would feel like, he made it to the bed, sliding as slowly as he could inside her heat.

Whatever fantasy he'd concocted in his head, nothing compared to the viselike grip she had on his cock. She hadn't mentioned if she'd had any partners since her divorce. By the way she was strangling his cock, he doubted it.

All he wanted to do was dive in until he was balls deep inside her. Except concern over whether she could take that demanded he take his time. He slowly slipped in and out, each movement taking him deeper inside her tight walls.

She buried her fingers in his hair, gripping the strands just tight enough to bite.

"I won't break, Michael. I don't need you to treat me like I'm glass."

Something in him snapped, and the thought of mustering any restraint was gone. He tilted his head, staring at her for a moment before he spoke.

"You sure about that?"

"Positive."

It was the only thing he needed to proceed. He flipped her over, her gorgeous ass in the air, taunting him like a red flag in front of a bull. He slid his fingers inside, scissoring and stretching to make sure she was prepared.

Satisfied that the woman knew what she wanted, he removed his fingers, loving the desperate and bereft whine that escaped her lips as he did. He paused for just a second more before he sheathed himself to the hilt inside her.

He stayed there, fully seated. Grabbing a handful of ass before sliding his hand down her back until he reached the delicate curve where her shoulder met her neck.

He applied pressure, not enough to hurt, just enough to make sure she couldn't move unless he wanted her to. He pulled out, thrusting his cock in fast and deep, and watched to see how she responded. The deep mewling into the bedding and the fact that her pussy was gripping him tighter was the perfect reason for him to do it again and again.

God, she was hot and tight, meeting every thrust with one of her own, taking him deeper as he pressed harder and harder into her body.

He felt delicate fingertips caress his balls, sending lightning directly to his dick, bringing him closer to his breaking point. Determined that she topple over with him. He pulled on her shoulder until she was upright, wrapping one hand around the front of her throat and sliding the other over her hot, wet cunt. The dual stimulation of his thrusts while thumbing her clit sent her over into ecstasy.

A split second later, he howled. That first jet of cum ripped from him like a bullet through the barrel of a gun. He tightened his hand at the base of her neck, biting down onto her shoulder as spasms racked his body until he barely had enough strength to keep from falling over.

He removed the condom and tossed it toward the small trash can at the side of the nightstand, hoping it actually made it inside. And as he fell back onto the plush pillows, the only thing he could concern himself with was pulling Vanessa's spent, naked form under the covers and into his arms, where they could both sleep off their post-sex weakness.

Chapter 14

"WOW, THIS IS EVEN BETTER TODAY THAN IT WAS YESTER-day." Vanessa looked around the splendor of Main Street, amazed at its transformation. Last night when they'd left, there'd been a few decorative lights up on shops, but nothing as detailed as what she was witnessing now.

The lampposts were bound in ribbons of lights. Huge bows anchored by them, welcoming everyone to the festival. Each shop they walked past had some kind of unique and festive display that invited passersby to stop and take in the spectacle of it all.

"This seems to surprise you."

It did. "I live in a gated community with a strict HOA. They do not do decorative lights."

"Not even for holidays?"

She shook her head. "In Edencrest, it's considered garish. It's not allowed at all."

"That seems cold."

It was. Before this moment, though, she'd never noticed how much. This wasn't just festive, it was warm, making her feel like she was somehow part of or welcome to everything around her. Edencrest was a cold mausoleum in comparison.

"Well then." He placed a hand at the small of her back, pulling her closer to him. "I guess we'd better make sure you have as much fun as you can before you go back."

His words were tinged with just the right amount of mischief to make her want to see what he had in store. "Aren't we here to work, though? What about Cindy's shop?"

"Sarah, Cindy's employee, is covering it right now. I told her we'd be there in about two hours to take over. So until then, we get to enjoy the festival."

She looked around, taking a breath and loving the scent of buttery popcorn, roasted nuts, and cotton candy filling the air. She looked at him and felt a giggle bubbling up in her chest she knew had nothing to do with the snacks she intended to buy. She was keenly aware that the man whose company she was privileged enough to have was certainly responsible for the lightness she was experiencing.

He took her to all the shops, giving her a chance to talk with the vendors. Each one connected to their stores in a way that was so much deeper than just commerce. It was like these small boutiques and storefronts were part of them, or at the very least a reflection of them.

They neared the cotton candy stand, and she moaned so deeply it could be heard above the music blasting from the loudspeakers throughout the strip. "You want some?"

"I shouldn't. I've already eaten roasted nuts and had some of those sweet rolls from Ms. Sonia. I really shouldn't."

"Yeah, but you will." He maneuvered them through the crowd to get them to the stand, slipping his hand into hers with natural ease, as if he'd done so a million times before. "And I promise you won't regret it once you taste it."

Too caught up in how good his skin felt against hers, she willingly walked into temptation. Besides, the excitement etched into his wide smile over something as simple as cotton candy was so intoxicating, she couldn't have resisted if she'd wanted to.

She chuckled as she watched his gaze follow the winding path the vendor was creating with his metal sugar spoon.

"What?" He stitched his eyebrows together into a deep V, which amused her enough to turn her chuckle into a full-blown laugh.

"For someone who appears so stoic most of the time, you light up at the simplest pleasures in life."

He opened his mouth to speak, but the line moved up and it was their turn to order.

"Hey there, Sheriff," said an older white man with a long full beard and kind eyes. He was stout, wearing a plaid shirt, denim overalls, and a faded red baseball cap. He looked like a mix between Santa Claus sans his red suit and Uncle Jesse from *The Dukes of Hazzard*. "It's nice to see you outta uniform mingling with the rest of us."

Michael groaned and nodded. "I know, Mr. Preston."

"You work too much. The Mrs. said the same to me a few days ago." He pointed a finger at Michael and narrowed his gaze in mock disappointment. Yet no matter how hard he attempted to look stern, the edges of his mouth crinkled into smile lines, tugging his mouth into a warm grin. "Matter fact, we were gonna invite you over for dinner tonight to make sure you were eating more than diner food. You look thin and the Mrs. worries you ain't eating right."

Vanessa caught the embarrassed look on Michael's face and smothered a smile behind her hand. He didn't seem to mind, though. His face lit up as he gave her a nod.

"Thanks, Mr. Preston. I'd love to, it's just, I already have plans." He pulled his gaze from hers and returned his attention to the cotton candy vendor. "My friend Vee came to visit with me for the festival. Vee"—he reached for Vanessa, opening his arm and beckoning her to stand closer—"this is Mr. Preston. He owns and operates the best orchard in Monroe Hills."

The older man extended one hand to her and removed his hat in a display of suave, old-school manners. "Hello, dear. It's very nice to meet you." He playfully smacked his hat against Michael's arm and grinned at her. "What are you doing running around with this sourpuss?"

A look passed between her and Michael and she could see the concern popping up in the faint lines on his forehead.

"Michael said the festival's spectacular, so I figured I'd come out and give it a try."

"Well, welcome." Mr. Preston nodded as he released her hand and put his hat back on. "You make sure he shows you a good time. If he doesn't, you come find me and I'll set him straight. Ya hear?"

"Hey," Michael protested. "You've known me all my life. You're supposed to take my side."

"Son," Mr. Preston said with a laugh. "When a woman this beautiful is around, there's only one side to take: hers. Maybe if you'd learn that, she wouldn't be the first friend you'd brought 'round these parts."

Michael blew out an exasperated breath and threw up his hands, shaking his head in exaggerated frustration.

"Can I just have the cotton candy, please?"

"She certainly can," Mr. Preston began as he grabbed a paper cone and began twisting and scooping up the sugary blue treat. He smiled and handed Vanessa what looked like a triple-size portion that made Michael's jaw drop.

"Thank you, Mr. Preston. This looks delicious."

"I hope you enjoy it. Hopefully Michael will bring you by the orchard so you can try some of our homemade apple pie and cider. We'll be serving them up tomorrow at the gala. But they're always best fresh."

"Michael, will you?"

He didn't have time to answer before Mr. Preston jumped in. "If he wants the pie and the jug of cider we always give him to take home, he'd sho' nuff better."

Michael nodded with no hesitation. "I'll bring her by around lunch. Maybe Mrs. Preston would take pity on us and add a jar of her homemade caramel to her care package."

The older man picked up a second paper cone and swirled it in the steel bowl. He covered it with a puff of blue cotton candy, handed it to Michael, and said, "I think we can definitely work that out."

Michael paid for their treats, and they said their goodbyes to the friendly cotton candy peddler. As they walked, Vanessa tore off a piece of the confection and shoved it in her mouth. Cotton candy was one of those things you never thought of eating on any given day. Yet when you were surrounded by a crowd of people, loud music, flashing lights, and amusement rides, it was impossible not to indulge.

"Is it always like this in this town?" Even though she managed to garble the few words as she chewed, he understood what she said.

"Like what?"

"People being so invested in your well-being?"

"Is that how you saw that?" Sarcasm laced his reply, amusing him. "I call it nosy busybodies."

She bumped into his arm purposely. "Come on. That old man was so sweet. It's obvious he cares a great deal about you. I admit," she continued as she stopped to pop another puff of cotton candy in her mouth, "I thought it would annoy me to have people be so familiar. But that was actually kind of nice, to see the way he teased you like a favorite uncle."

"Nice for you, maybe," he grumbled, falling back into that grouchy persona he tried so hard to convince her was his true self. But with each passing moment, she doubted that more and more.

"I'm serious. I'd give anything to have someone worry about whether I was eating enough and to fix me pie and cider just because they were thinking of me."

"It is nice in a way," he answered. "When my parents died, things were a mess. I was so busy trying to get everything settled while taking care of my sister, I would forget to eat. So Mrs. Preston started dropping off care packages to me and Cindy until I could get my bearings."

She thought about how hard it was to lose her father four years ago and how having that kind of support would've meant the world to her.

"It's easy to forget about yourself when you're dealing with the business of grief."

"You sound like you know a little something about it?"

She huffed. "Yeah. Firsthand experience. My mom died when I was little. I barely have memories of her. My dad died four years ago. I had to handle everything by myself." She pulled her eyes away from his and dropped her gaze to the sidewalk. "Karl was away on business. He made it home for the funeral. Unsurprisingly, no sooner than the door to Dad's mausoleum closed, he was gone on another business trip."

Michael reached for her hand, running his fingers carefully over her knuckles. "He left you alone to bury your father?"

She dared to lift her gaze and saw dark brown eyes filled with compassion, empathy, edged with anger. "I was used to it. Karl traveled quite a bit."

He lifted her hand to his mouth and pressed a gentle kiss on the back of it, his gaze burning into her, seeing beyond her calm facade.

"If you were mine, there's no way I'd ever let you go through something like that without being by your side."

The deep timbre of his voice heated the brisk air the early fall weather brought.

"It . . . ah . . ." She stumbled over her words, getting caught up in the intensity of his dark gaze. "It wasn't easy. It taught me to treasure those who support me, though. That's why I love Janae and Cree so much. They're the siblings I never had and the support system I always wanted."

Her heart sped up as he rubbed his thumb in circles over the back of her hand where his lips had just touched her.

"Apparently," she continued, "it's something that's particular to residents of this town. From what I can tell, good people live in Monroe Hills."

He stared at her silently, his eyes searching for something she wasn't necessarily ready to give. After last night, the idea of being physically intimate with Michael was an easy decision. Yes, please, and thank you. Except the way his gaze bore through her, asking for entrance into her core, made her uneasy.

Uneasy was a misnomer. She was downright unhinged by the way he seemed able to sneak past her defenses. She'd kept her cold exterior for so long, letting no one other than her girls know how heartbreakingly lonely her marriage was.

Yet as he looked at her with that deep dark gaze, all she wanted to do was swing the doors open and give him the access he was silently asking for.

Not today!

She shook her head, breaking free of his hold. Giving into desire was one thing. Letting him really know her? Nope, that wasn't an option on the table at all.

Hopefully she remembered that the next time he was bringing her to ecstasy or gifting her with the warmth of his kindness.

"What's going on here?"

Michael stopped and followed the direction of Vanessa's pointed finger until he saw Mr. Montgomery's shop. It stood in the middle of Main Street, undecorated with the gates down and locks firmly secured.

"That's Mr. Montgomery's accounting business."

"The lights are on but the gates are down. Is he the only person in this town who hates festivals?"

As folks walked around them on the street, he placed his hand at the small of her back and guided her to the storefront.

"No, Mr. Montgomery adores festivals, especially this one. His son lives out in Virginia. He and his husband just had their first child, so Mr. Montgomery's decided to retire and move down there to be closer to them. According to him, he wants to be a hands-on grandpa. That little girl will be the most delightfully spoiled child to ever live."

A slim older white man with a clean-shaven face with white hair cut into a tapered style saw them looking through the window and waved before coming to the door and welcoming them inside.

"Hey, Michael, I'm glad I got to see you before I left. I'll be on my way to meet my grandbaby first thing in the morning."

"Have Mark and Kenny decided on a name yet?"

The older man's face lit up bright. "They have! They won't tell me until I get there, though. They wanna surprise me. Tell you the truth, I don't much care what they call her. Whatever her name is, she's my grandbaby and that's all that matters."

Michael could see the slightly sad tinge to Vanessa's face and he imagined she must be thinking about her own grandparents, especially the grandmother she spoke so fondly of.

"Mr. Montgomery. This is my friend Vee; she's an accountant too."

She extended her hand, sharing a broad smile with the gentleman. "Hello, Mr. Montgomery. This is a lovely shop you have here." She turned to look at the small office space. "My grandparents used to own a shop about this size. That's where I learned my love of numbers and finance. Michael tells me you'll be leaving it soon."

"Yes," he answered with a twinkle of excitement in his eyes. "I signed the papers today to officially put it on the market."

"I certainly understand your zeal to get away. A new baby is a great reason to make a move like this. Still, there is a part of me that's a little sad every time I hear a place like yours that helps everyday people is closing."

He pushed his hands in his pocket and nodded. "You sound like someone who's spent one too many years working in a corporate setting."

Michael watched a somber curtain fall over her face, making him ache to pull her into his embrace.

"Unfortunately, you're right. I worked in corporate accounting for twenty years. I'm thrilled to be out of it."

Vanessa scanned the room again with a longing gaze and Michael could tell her mind was taking her back to that simpler time, before the complications that eventually took over her life.

"Just out of curiosity." Mr. Montgomery tilted his head as a crooked smile curved one side of his mouth. "Are you in the market to buy a small accounting business? 'Cause if you are, I actually have one I could sell you."

Michael didn't know why the idea of Vanessa owning this shop, working just a few doors away from him at the sheriff's office, made something warm and bright bloom in his chest.

"That's actually not a bad idea, Vee. You should exchange information with Mr. Montgomery so the two of you can talk about this."

Michael was so caught up in the idea, he almost didn't notice the slight tension in Vanessa's body as Mr. Montgomery extended a business card to her.

She took the card, dropping it inside her bag and exchanging one with the new grandfather. "Your shop is lovely. Unfortunately, I'm just visiting Monroe Hills."

"Well." He shook his head from side to side. "You visit long enough and you just might end up staying."

Michael and Vanessa said their goodbyes before stepping out onto the sidewalk.

"How long has he been here?"

"Forever," Michael answered. When she folded her arms and tilted her head, he realized she was looking for an actual numeral.

I guess accountants are always serious about their numbers.

"He's been here since before I was born." It was true. Michael didn't know who the town accountant was before Mr. Montgomery.

"To be in business that long, he must have been good at what he did and trusted by his clients."

"He's still good at what he does. The town is definitely gonna suffer with him leaving. You know, it really isn't a bad idea to consider buying his business. It could be a good thing for you."

She didn't answer, just stared at him with her brows pinched together as she tried to figure what he was getting at.

"You said you've been restless, looking for that next thing you're supposed to do with your life. You even talked about starting up a small accounting business. If you bought Mr. Montgomery's place, you'd have built-in clientele, and you wouldn't have to start from nothing. You should definitely look into it."

Her brain was still turning; he could tell from the way she kept glancing back at the building. Watching her like this, distracted, not worried about anything in particular, it was somehow refreshing. Not that he'd known her long enough to truly be able to name her expressions; he was still working on that. Right now, though, she looked almost whimsical, as if she were in another world unconcerned with the troubles of today.

He reached out and tucked the sleek lock of hair behind her ear, bringing her out of her musings. When she turned her gaze to him, he cupped her cheek.

"Everything okay?"

She blinked. When her dark eyes were clear, she zeroed in on him. "Yeah," she answered. "I was just thinking accounting has become such a corporate thing lately, it's kinda nice to see an old-fashioned place like this made for real people. In New York and New Jersey, you have these pop-up businesses that work from about January to

April doing taxes. Regrettably, there aren't very many accounting and bookkeeping places that work year-round helping their clients build lasting financial stability. We've lost that personal touch."

"Have you ever worked in a place like this?" He dropped his hand to her arm. He would've loved to keep his palm against the smooth skin of her face. Considering they were standing on the street, however, he thought it might seem a bit odd.

Yeah, as if standing in the middle of the sidewalk rubbing her arm isn't weird. Who do you think you're fooling?

"I told you my grandfather came from a family of jewelers, right?" He nodded, and she continued. "Well, my grandfather started his small accounting firm and hired my grandmother as a secretary. Soon, he realized she had an affinity for accounting too, and he promoted her, eventually making her a partner in the business. Not long after that, they married and had my dad.

"I used to go to their shop all the time and watch the two of them with their old-fashioned counting machines. I always wanted one. When my father took over the company, he didn't share their vision of a small family business. Instead, he worked tirelessly to turn their mom-and-pop operation into this impersonal conglomerate."

"So you still run it?"

She shook her head. "No. It was too much like what I had at Karl's company, and I just didn't want to commit to some soulless entity. I let his partners buy me out instead."

He let his hand slide down to her hand, taking one, then the other into his. "Do you regret it?"

She looked back at Mr. Montgomery's shop before meeting his gaze. "No," she answered. "It was nothing like I remember my grandparents' shop being. It lost the thing I loved about it."

"What's that?"

She took a breath, sadness filling her eyes. "Heart."

"Yet another reason for you to talk to Montgomery. You'd be perfect at running your own firm."

"Michael." His name was a labored sigh, drawing his concern as he stepped closer to her. "I know you're just trying to help. But please, stop trying to sell me Mr. Montgomery's business. I'm not interested, and if I were, I'm more than capable of doing it without being nudged by a man I've only recently become acquainted with."

Her shoulders slumped with an invisible burden and he fought against the voice in his head, telling him not to let himself get pulled in any further. He wasn't strong enough for that. The need building in him overtook good sense, and he pulled her into his arms, hoping she'd take whatever she needed from him in that moment.

"I'm sorry, Vanessa." He hoped his voice conveyed his sincerity. He was sorry he'd somehow offended her, even if he couldn't figure out what was so terrible about helping her see what he was fast becoming aware of: Vanessa could definitely fit into Monroe Hills. After all, she fit right in with him. Especially as he pulled her into the cove of his arms.

"Hi, Michael, fancy seeing you here."

The familiar voice made his entire body tense. Even Vanessa noticed it, because she pulled her head from where it rested against his shoulder and looked up at him with unanswered questions floating in her eyes.

He turned to the voice, and when Vanessa attempted to step away from him, he kept one arm around her shoulders and pulled her closer to him.

"Amanda Sayers." He pasted on his friendly but professional smile and greeted her. "It wouldn't look right for the sheriff to miss the biggest event this town holds all year. How've you been?"

Amanda, a tall, slender woman with blond hair and blue eyes, stood directly in front of them. Although she was talking to Michael, she was staring directly at Vanessa.

"I've been busy," she responded. "Seems like you have too." She extended her hand to Vanessa. "Hi, I'm Amanda. Welcome to Monroe Hills."

Vanessa glanced up at Michael before she extended her hand to Amanda.

"Hi Amanda. I'm Vee. I'm a friend of Michael's."

"I hope our sheriff is showing you a good time. He can be sort of single-minded about his work sometimes, completely forgetting life exists outside of his office."

Michael stared at Amanda through the narrowed slits of his eyes. That was a definite slight, no matter how friendly Amanda's voice sounded. He didn't take it personally, though. He'd been turning down her invitations to get to know each other better since he'd returned to Monroe Hills. Seeing how Amanda didn't always think the word "no" applied to her, she didn't seem bothered by him consistently declining her invitations.

He could feel Vanessa's arm lift and circle his waist, and somehow the possessive nature of their embrace felt right.

"Well, I'll have to do my best to keep him otherwise occupied, I guess."

The false smile on Amanda's face slipped a little, and Michael had to fight himself not to snicker.

"Well, good luck with that." Amanda nodded in Michael's direction as she stepped around him. "See you at the auction tomorrow," she threw over her shoulder. "I've got my paddle ready to go."

Michael suppressed the groan sitting in the middle of his throat.

"She seems a bit . . ."

"Jealous?" Michael countered as he closed his eyes and pinched the bridge of his nose.

"I was gonna say possessive," she answered, "although jealous works too. She was definitely trying to mark her territory. Something you wanna tell me? I know I don't have any hold on you. It's just . . . considering you kissed me in the middle of your sister's shop yesterday and screwed me until the wee hours of the morning, I'd at least like to know if I'm stepping on another woman's turf."

He pulled her tighter into his arms, keeping her flush against him as he looked directly into her eyes.

"Like I told you when we were talking about the auction, Amanda is ambitious and won't take no for an answer. She only wants me because she thinks dating the sheriff will up her standing among Monroe socialites. I'm not interested."

"You sure?" The crooked grin on her face was enough to let him know she was teasing him. And the spark of something deliciously sinister in her eyes did more than amuse him. If he was honest, it was damn well turning him on and that was something he definitely didn't need in the middle of the street.

He lifted three fingers in the air as validation. "Scout's honor."

She shook her head. "If anyone else had said that to me, I'd laugh until I cried. Yet somehow, I get the feeling growing up here in Mayberry, you probably were a Scout."

"I promise if you keep trashing my town, I'm gonna forget all those lessons on good manners and duty the Scouts taught me."

"Someone's sensitive about his small town."

He took a deep breath to answer her and held up a pointed finger to playfully make his point. "There you go, badmouthing my town again."

"Badmouthing is a strong word," she responded. "Especially considering *The Andy Griffith Show* made Mayberry everyone's favorite place."

"So, you're saying Monroe Hills is your favorite place?"

The air heated around them, and suddenly the amusement in him faded. He'd said it with just enough lightness that she'd think he was joking. Deep down, though, something he couldn't name was tightening around his chest, making it hard to breathe while he waited for her answer.

She looked at him, her smile wide and her lids lightly closed with her long, dark eyelashes fluttering against her full cheeks. She played the coy, bashful role well. Then, when she finally lifted her eyes to him, he knew he'd lost the game they were playing.

"I'm saying," she said, as she tugged the corner of her bottom lip between her teeth and that invisible band around his chest closed another notch, "Monroe Hills certainly has its attractions."

His heart thumped harder and faster in his chest. If he wasn't careful, her wordplay would be the death of him.

He shook his head, trying to remember this was only for fun. That's all it could be considering who they were.

"Playing with fire gets you burned, Vanessa."

His throat was raw and his voice like gravel. The sound should've been a warning for anyone close enough to hear. Instead of fear or retreat, however, he saw temptation swirling in the depths of her chocolate gaze.

She grabbed his hand, then looked up and winked at him before she responded, "Promises, promises, Sheriff," before she tugged him toward his sister's shop. And like the catch of the day caught on a shiny hook, he followed in her wake.

Chapter 15

~

"MICHAEL, ARE YOU AWAKE?"

A few seconds after Vanessa lightly tapped on the door, she placed her ear to it to see if she heard movement. From what she knew of Michael so far, he was an early riser. Therefore, when she hadn't found him downstairs after she'd showered and dressed, she thought she'd knock on his door to check on him.

With her ear still pressed to the door, all she heard was silence until the very last moment when the door suddenly fell open. She tried to prepare for kissing the hardwood floor, then unexpectedly found herself pressed against a wall of hard flesh instead.

Quick yet familiar hands wrapped around her waist, steadying her so she didn't end up in an embarrassing heap.

"Morning to you, too."

His voice was rich and deep, as intoxicating as a shot of brandy in her coffee. Though it was the feel of his bare chest, covered slightly with a gentle smattering of fine, dark hair across his pecs, that made her forget exactly why she'd shown up in front of his bedroom door in the first place.

That and how good he smells. Why does he smell so good?

She inhaled deeply and the faint scent of something earthy

tinged with spice filled her senses and she relaxed against him, taking another long sniff of the glorious scent.

"Are you smelling me?"

She didn't even have the shame to pretend he hadn't busted her. Nope, she fully committed and pressed her nose impossibly close to his skin and sniffed again.

He chuckled and said, "I guess it's a good thing I just showered, then."

She found enough of her pride left to pull her face away, but when she attempted to separate herself from him completely, he tightened his hold around her waist.

"I don't think I've ever smelled that particular brand of cologne before. It's very . . . nice."

He hitched his mouth up on one side with a cocky, knowing grin. "I'm not wearing any cologne. Just soap and water."

She closed her eyes and groaned. Him standing under a spray of water glistening with soapsuds wasn't an image she needed in her head right now. That didn't stop her brain from conjuring up the image, anyway.

"That's . . . um . . . that's some . . . good soap, then." Even she had to chuckle at her inarticulate response.

"Did you need something?"

Still slightly embarrassed at her reaction to his feel and smell, she lifted her gaze in a side glance to meet his eyes.

"I just wanted to make sure you were okay. You're usually up before me and I couldn't find you downstairs."

"I went for a run in the neighborhood this morning. I'm usually gone and back before you get up. After all our fun at the carnival, though, I got a late start."

She slid her hands from his chest, down his arms, until they were prying his firm hands from around her waist. This kind of proximity was messing with her head, and as much as she liked the feel and smell of him, she had come in here with a purpose.

"Well, Cree and Janae are going to pick me up in a little while so I can find an outfit for the gala. I wanted to let you know I was leaving."

He placed his hands on his hips, drawing her eyes to the sharp vee peeking out above the waistband of his sweatpants.

Do not look below his waistband. Do not look below his waistband.

"Vanessa, you've decided to attend the gala?"

Thank God for small mercies.

"Ummm . . . yeah." She stumbled over her thoughts, fighting to connect the words so they'd make sense when she spoke them. "I . . . I thought it would be fun. So, I'm going out with the girls to get my hair done and go shopping for an outfit. Remember, I wasn't supposed to be here this long. I don't have anything appropriate to wear."

He stood there nodding, with his hands still sitting low on his hips, looking like a cross between Superman and a male underwear model.

"I just wanted to see if you'll be all right handling the store alone today."

"Yeah," he responded. "Cindy's assistant is going to be there. Considering tonight is the gala, I'm sure the salon and the stores will be packed. Have the ladies bring you back here instead of the shop when you're done. We'll leave as soon as you get back."

She tipped her head in agreement, then turned to leave. Before she could move, however, his hand was on her forearm, stopping her. "Vanessa."

She turned, reminding herself to keep her composure. Yes, she'd agreed to let herself have fun. That didn't mean she needed to seem desperate for his attention, though, even if she was.

"Despite being put on display like a flat-screen TV on Black Friday, this year doesn't feel so bad. For the first time, I'm looking forward to going to the gala."

"Why's that?"

She didn't know what he'd say, she just hoped it was something that was going to make her heart beat even faster than it already did.

"Because I'll have the most beautiful woman in town on my arm. I'd be an idiot not to celebrate being such a lucky bastard."

Yeah, that was it. The wonderful thing that was going to make her heart beat so fast she thought she might have a cardiac event. His words leaving her mouth dry, she swallowed, then cleared her throat.

"For a small-town sheriff, you sure have big game, Michael."

He crossed his arms and lifted his brow. "Is it working?"

She nodded enthusiastically, "Oh, it's working. That's for damn sure. Let me get out of here before my girlfriends catch us in a compromising position. Wouldn't want to feed the gossip mill. Would we?"

"With you," he said as he leaned closer, placing a finger under her chin, "I'd be willing to risk it." He placed his lips on hers and her body quivered as if it were more liquid than flesh and bone.

His lips were soft and full, yet still so strong. Guiding her, tempting her, making her chase him for what she wanted. If temptation was a field of study, he had to have a doctorate. Because there was no reason a simple kiss from a man she'd only known a handful of days should make her body burn with need this way.

Okay, she'd slept with said man, yet even so, she shouldn't be affected by his game.

He lifted his head, smiling down at her with this "Yeah, I know you want this" look in his hooded eyes.

His presumptive gaze should've offended her. Yet, to no one's surprise—especially not her own—the only thing she felt coursing through her veins was hot, scaring desire.

"Have fun," he whispered after giving her one final peck and stepping away from her.

She blew out a breath and nodded. "Yeah . . . fun. That's exactly what I'm thinking about having now."

"Vanessa, what are you doing in there?" She cringed at the shrill sound of Janae yelling her name in the small boutique. She was currently standing at the mirror in a dressing room, trying on what felt like the millionth outfit the store owner had given her.

"Vanessa," Cree said, joining in the chorus. "Come on, it can't be that bad."

"Says the woman with hips and boobs for days. These dresses make me look like I'm living in a bad eighties high school dance movie. I'm forty, not a teenaged prom queen."

She stepped out of the dressing room and caught her friends fighting to keep their laughter at bay. When Vanessa stepped forward and nearly tripped over the large taffeta skirt of the dress, they understandably lost control and crumpled in laughter.

Vanessa turned around to look in the larger mirror and fell into a fit of giggles with her friends. Layers of peach taffeta covered her, and although the color looked great against her dark brown skin, she would not be caught dead outside this boutique in it.

The boutique owner tried hard to keep a professional demeanor, but when Vanessa glanced over at her, her shoulders began shaking with laughter too.

"I'm sorry. All of our more cosmopolitan options were purchased ages ago. I'm afraid this and a tuxedo are all we have left in stock in your size."

Vanessa's gaze collided with her two friends' and all three of them said in unison, "Let's see the tuxedo."

Vanessa gladly peeled the peach monstrosity off and pushed it over the top of the dressing room door to Janae. Soon, the boutique owner was sliding her a black garment bag through the same opening. She hung the bag on a nearby hook and stared at it with trepidation inching up her spine.

"If this thing has a ruffled shirt and a cummerbund, I'm going to lose my shit."

She slowly unzipped the bag, pushing it back until the tuxedo was visible. Navy blue with black satin lapels jumped out at her and hope built slowly in her chest. "So far, so good." She was cautiously hopeful that she could wear this and not look like a fool tonight.

Excited, she put the clothes on, refusing to look at herself until she was in the larger mirror outside. When she stepped out of the room, her friends' chatter stopped, and for a second, she thought retreat might be the best option. Except this was the last chance she had and she knew she had to at least look at herself before she vetoed it.

She turned to the mirror on the wall and released the breath she was holding. The black rouched bustier made her girls sit pretty and gave her stomach the illusion of flatness she knew didn't exist.

The slender navy blue pants with satin piping down the side of each leg made her legs look long, paired with the gold, sequined heels the saleswoman had just brought over, and she looked like a runway model. The single-breasted two-button jacket gave her sharp, strong shoulders, taking the outfit overboard from nice to sexy as hell.

She turned to her friends, holding her hands out as she spun in a slow circle. "So, ladies, is this it?"

Neither spoke, both nodding slowly with their gazes fixed on her. "Well, if you two have nothing to stay, I must be stunning." She found her reflection in the mirror, running her hands slowly down the front of the form-fitting jacket and bustier, sticking her leg out to one side and jutting her hip out to the other while she tucked her hand into her pants pocket, pushing the jacket flap behind her, exposing the rounded mound of her breast. Yeah, she was serving stunning with a side of sexy as hell with this look. This was perfect for her first and probably only official date with Sheriff Michael.

"You're about to put a hurting on that man, aren't you?" Janae's question made her hitch her mouth into a confident grin.

"I certainly am."

Cree came to stand next to her and gave her an appraising stare through the mirror. "Chile, he doesn't have a clue what he's up against, does he?"

Nope, he didn't. And she didn't feel the least bit bad about catching him off guard.

Chapter 16

～

"MICHAEL," VANESSA BELLOWED FROM DOWNSTAIRS. "The cliché is that the woman is supposed to be the one taking forever to get ready. Are you purposely trying to make us miss the gala?"

Yeah.

Even though he wouldn't say it out loud, he knew it was the truth. He hated this thing and always waited until the last possible minute to get dressed and get on his way. Usually, Cindy was there to kick his butt in gear and get him situated so he'd leave on time. She was also here to tie this blasted bow tie he couldn't get right if his life depended on it.

"Fuck it." He threw up his hands, grabbed his wallet, and headed downstairs. He'd just have to go sans tie. He couldn't spend another fifteen minutes trying to get this shit right.

"Michael!"

"On my way!" he hollered from his room. He thought about pulling the tie from his neck and leaving it on the dresser. However, as he glimpsed the untied ends hanging on either side of his neck, he thought perhaps he could pull off that "I'm too cool to tie my bow tie" look.

Determined not to fret over it any longer, he made his way down the stairs to find Vanessa standing by his fireplace on the other side of the living room.

She turned around to face him, and he damn near missed the bottom step by focusing on her instead of his feet. She was wearing a tuxedo that fit every curve she had and made him ball his hands into tight fists for fear he wouldn't be able to keep them to himself.

Her sleek bob had been curled into beach waves with one side pinned back, exposing the elegant curve of her neck. Her jacket was open, and the sight of her plump breasts essentially standing at attention for his viewing pleasure made his tuxedo pants more uncomfortable than the stiff material usually would.

"That bad," she said with a playful grin. She knew damn well there was nothing remotely bad about her look or her outfit. Everything about it said Sexiest Boss of the Year.

"Yeah," he choked out. "Perhaps we should stay in and discuss my thoughts on what you're wearing."

She walked closer to where he stood, pushing both hands in her pockets, which gave him a better view of the beautiful brown skin of her chest and bosom. She was definitely not playing fair.

"Really?" she questioned, lifting her brow in mock confusion. "What exactly are your thoughts?"

He somehow found the strength and focus to make his legs and feet work to step down off that bottom step that led into the living room. "I'm afraid what I have to say might offend your delicate nature. Getting slapped right before an event may depreciate the value of the goods I have to put on display to get people to part with their coins."

"And if I promise to keep my hands to myself?"

He stepped closer until they were almost touching. "That's the problem." He looked her up and down before bringing his gaze back to hers. "I don't want you to keep your hands to yourself."

He waited to see if she would back away. If she showed even

the slightest bit of hesitancy, he'd pause this game they were playing. Yes, he wanted her again. But only if the desire was mutual. His ego couldn't take it if he didn't see the exact same need in her eyes.

"You see that as a problem?" She shrugged her shoulders and folded her arms, pushing her tits impossibly high, making the delicious vee of her cleavage more pronounced and tempting. "I see it as a goal."

"I keep telling you you're playing with fire."

"And I keep telling you, I like the heat. What's the problem, Sheriff?"

He groaned, closing his eyes and running his hand down the length of his face. "If I didn't know I would end up having to deal with the mayor's bullshit behind my absence, I'd strip every layer of clothing from your skin. Since that's not an option right now, how about we get on with this shitshow so I can eventually be put out of my misery?"

She raised a slender finger to make sure she had his attention. It was pointless since her breathing was enough to catch his notice.

"I have a counteroffer. How about we go to the gala and make an attempt to enjoy ourselves? And if you make a real effort to have fun, I promise to reward you handsomely when we return."

The way the word "reward" slipped off her lips made his cock twitch. And if he wasn't cautious, he would not be fit to be in public. He carefully grazed his eyes over her form to make sure he was reading her signals correctly.

"I promise," she spoke softly while raising her hand and cupping his chin, "your reward will involve you peeling every layer of clothing from my skin, just as you proposed."

He could feel his blood heating and was certain she could see the damnable blush that colored his skin whenever heat, be it natural or sexual, spread through him.

"Then I guess we'd best be on our way."

She stepped away, grabbing a small clutch purse from a nearby table. She turned toward the door, then stopped to face him again. She put the clutch between her knees and reached up to his neck.

"First, let's get this tie correctly knotted. Despite what you might see in magazines, bow ties are not meant to be worn like this."

It took her a few seconds to complete what he'd spent nearly twenty minutes trying to get done. There was obviously something magical about her fingers, and he had every intention of exploring that hypothesis again when they returned.

"Now," she huffed as she straightened his tie, then looked up and smiled at him. "It's time for you to take me to the ball."

Vanessa walked into the town catering hall, not sure what she was expecting. Taking a long glance around the space, she admitted that crystal chandeliers and marble staircases probably weren't it.

Check your privilege, Vanessa. Just because it's small doesn't mean it's rinky-dink.

Michael placed a gentle yet firm hand at the base of her spine before looking down at her. "Are you ready?"

"For what exactly?"

"It's one thing for you to walk on the street with me at the festival," he whispered, trying to make sure she was the only one who heard him. "Being here with me like this almost ensures the town will see us an item, though. You okay with that?"

She was too okay with that. That was her problem. She enjoyed being in Michael's company. She liked the playful way they interacted. Still, by the very nature of their connection, she also knew it could never be more than these few moments they'd get to spend while she waited to speak to Cindy and for her car to be repaired. There was nothing that could happen after that.

Her life was waiting for her in New Jersey.

What life exactly is that?

The one she was supposed to be rebuilding. The one she'd promised herself she'd have, despite how listless she felt.

She looped her hand around his waist and plastered on the widest grin she could. "I'm perfectly okay with people making assumptions about our relationship. It's not like I'll be here. What do I care?"

She felt his body tense slightly next to hers. Unsure of what that meant, if anything, she searched his gaze for clues. Something dark was there. Not quite anger, not quite sadness, yet something she'd said had put that look there.

"Everything okay, Michael?"

He sighed deeply, pulling his gaze away from her in the process. "Nothing. Just ready to get this show on the road so I can be done with this ridiculousness."

He moved them toward a set of double doors. Standing there, she could hear the muted sounds of music coming through them. He reached for the doorknob, opening the door to the amplified sounds and a flurry of people moving throughout the dimmed room.

They stepped inside, and all heads turned their way. It became quickly apparent that Michael wasn't kidding about the attention. With so many people packed into the immense room, she wagered that most of Monroe Hills was present and accounted for.

A glimpse of waving arms caught her attention, and she spied Cree and Janae motioning them to a table in the back of the room.

"This way. Cree and Janae probably saved us seats."

He nodded, dropping his hand from her back and slipping her hand into his. He led her through the throng of people, watching them as they moved to their intended location. When they arrived, a dark-skinned Black man with smooth, rich skin, thick, close-cropped curls, and a goatee stood.

"Thanks for showing up. I had a bet with Adam you'd find a way to back out. I knew you wouldn't shirk your duty."

Michael released Vanessa's hand to shake the stranger's. "I hope your stake was high. Knowing he has to forfeit cash because he bet against me makes dressing in this damn tuxedo worth it."

Michael turned back to Vanessa briefly before talking to the man again. "Vee, this is my good friend Derrick Lattimore. Derrick, this is Vee."

She saw the strange look pass between Cree and Janae sitting at the table and gave her head a brief shake to keep them from voicing their confusion.

"Derrick, it's lovely to meet you."

"Same to you. I wasn't expecting Michael to bring a date to this thing. He always goes stag."

"Well, I'm only in town for a few days, so we figured what's the harm."

His lips curved into a broad grin, showing a mouthful of white teeth. "In that case, let's hope you have a good time, then." He turned to the table and back to them. "I'm headed to the bar for a drink run. Anyone want anything?"

Janae and Cree asked for wine, and Vanessa and Michael declined. When Derrick left, Michael walked over to Cree and Janae, kissing them each on the cheek and waiting for her to do the same before he pulled out a chair next to Janae. Once Vanessa was seated, he took the one directly next to her.

"Who is Vee, and why is she here and not Vanessa?" There Janae went, speaking her mind before anyone served her a line of bullshit.

"Michael mentioned Vanessa to his friends, only when Cindy's travel plans changed and I was marooned here, we thought it might be best if as few people as possible knew who I actually am."

"Yeah." Michael leaned in. "We don't want anyone to spill the beans, even accidentally, about why she's here."

Cree giggled. "And you know your man Derrick can't hold water. Is that it?"

Michael chuckled, and a youthfulness fell over his face. "You've known him just as long as I have. You know the answer to that question."

They all shared a group laugh as Derrick returned to the table.

"What's so funny?" he asked as he placed the ladies' drink orders in front of them. They all shared a knowing look and tried to keep their faces straight.

"Nothing much," Vanessa answered. "Just talking about how useless Michael is at tying a bow tie."

Michael leaned in closer at the sound of his name, rubbing his shoulder against hers. "Thank goodness Vee rescued me from my torture."

"That's noble of you, Vee." He lifted the tumbler he was holding to his mouth and took a sip of the amber liquid. "I guess it's lucky he found you. Speaking of," he said as he put his drink down and leaned his elbows on the table. "Where did he find you?"

Michael put his arm around her and pulled her closer, his nearness throwing her off her game slightly. The way that man smelled made her want to plant her damn nose in his neck. Regrettably, that wasn't appropriate at an event like this.

"Do I cross-examine your dates, D?"

Derrick didn't take his eyes off her, despite Michael's effort to deflect. Most people would feel nervous under this kind of pressure. Not her, though. He assumed it was because she'd spent a lifetime navigating fancy parties such as these, so hiding within plain sight was second nature. She put on a friendly smile, straightened her shoulders and looked directly at Derrick.

"At my favorite coffee shop." She felt Michael's body tense next to hers. She put a firm hand on his thigh and squeezed lightly, hopefully giving him something else to focus on than his friend's interrogation. "It was packed, and he had an unoccupied seat in his booth. I asked if I could share his table and he said yes. That conversation led to me coming out here to visit."

Derrick looked between them with a look she instantly recognized. It was the "This sounds plausible, but I'm still looking for any trace of bullshit in your statement" look. Too bad he wouldn't find anything there. The best lies were peppered with truth. He'd never catch her unless she wanted to be caught.

When you'd survived the hell she'd gone through at the hands of Karl, you learned to cover your tracks pretty well to fool the outside world.

"Amazing how your coffee addiction ended up paying off."

Michael didn't respond. He simply leaned in and kissed her temple gently, making her wish this event were over and they were already back at Michael's house. There they would get to the entertainment portion of the evening.

Derrick took a breath, poised to say something else, when the music quieted and the DJ's voice came over the speakers instead. "Good evening everyone, please take your seats as our host, Mayor Healy, comes to the stage."

A tall, South Asian man with broad shoulders and dark hair stood at the podium just to the side of the runway at the front of the room. A large round of applause greeted him, and Vanessa figured this town either really loved their mayor or they were good at pretending to be enthusiastic about their elected officials.

"Good evening, Monroe Hills. I'm thrilled to be your host once again for our annual singles auction. There are two ways to place your bids. The first is through your bidding paddles at the center of your tables. The second is by going to the business office across the hall and placing your bid in advance. Once bidding begins on the single of your choice, advance bidding is closed. The highest bidder wins a friendly date with one of our eligible singles. Please make certain you stop in the business office across the hall to complete all promissory notes before the end of the gala. The action starts in fifteen minutes. I'm asking all participating singles to take your place backstage at this time."

Vanessa looked around the room. Although there was quiet as Mayor Healy spoke, there was an anticipatory hum of excitement that seemed to generate an almost audible buzz.

"By the look of this room, the crowd seems pretty primed. Do they really like this sort of thing?"

Everyone at the table nodded in unison. "People claim they do it for the good of the university," Cree said.

"Yeah," Janae continued. "Some of them are genuinely interested in helping send kids to school. I'd say most of them do it because it's a chance for a date with their secret crushes." Janae's candid assessment seemed to be shared by the five people seated with Vanessa as they all nodded in unison. "But either way, it's the biggest fundraiser of the year and it sends at least five kids to school on a full four-year ride. Can't be mad at that."

Vanessa turned to Michael to find the line of his jaw tense and muscle ticking.

"I guess that means your suffering begins now?"

He groaned, making each of them chuckle as he pushed his chair back and stood. "Pray for my return. Some of these bidders can get . . . aggressive."

He walked from their table and headed through the curtain at the side of the stage.

"He really hates this, doesn't he?"

Derrick's shoulders shook. "Although Michael's never been one for putting on a show, I think he hates this specifically because of who always ends up winning a date with him."

She narrowed her gaze, waiting for him to continue.

"Amanda Sayers," Derrick continued. "She always manages to put down the winning bid and forces Michael into the date he won't willingly give her any other time."

Vanessa remembered the aura of entitlement Amanda wore when they briefly met during the festival. Maybe it was because she knew Michael wasn't into her, or perhaps it was just simple jealousy.

Whichever it was, Vanessa felt extra petty, which meant Amanda had a surprise coming her way.

"Would you all excuse me for a moment? I need to powder my nose."

When Janae and Cree rose too, she lifted her palm, stopping them. "It's all right. I don't need company this time."

The two shared a strange look before glancing her way and nodding. She walked out of the room, looking in each direction before she headed across the hallway to a smaller catering room that was being used to process payments.

The room was empty until Mayor Healy stepped inside. "Can I help you?"

"Yes, I was looking to make an advance bid on one of the singles, however, I don't see anyone here to complete my transaction."

He smiled kindly and walked her over to one of the empty tables. "That's all right. I think the folks handling this part are taking bids from the participating singles. They'll be over shortly. I can help you, though."

He reached across the table and grabbed a bidding sheet and handed it to her. "Just fill that out and give your donation, and your bid is placed."

She pulled a pen from her clutch and began filling out the form. When she finished, she handed it to the mayor. He gave the form a cursory look until his eyes widened and his gaze slammed into hers.

"I think you may have written the wrong number. Are you sure you meant to write this much?"

He gave her back the paper, and she counted the zeros, making sure she hadn't made a clerical error. When she was certain the number was as she'd intended, she handed the form back to the mayor.

"The number is correct."

He leveled his gaze at her and she could see suspicion contorting his face with pursed lips and a raised brow.

"Is this some kind of game? You do know it's a crime to render false bids, don't you?"

"Mayor Healy," she began softly, attempting to assuage his worry with her calm voice. "I can promise you that bid is very real. If you have concerns about whether or not I can make the payment, tell me how I can submit an electronic donation and I'll wire the money this instant."

He regarded her carefully, tilting his head as he contemplated her offer. He shoved his hands in his pocket and nodded.

"Okay," he agreed, giving her the information and standing with his arms crossed as she completed the transaction on her phone. Before she pressed send, she looked up at him.

"Mayor Healy?" His cautious gaze clashed with hers. "There's only one condition to the donation. It has to remain anonymous. I know secrets aren't necessarily a big thing in Monroe Hills, and under usual circumstances, I wouldn't mind. In this instance, though, it's important that I keep my anonymity."

"Don't you want the recognition?"

She shook her head. "No, I just want to make sure that more children have an opportunity for quality education. I'm assuming that once I complete it, I'll get a receipt for tax purposes, right?"

He nodded.

"Good, that's all I need. That and your promise that no one will know who the donor is. Do I have it?"

He searched her face and after a moment of disbelief, he finally nodded and gave her his hand. "You have it. I'll keep your name a secret. Just know that if that wire transfer is rejected, I'll plaster your name all over this town and beyond. Are we clear?"

"Perfectly," she answered before hitting submit on the donation page. "There," she huffed. "It's done. I guess I better get back there. I don't want to miss the show."

"Miss . . ." He looked down at her original printed form and walked over to one of the tabletop shredders. "Jared, do you want me to just announce you've won?"

"No." She shook her head. "Let people feel as if they have a chance to win. I'm betting the excitement of the show makes the giving that much more enjoyable."

He shredded her document and smiled at her. "Thank you for your generous donation. You're gonna put a lot of kids through school."

"You're more than welcome, Mayor. See you back inside."

The grin on her face spread like butter against warm bread. She reentered the ballroom and walked over to the table.

"That was a long powder-room break. Everything okay?"

Vanessa smiled at Cree. "Of course. You know what a perfectionist I am when it comes to my makeup." She waved her hand, dismissing Cree's concern. "Did Michael walk yet?"

"Not yet," Derrick answered quickly. "I hate to burst your bubble. Michael is an extremely popular draw at this thing. If you're planning on betting on him, you've got a long line and a lot of money ahead of you. He's usually the most sought-after single. Donors usually make their bids in advance and the same person ends up outbidding everyone every single year."

She snuck a careful glance at Cree and Janae and nearly lost it when she saw their smothered amusement.

"Is that a fact, Derrick?" When he confirmed his earlier statement, she shrugged her shoulders. "Well, may the best person win. Regardless of who places the winning bid, the only real winners tonight are the kids that get to go to college after this event."

The mayor, taking his place on stage again, brought their conversation to an end. Like any other auction, the auctioneer's calls for bids were one of the most entertaining parts. He kept the crowd laughing and the well-dressed volunteers parading on the stage kept the fundraising money coming.

They'd made it through a few trips to the buffet table and bar as the auction continued. Now they were nearing the end, and Michael still hadn't walked yet.

"Everyone, we've finally reached the moment we've all been waiting for. The moment our most eligible single takes the stage. He is our trusted sheriff. His duty is to serve and protect Monroe Hills, and I can tell you, he takes his job very seriously. How much are y'all willing to pay for a date with a genuinely good man who has his own pair of handcuffs?"

The crowd's collective laugh filled the air and anticipation made her heart beat faster inside her chest. It wasn't like she hadn't already seen him tonight. He was gorgeous in a T-shirt and sweats. Wearing a tux, he was lethal, a danger to her peace of mind and her undersexed body too.

When he stepped out from behind the curtain, covered in the spotlight and confidence, her mouth went dry. From his dark tapered hair to the pointy patent leather shoes that reflected the gleam of the spotlight, he was sexiness personified.

Someone at the front of the room yelled out, "Five hundred dollars." And from there, the bids flew back and forth, side to side, as the residents of Monroe Hills seemed ready to spend their last spare dime for a date with the unattached sheriff.

"Two thousand dollars."

The number was large enough to get her attention, so she searched the room until she found the only paddle still remaining in the air. It was attached to the hand of none other than Amanda Sayers.

"Do we have another bid?" When no one answered, the mayor looked around the room until his gaze connected with Vanessa's. She gave a brief nod, and he did the same in acknowledgment.

"Going once, going twice . . ." She watched Amanda stand up, looking quite pleased with her perceived win. "Wait." The Mayor lifted his phone in his hand. "I've just been informed we've had an advance bid come in for our dear sheriff to the tune of two million dollars."

There was a collective gasp throughout the room and Vanessa could feel Cree's and Janae's gazes burning into the side of her face. She refused to turn her head and acknowledge them, no matter how badly she wanted to. This night wasn't about her. It was about doing something good for a worthy cause, and to put a man at ease who was somehow making himself more and more necessary in her life.

"Going once, going twice . . ." He waited a beat longer, and when Amanda stormed out of the room, he banged his gavel and yelled, "Sold to an anonymous donor."

The room was still quiet, its shocked attendees looking from one to another or tracking their gazes around the room to see if they could figure out what had just happened.

She made the mistake of looking at Janae and the woman pinned her with a steely gaze that said, "You ain't slick."

Janae lasered her suspicious stare at Vanessa for another moment before she started a slow clap that eventually caught on in the room like a contagious wave at a sporting event. Vanessa could concede that this bidding game was a bit of sport, in a way. She'd done something good for Monroe Hills, kept Michael from doing something he didn't want to do, and blocked Amanda from forcing Michael into a date he didn't want all in one strategic move.

The crowd swelled, and Vanessa was infinitely more pleased with herself until she saw Michael's hard glare land directly on her from the stage.

The music began, encouraging people to dance the remainder of the evening away. Vanessa remained planted in her seat as she watched Michael walk toward her with intention in every step. When he arrived at their table, he said nothing, simply held out his hand to her and waited expectantly for her to take it.

She didn't disappoint. Rising quickly, she nodded to the rest of her tablemates and placed her hand in Michael's, allowing him to lead her onto the floor.

He said nothing, simply pulled her close to him, securing his hand at her waist and placing his mouth next to her ear. The mixture of the sweet yet spicy scent he wore, the circular motion of their dancing, and the heat of him plastered against her—it was almost too much.

She was lightheaded. Her heart was beating so fast she was certain he could both feel and hear it, considering how tightly he held her.

"Why did you do it?"

She cleared her throat, trying to steady herself enough so that chill she felt traversing her entire body didn't turn into a full-body shiver.

"I'm not sure I know what you mean?"

He tightened his hold on her, and the pressure of his hard body, firm and tempting against hers, made her miss a step.

"You know exactly what I'm talking about. How long do you think it's going to take anyone in this town to jump to the conclusion that the incredibly generous donation we just received is because of the beautiful stranger who arrived in their town at the same time?"

His voice was deep and steady. She couldn't tell if that was a sign of his anger or confusion. She pulled back slightly to stare up at him.

"Are you upset?" When he didn't answer immediately, she felt the hairs at her nape prickle her skin. "Michael, I only wanted—"

"Can you afford this, Vanessa?"

She stared at him, tilting her head. Of all the things she'd expected him to ask, that wasn't it.

"You did a background check on me before you arrived on my doorstep. You tell me."

He shook his head. "I didn't look into your financials, Vanessa. Even if I'd wanted to, I couldn't without a warrant. No judge would grant one without cause. I don't know how much money you're worth. I assumed from the exclusive neighborhood, the designer clothes, and the luxury car that you're not hurting for cash. Not hurting isn't the same as being able to spare two million dollars like I'd give away a five-dollar bill out of my wallet."

She stiffened in his arms, trying to pull away. Her resistance seemed to make him tighten his grip as he kept his arm fastened around her waist, keeping her right where he wanted her. Memories of him doing the same thing in bed, pinning her just where he wanted her so she couldn't run from all the pleasure he planned on doling out, assailed her.

She shook her head, trying to clear her mind so she could focus on the conversation at hand. She needed to deal with this. It was one thing for him to boss her around in bed. That she wanted more than her next breath. This thing he did where he was trying to police her life, that didn't feel good at all. It reminded her too much of the life she'd fought so hard to leave behind.

"Vanessa, I'm not angry with you," he began, some of the tension bleeding out of his features. His eyes were aglow with something akin to . . . worry. "I just don't want you to end up doing something to help me that will end up hurting you in the end."

The softness of his eyes in that moment tugged at her heart, making regret spread through her faster than a tipped-over cup of black coffee onto white clothes. Michael wasn't Karl. She needed to stop comparing them.

Finally gathering hold of herself, she leaned in, pressing her lips gently to his. "This gallant knight thing you have going on is the real deal, isn't it?"

A light pink flush colored his cheeks as he smiled down at her. "If you're asking me if doing the right thing and worrying about people is important to me, yeah, it's the real deal."

She threaded her fingers through the shaved hair at the base of his hairline, and the tingling sensation made her repeat the action.

"Listen, I know you're trying to help. I'm realizing that's your nature. It happens to be one of the things I like most about you. I just need you to remember, I make my own decisions. If I want to give away every cent I have, that's my choice to make. I get that you take protecting people seriously. But you gotta stop. People have to make decisions for themselves. Even when they're bad ones."

She could see acceptance reluctantly taking root in his eyes and decided to throw him a bone. "Just to put your mind at ease, I could make that donation several times over for a long time and still touch none of my considerable assets. My divorce attorney was the best and I'm a pretty decent accountant."

He chuckled, biting his lip to suppress amusement while looking sexier than any runway model she'd ever seen grace a catwalk or print ad. "Besides." She cleared her throat. "It's a tax write-off. And since I don't have any dependents or business expenses yet, this is a good thing in the eyes of Uncle Sam. Mostly, though, I wanted to do it because it was a noble cause. If you were willing to sacrifice yourself to that auction, the least I could do was to part with some disposable cash."

He stared intently, his gaze sliding over her slowly before reaching her eyes again.

"You're really something, you know that, right?"

"Yeah, pretty much." She secured her hands around his neck, and he surrounded her in his solid arms. She smiled, and breathed in deeply, treasuring the feeling of security she couldn't remember experiencing before.

"What am I going to do with you, Vanessa?"

"If you really want an answer to that, take me home and I'll show you."

Even over the music, she could hear his deep, throaty groan.

"I'm wearing the wrong kind of pants for you to say shit like that to me in public, woman."

She shrugged, pressing herself against the semi-hard-on she could feel at her belly.

"Take me home and the only thing you'll have to worry about is how quickly I can get you out of those offending pants."

He didn't respond, simply grabbed her hand and pulled her toward the table to get her clutch and say their goodbyes to their friends. As they turned to walk away, she could hear Cree saying, "Don't hurt nothin'."

Neither of them stopped as the snickers from their friends became full-on howling. With their arms looped around each other's waists, they headed for the valet with a singular purpose in mind: getting back to the house as soon and safely as possible.

Chapter 17

MICHAEL PULLED INTO THE GARAGE AS HE HAD A MIL-
lion times since he'd purchased this house ten years ago. Yet tonight,
somehow everything seemed new. He was giddy, as evidenced by
the smile he had to keep fighting so he wouldn't look like a high
schooler so happy to get some he couldn't keep his chill.

Well, he was happy at the potential. He hadn't made it to
Philly in . . . a while for one of his discreet hookups. They'd kind
of lost their draw about six months ago. He didn't know why. He
couldn't attach it to any particular occurrence. All he knew was
that it had become more of an effort to go to Philadelphia for sex
than it had in the past, and his trips had become fewer and fewer
until they'd altogether stopped.

He helped Vanessa out of the car and held the door open so
she could enter the mudroom. He followed behind her, unknotting
his tie and shoving his hands in his pockets as they stopped in the
kitchen.

"Everything okay?" she asked, her eyes filled with concern. "If
you've changed your mind, it's okay."

"Changed my mind?" His bark turned into full-on laughter. "I'm
so wound up and ready to be with you I'm standing in the middle

of my kitchen with my hands shoved in my pockets to keep from mauling you."

She shrugged. "I thought that's the reason we came back here in the first place."

"It is," he replied. "I just don't want you to think that's all I care about. I like sex as much as the next person. I just don't want you to think that's all I want."

She dropped her clutch on the counter and unbuttoned her jacket, letting it slip elegantly from her shoulders before she threw it on the counter next to her purse.

"What if I'm okay with you only wanting sex from me?" she asked quietly as she stepped backward, heading toward the door that separated the kitchen from the living room.

When she was on the other side, making her way to the back of the couch, she leaned against it, stepping out of one pointed stiletto and then the other.

"Would you stop holding back if I told you I'm okay with whatever you have in mind tonight?"

He didn't answer immediately. Instead, he removed his jacket and threw it on the nearest level surface he could find. Next, his tie followed, and then his cuff links. He unbuttoned his shirt, pulling it out of his pants and leaving the flaps to hang open.

He stepped closer to her, wrapping his fingers around the back of her neck as his thumb stroked against the curve of her jaw.

"You have no idea how much I've wanted you since the first day I saw you."

His voice was almost unrecognizable to his own ears. He'd barely touched her, and already his skin was tight and hot as his body responded to just the idea of having her again.

"I knew I was dead wrong. I knew I'd come there for a totally different reason. Only once I saw you in that sweater dress and those boots, watching the way you moved, all I wanted was to know what it was like to touch you, have you any way I wanted you."

It was true, and because he didn't have words that could truly express the intensity of his need that day and every day since, he kissed her, pressing so hard against her lips he was certain the delicate flesh would bruise later.

His fingers found the clasp to her pants. He made quick work of unzipping them, stepping away from her briefly to pull them down her legs, leaving a trail of kisses down her flesh as he disposed of the offending garment.

When he stood up, he watched her reach for the side zipper of her bustier. He put his hand on top of hers to stop her, looking down at the tempting silhouette it provided.

"Don't," he ground out. "Leave it on."

She dropped her hand, standing still before him. He could see the pulse at the base of her throat jump. He traced his thumb there, pressing slightly to feel it throb against his digit.

"Is this a sign of nervousness or excitement?"

She dropped her head, bringing her eyes back up to his after a moment. A bit of embarrassment shone there. He was grateful she didn't try to hide it from him. He wanted to see it all, the uncertainty, the need, the excitement, everything that came along with connecting with a new person in this way.

"A little of both. It's been a while since I've done this. In theory, it seemed like a great idea. But now . . ."

He stood up straight, pulling slightly away from her as he regarded her carefully.

"We've done this before, Vanessa. Or was it so forgettable you don't remember?"

She dropped her eyes, the deep brown skin on her face morphing into a mauve blush.

"I haven't forgotten. It was . . . incredible."

Her voice was breathless, as if she were having a hard time controlling the air in and out of her lungs.

"Are you having second thoughts? We don't have to do anything if you don't want to."

"No." She raised her hand to his chest, parting the open flaps of the material covering it, and resting her palm against his flesh. "I didn't mean for you to stop. I just meant it's been a long time since I've done this."

She rubbed her hands up and down her upper arms as if she were suddenly cold. "That night in your guest room was fantastic. It wasn't planned, though. It kind of happened out of the blue. And it might've been a fluke that it was so good the last time."

She looked up into his eyes, granting him the chance to see the vulnerability in them. "It's been a long time since I've planned a seduction, and even though I know I started this back at the catering hall, the reality kinda hit me when I walked in the door. I was sort of hoping to follow your lead so I wouldn't goof it up too much." She huffed, wrapping her arms around herself before she spoke again. "I just don't want you to be disappointed. That's all."

He kissed her again, placing his forehead against hers as he chuckled a bit.

"In case you didn't know, before that night in the guest room, it'd been a while for me too." He wrapped his arms around her waist, drawing her to him, bringing her fully against his body. "Our mutual dry spells aside, after knowing what it's like to be inside you, to have you so hot and tight around my cock I could hardly breathe, I don't think we need to worry about how this is gonna turn out."

"Really?"

He could feel the lines of his forehead bunching together in confusion. Then he realized she was serious. She honestly didn't know how absolutely irresistible she was.

"I've been half-hard all night thinking about sliding into you. I don't care how out of practice either of us are, the reality will always outdo the fantasy."

"Fantasy, huh? Care to share?"

There she went again. Teasing him with her words. In the time he'd known her, he was learning so much about her. She was playful with him when she felt comfortable, shy when she was uncertain, and pensive when she was vulnerable.

They'd been in this house less than ten minutes and he'd seen her run the range of those emotions. She felt deeply, even when she tried to hide behind her posh veneer, all her emotions rooted down into the depths of her soul. And in this moment, he was the man fortunate enough to get to see it all play out.

"I've had a million fantasies about you since that first meeting in Jersey. Hell, since the night you let me touch you. All of 'em on replay, trapped in my head with nowhere to go." He let his fingers grace her shoulders, relishing the shiver she gifted him with when his flesh met hers.

She was such a responsive lover. And as evolved as he should be as a grown-ass man, his ego relished every shiver, every moan she offered him. He treasured every reaction she blessed him with when she was naked beneath him.

"My favorite one to date was sitting on my couch watching those beautiful lips of yours wrapped around my cock."

She fanned herself quickly with her hand, before looking at him. "It's suddenly boiling in here."

"Well, I could open a window." He smirked as he moved in closer. "But considering how vocal you were the last time, I don't think we want to give my neighbors that kind of show. Or maybe we do. You tell me."

He reached for her waist, pulling her to her feet and into his arms. He laced his fingers through hers and headed toward the steps, but halfway there he felt resistance from her. He turned around and found her staring up at him with a grin that was just this side of mischievous.

"Everything okay?"

She nodded. "Yeah. I just thought since there's a perfectly good couch here, we'd spend a little time working on your fantasy."

And just like that he went from half-hard to painfully so, his cock trapped behind his zipper, begging to be free.

Without a word, he course-corrected and cut a path to the couch. He removed his shirt slowly, giving her time to change her mind. To say it turned him on when, instead of backing away, she stepped closer to him was an understatement. She was grabbing at the placket of his tuxedo pants and undoing it with great ease, all the while setting his body aflame.

He watched her watching him. She seemed to take a perverse sort of pleasure in the slow glide of his zipper down his bulge. She rested a warm hand on his abdomen, making him ache for the moment she'd slide it down and take hold of him. Instead of giving him what he wanted in that drawn out second, she slid her hand up his abs, between his pecs and snaked it around the back of his neck until her fingers found their way into his hair grazing against his scalp.

Her mouth latched onto his in a hard press of lips. It was a simple declaration that she didn't come to play, and he was here for it. In her head, Vanessa might question her ability to turn him on, but nothing about the way she was owning his fucking mouth said, "I'm nervous." This woman was going to sap every bit of his strength with something as simple as her kiss.

She released him as quickly as she grabbed him. Giving a gentle push to his chest, making him take a seat on the sofa cushions.

The determination that flashed in her eyes made his cock jerk. She wasn't fucking around and neither was he, so he quickly pulled his tuxedo pants and boxer briefs down in one swift move. Apparently, that wasn't enough, though, because she knelt down and removed them from him, tossing them to the side of her as she leaned in between his legs, pushing at his knees to make him spread his legs wider.

He could feel her heated gaze slide down the length of him. It should feel obscene for him to be this exposed, yet all he wanted was for her to give him everything her eyes promised he'd have.

She wrapped elegant fingers around his base, the warmth of her hand making him jerk again in anticipation of her next move. She gave a gentle tug, and he saw spots in his vision. Possibly because he'd been holding his breath while she took her slow time to make that first move. Once he felt her caress, he knew the cause was that he was so damn turned on, a simple touch from her had him ready to explode.

She let go of him, moving her hands up and down both of his thighs as her raspberry pink tongue darted out, taking one long stroke from his balls to the rounded dome of his circumcised cock.

By the time she slowly licked around the head, his skin was on fire, and he was certain the flames would consume him. She looked up at him and he could see she was enjoying what they both knew was going to be his undoing.

She opened her mouth and took him into her wet heat, and the only thing he could do was moan into the impossible pleasure overwhelming him.

As much as he didn't want to miss this visual, the feel of her mouth on him was almost too much to bear. Her movements were still shallow, only taking him part of the way into her heat. It was good, yet it wasn't good enough. He wanted more.

He threaded his fingers through her hair, tightening just enough to guide her where he wanted her. The next time she released him, he held her in place before she could descend upon him again.

Grabbing the base of his cock and stroking up once, he took the head and brushed it across her lips, loving the red smear of her lipstick depositing onto his skin. When he finished amusing himself, he slid his hand down to the base again and pulled her forward.

"That's it," he half hissed, "take me as deep as you can." Applying gentle pressure, he kept encouraging her forward until she had nearly half his length enveloped by the burning inferno of her mouth.

He didn't know which was better, the indecent picture she made on her knees between his legs with a mouthful of his cock, or the actual sensation of wet lips and the hot walls of her collapsed cheeks rubbing against his flesh.

Either way, his fucking balls were so tight and high, they'd probably climb up to his throat before she was done. He was so damn close, the pressure building incrementally, requiring more and more of his will to keep from spilling down her throat.

Shit.

He immediately chastised himself, because now he couldn't stop thinking about watching her drink his spend down like her favorite beverage.

He battled within himself for a few more moments before he tugged her off of him, grabbing her by the chin and licking into her mouth. Tongues tangling, teeth clicking, their lips were going to be raw by the time this was said and done. It was a small price to pay, in his opinion. He'd stock up on lip balm because there was no way he was gentling this kiss, not when he felt like molten lava was running through his body, turning his organs to ash.

He tore away from her mouth only because his body demanded air. He used that reprieve to reach down for his tuxedo pants, rooting around for his wallet in the pockets.

"You keep a condom in your tuxedo pants?"

"Technically, it was in my wallet. But, yeah." He said it as if that should be obvious. Because it should be obvious that there probably would never be an occasion when he wouldn't want to bury himself inside her welcoming body. "Especially when I've had designs on being inside of you all damn day. Hell, fuck around and there might be one in the kitchen cabinet too."

She licked her swollen lips and chuckled. She might think he was teasing. The joke was definitely on her because he was dead serious.

He covered himself, pulled her up, and had her straddle him. "It's all you, baby."

Lifting a brow, she accepted the gauntlet he'd just thrown down, taking hold of the base of his cock, guiding it to her slick folds where she rubbed it at her wet entrance before sliding slowly down until his entire dick was enveloped by her hot, slick flesh.

She canted her hips, and he instantly dropped his head against the cushions, overwhelmed by how deep he was inside of her.

He grabbed onto her shoulder, pulling her forward, nipping at the tender skin between her neck and shoulder. When she shivered, twirling her hips in response, he moved his mouth to her ear. "Fuck, Vee," he hissed through clenched teeth. "Ride this shit like you own it."

He didn't know if it was his demand, or possibly just that she was in the mood. Whatever it was, she did exactly as he'd told her. She secured her hands on the back of the couch on either side of his head. That should've been his first clue that she was about to destroy him. He was so far gone, however, it wasn't until her hips set a fast and brutal pace that he realized she truly did own him.

Her slick walls were squeezing him like they were trying to milk him of not just his pending orgasm, but his very essence, the soul that made him who he was. And in that moment, he'd gladly part with it if it meant she'd keep fucking him so good every nerve in his body was so raw he couldn't tell the difference between pleasure and pain.

She rode him for everything he was worth, and her rhythm didn't falter until her building climax peaked.

He planted his feet and grabbed hold of her ass as he pistoned inside of her, keeping her on the edge of release, drawing it out until coherent words weren't possible. All she could do was scream until her throat was raw and there was no sound left.

Watching her give into their pleasure and her still-spasming cunt ignited his short fuse. He held her so tight he'd have to check for bruises later, much later. As his orgasm took control, his muscles locked involuntarily, and he couldn't have let go if he'd wanted to.

He buried his face into her bosom, smothering the animalistic growl in between her ample tits. And when the last wave of his climax finally passed over him, he dropped his head back against the couch cushions. Lifting his fatigued arms until his shaky fingers reached her face, he combed back the now sweat-limp curls and smiled.

Breath still ragged, he spoke in choppy words. "Doing . . . that . . . again." And he would. He just needed hydration and maybe a nap before he could.

"That was amazing." Vanessa stretched like a satisfied cat coming down off a catnip high. When she opened her eyes, Michael locked his elbow, perching his head on his hand, staring down at her with pride shining in his eyes.

"Thank you for the high praise." He slid his arm around her waist, pulling her closer against the solid wall of his body. "I do aim to please. In fact," he said as he let his thumb stroke back and forth over her lower belly, teetering dangerously close toward her mound, "I think maybe we should go for a second round just to make sure I didn't miss anything vital the first time."

She turned around in his arms, which took a bit of doing since they were two grown people smashed together on a couch. "I applaud your commitment to thoroughness."

"It's that old Boy Scout training kicking in." He relaxed his face with just the slightest hint of a smile on his pink lips. "In the Scouts, the job isn't done until it's done right."

She ran her fingers through the light dusting of dark hair on his pecs and let her vision linger there for a minute before meeting his gaze again.

"Maybe the Scouts will get my next charitable donation. Because your attention to detail is a thing of beauty. That kind of work ethic should definitely be encouraged."

"Yeah?" He dipped his head down, stealing a quick kiss before he ran his hand down her back, re-electrifying all the nerves that had just begun to simmer since their first session ended.

By the time his wide, rough palm reached the curve of her ass, she'd wrapped her arm around his neck, pulling him down on top of her. The feel of his thickening flesh against her soft, tender folds made her hips swerve as they involuntarily sought more contact, more sensation, more satisfaction.

"Not that I don't want this to continue." He kissed her as he ran his hand down her abdomen until his fingers slipped between her folds, sliding easily against her flesh. "But I don't have any more condoms down here." Her legs spread wider and before she could catch her breath, he'd dipped two fingers into her slick opening. He kept sliding his digits in and out until all she could do was moan in response. "And even though I could spend an entire night watching you ride my fingers, I'd be lying if I said I wasn't aching to slide inside you again."

She closed her eyes. She couldn't watch him pleasuring her and not spill over into bliss within seconds.

"If you plan for us to make it upstairs," she huffed through clenched teeth, "then you'd better stop now."

He settled back behind her, continuing manipulations. "Not yet," he whispered in her ear, biting the tender flesh of her lobe. "Not when I know you're so close to coming." He let his thumb slide over the sensitive flesh of her clit and the first spasm of climax made her clamp down on his fingers.

"That's it, baby," he whispered as his fingers continued to move inside her, twisting and teasing until she was so close every nerve in her body was on fire. "Come all over my fingers and we can take this party to my bedroom."

His thumb and fingers working in tandem against her clit and inside her walls carried her into bliss. As her pleasure climbed higher, locking every muscle in her body as her climax seized control of her, she broke apart for him.

And through it all, he continued to whisper sweet, sexy things in her ear that wouldn't let the powerful orgasm abate. Instead, he continued to stroke her, continued his litany of the filthy things he wanted to do to her when they were upstairs, until she was so spent, all she could do was lay there like an overcooked noodle.

"You are entirely too good at that." She was out of breath, as if she'd run some type of marathon instead of orgasming on this man's couch.

He sat up, then tugged on her arm until she followed, straddling him. "Trust me, I get just as much pleasure from doing it as you. I could watch you come all night."

"And I'm certainly not against letting you try." She kissed him, loving the lazy way they enjoyed each other without frenzy, nor care of when the next act of their lovemaking would occur. She knew he was ready to begin their next round by the hard cock she was sitting on top of.

Instead of rushing her upstairs so he could have what he'd said he wanted, he took his time palming her ass and kissing her to within an inch of her life as he ground his hips against hers.

The distant sound of metal clinking against metal tugged at her consciousness. Not enough to make her give up the sweetness of his lips and the tongue stroking against hers, but enough that her focus became slightly split between what Michael was doing to her and that sound.

Michael ripped his mouth away from hers just before spouting, "Oh, shit!"

Before she could process what was happening, she looked up in time to see the front door opening and a young woman with features similar to Michael's walking in the door.

"Cindy, don't come—"

Already inside, and the large looming figure behind her stepped into the light.

"Vanessa?"

The sound of Karl's voice made Michael's body tense against hers, wrapping protective arms around her.

"Get out!" His booming voice rumbled through the room. It was too late, though. Cindy and Vanessa's ex-husband, Karl, were already inside with a partially obstructed view of Michael and Vanessa naked as hell on the couch.

Chapter 18

MICHAEL KEPT HIS ARMS WRAPPED TIGHTLY AROUND Vanessa until he heard the click of the door close.

"You okay?"

"My ex-husband just walked in on me naked with my new lover. What do you think?"

He regarded her carefully and nodded, releasing her from his grip. "Go upstairs and get dressed. Seems like we're having this conversation a lot sooner than we expected. We'll be in the kitchen when you're ready."

She closed her eyes as if she needed to gather her strength before she found the will to disengage her body from his.

She didn't look at him, just scurried around picking up her clothing strewn all over the floor, and rushed off so quickly, he was surprised he didn't see the accent pieces on his tabletops and walls flying behind her in her tailwind.

With no time to linger, he found his underwear, pants, and shirt, putting them on quickly and walking to the door. He snatched it open, more than a little annoyed that his time with Vanessa was interrupted, but utterly angry that Karl had found her exposed like that.

He should've protected Vanessa better. That he'd been so wrapped up in making love to her he'd let his guard down meant a great deal of the angry heat building inside of him was directed at himself.

"Cindy, we're obviously interrupting. Let's just leave."

"What's the matter, Karl?" Michael stood in the opened doorway with his arms folded. "Don't you want to explain to my sister how you know Vanessa?"

Even though the darkness muted his features, Michael could see the lines of the man's face harden.

"You did this?" His voice was a low whisper meant to threaten. Karl's attempt at intimidation fell flat. In fact, Michael saw it more like an invitation, since Michael would relish the opportunity to drag this asshole across his front porch and lawn.

Michael answered, "You're damn right I did."

Cindy looked back and forth between them with unanswered questions in her eyes. Her obvious concern about the rising tension between her brother and the man she planned to marry aged her in ways that tugged at Michael's heart. His need to spare her feelings notwithstanding, Michael had to do what was best for her. Marrying a con artist like Karl would do more than hurt her feelings. It would ruin her. Michael couldn't allow that.

He stood back, ushering the two in. "The kitchen" was all he said before leading them to their destination.

The kitchen door hadn't swung closed behind them before Karl turned around, pointing his finger in Michael's direction.

"You had no right!"

"She's my sister. I had every right."

Cindy stood in the middle of them with her hands pushing outward to keep an imaginary wall between the two of them.

"Michael, what's going on? Who is that woman? Karl"—she turned to her fiancé—"how do you know her?"

"Go ahead," Michael goaded Karl. "Answer her question."

Michael could see the angry red flush crawling up Karl's neck and he reveled in the fact that he knew Karl was pissed because he'd caught him.

"What is it, Karl? Are you trying to come up with a believable lie to explain the truth of who's currently in my guest room?"

"Karl, Michael!" Cindy yelled, drawing both their attention to her. "Who is this woman?"

Before Michael could open his mouth, he heard the creak of the bottom step that led into his kitchen.

"I'm Vanessa Jared." She walked carefully until she was standing next to Michael. "I'm formerly Vanessa Scott." He could see the worry on her face as she looked up into his eyes for permission, or maybe encouragement. She was silently asking, *Are you sure you want me to do this?* When he nodded, she took a breath and faced Cindy. "I'm Karl's ex-wife."

Vanessa watched understanding creep its way into the furrowed brow of the young woman standing in front of her. She was calculating everything Vanessa had said and gathering the resulting meaning. Not just what the literal words meant, but how her world, her relationship was ultimately impacted by Vanessa's words too.

It was heartbreaking to watch understanding bloom in her eyes. The shock wearing off and giving way to anger. Although Vanessa could see her rage building, coloring the fair complexion of her face and neck with a ruddy blush, she didn't know Cindy well enough to tell who her anger was directed at. Was it Karl, Michael, or Vanessa? If she had to hazard a guess, she'd probably say it was a bit of all three.

"Michael, is this some kind of joke?"

Michael went to speak, but Vanessa intervened. This kind of hurt was going to ruin their relationship, and something about that seemed wrong to her. So in that instance, she silently volunteered to be the sacrificial lamb.

"It's not a joke, Cindy. I really am Karl's ex-wife. I know that's hard to hear because he's told you I was dead, but I assure you, I am very much alive." She lifted the folder she'd been holding in her hand, and clung to the small photo album she held in the other, nodding in the counter's direction, hoping Cindy would follow her.

When she did, Vanessa let a cautious breath slip from her lips. She pushed the album to the side and placed the folder directly between them on the counter, sliding it across to Cindy.

With a shaky hand, the young woman opened the folder and looked down at the documents in front of her.

"This is our marriage license." Vanessa spoke carefully, afraid if her voice were too rough, she'd fail to get through to Cindy. "This is our wedding announcement in one of the society magazines. And this," she said cautiously as Cindy unfolded the legal document, "is our divorce decree."

Cindy remained silent as she kept her eyes fixed to the papers in front of her.

"This is my birth certificate. And this—" She reached into the pocket of her jeans and slid two plastic cards across the counter as well. "These are both my driver's licenses. One in my married name, and the other in my maiden name, issued after our divorce two years ago."

Cindy closed the file, and when she lifted her gaze, Vanessa could see a single, lonely tear sliding down her pale cheek. The young woman turned to Karl.

"You told me she was dead."

"Trust me," he mumbled. "My life would be so much better if she were."

His steely blue gaze covered Vanessa, and she fought the chill settling into her bones. Tall, blond, straight hair with a runner's slim build, Karl stood before her in one of his designer business suits looking every bit the cold-hearted bastard he was.

"You took everything from me and you still have your grubby hands in my goddamn pockets, Vanessa."

From the corner of her eye, she could see Michael's fist clench. She held up her hand, hoping it would be enough to keep things calm. Michael looked at her for a long moment, finally nodding his head as he stepped away from Karl and walked to stand beside her at the counter.

"I took no more than I earned as your wife of twenty years. If you calculated the cost of everything I've ever done for you, the settlement I walked away with doesn't halfway cover it. I devoted my life to you and you repaid me by emotionally tormenting me and sleeping with every woman you fancied. You cared so little about me, were so certain of your control over me, you didn't even try to hide it, flaunting your infidelity like it was some sort of sick badge of honor. You'd made me into the perfect victim, so you had no reason to believe I'd ever fight back. I won't let you do the same to another unsuspecting woman who doesn't know any better—"

"Karl," Cindy interrupted, "is any of this true?"

Karl's hard face softened as he collected himself, something Vanessa called him getting into character all the times she'd watched him do it. With outstretched arms, he walked toward Cindy.

"Darling," he crooned, his voice rich with emotion Vanessa knew damn well he was faking. "Don't believe the bitter hatred she's spewing. Vanessa's mission in life is to make mine miserable. I gave her most of my fortune just to free myself from her tentacles."

Bull's-eye! Karl's aim was always perfect when it came to stomping on her confidence. And like all the other times, the arrow lodged deep into her self-confidence.

"You've got one more time to come out your face like that about Vanessa before I shut your disrespectful mouth for you."

Michael defending her was just as sexy as his sweet caress

against her skin. His protectiveness fortified her. Instead of shrinking back, she held up her finger to stop him. She needed to be the one to do this on her own.

Unlike before, she'd spent too much time in the presence of two great women who'd poured power into her for the last two years. The old Vanessa would've folded and crumpled with Karl's words. This Vanessa took the hit and regrouped, ready to come out swinging with a shot of her own.

"Karl, the only person who was ever miserable in our relationship was me." She turned her attention to Cindy before she continued.

"In the beginning, he showered me with gifts and attention. The type of praise was addictive the way he so liberally applied it." She closed her eyes and allowed the memories to sweep over her. The Karl of more than twenty years ago was just as charming and handsome as he was now. It was no wonder she hadn't discovered what a snake he was until many years into their marriage.

"It didn't take long for that to change. Soon, he began pulling the praise away and replacing it with criticism." She took a shaky breath as her life played like a highlights sports reel across her mind. "First, it was my hair. He didn't like it. It didn't matter if it was short or long, it wasn't what he wanted. It had to be tucked into a severe bun at the back of my neck. To him, it was elegant, and his wife needed to be elegant at all times to impress his business associates."

She watched Cindy move a trembling hand across the tight bun on her head and hoped her recount penetrated.

"Then it was my clothes. He didn't want to see me in jeans or anything form-fitting. And the only jewelry I could wear were my wedding rings and the pearl earrings and necklace set he'd given me."

Vanessa looked at Cindy's neck and ears and saw what looked like a carbon copy of the pearl set he'd given her twenty years ago.

God, you're such a bastard, Karl.

"Then, when my friends and family started questioning the changes in my appearance, Karl separated me from them. He moved us out of Denver to an exclusive neighborhood in New Jersey. He said it was so he could build his new business in New York. As you can probably imagine, that was just an excuse. The real reason was he wanted to isolate me from anyone who could recognize what was going on. And it worked."

She pressed her hand onto the solid granite of the countertop to gain purchase. Talking about this wasn't easy, but she could see by the way Cindy's gaze was fixed to hers, that she was doing the right thing, so she continued.

"He was conditioning me to be his willing victim, and I didn't recognize it before it was too late. Before I knew it, everything I did was because he liked it or it benefited him in some way. My wants or needs didn't enter into the calculation. That included who I worked for. I'm a credentialed accountant, who could've worked anywhere. However, the only job he allowed me to hold was working as an accountant for his company."

She stopped for a moment to take a breath. She told herself it was to give Cindy a chance to process everything she was saying. Vanessa soon realized that lie was to protect her and not Cindy. The truth was, reliving the memories of Karl's emotional abuse still hit her like a sledgehammer to the middle of her chest.

"Once I recognized how he'd victimized me, I knew I couldn't stay anymore. I needed to be safe and plan my exit. Once I was reasonably sure I could extricate myself from his clutches, I was angry as hell.

"My anger and fear that he would undoubtedly do this again forced me to seek a sizable settlement. With him as my only employer, I knew I'd never be able to work again. My husband was a philandering bastard and an abuser, but I was going to be the one that suffered professionally as a result of his behavior. I was nothing more than property to him. And there was no way he'd help me walk away. He wanted me broken and dependent on him so he could control me. To avoid that, I took him for all he was worth to make sure I'd be well taken care of if I couldn't find work."

Cindy searched Vanessa's face. Maybe she was looking for the truth, or possibly the lie. Either way, she never dropped her eyes from Vanessa's face, hanging onto her every word.

"Was he ever . . . violent with you?"

Michael moved closer to Vanessa, placing a supportive hand around her waist. The gesture was sweet. Vanessa hazarded a guess that depending on her answer, his motive was also to do something with his hands so they wouldn't be free to wrap them around Karl's neck.

"Did he ever hit me? No. But he terrorized me just the same. He backed me into corners while he yelled at me. He blocked access to my credit cards and bank accounts whenever he was mad at me, just to show me I couldn't survive without him. After the first time, I was smart enough to siphon off funds, so it never happened again. But I could only do it because of my experience as an accountant. If I hadn't had my education to rely on, I would've remained in a hell of his making forever."

"This is ridiculous, Cindy. Are you going to trust a perfect stranger over the man who loves you, who wants to marry you?"

Vanessa's anger rose as she watched her ex-husband use the same tricks and tactics he'd used to victimize her all those years ago. It was so obvious to see them for what they were now, back then, not so much. Fortunately, she was free of Karl. She didn't have to be afraid of how angry he would be.

"Why would he do all of this?" Cindy's question was painful to hear. It was partly, "I'm looking for a reason to believe him, while simultaneously trying to find out the truth."

"Money, is the simple answer," Vanessa continued. "I took Karl for all of his considerable assets. Anything that could be liquidated, including our six-million-dollar home, went to me. Karl was left only with his company and the assets attached to it."

Cindy narrowed her gaze at Vanessa. "It's a multi-million-dollar company. He's still rich."

"On paper," Vanessa responded. "He's what we call 'cash poor.' In order to get cash, he's going to have to either sell off parts of his company or the entire thing. I presume he's told you he doesn't want a prenup. He trusts you enough, and he's certain the two of you will be together for eternity."

She could see by the way color rose in Cindy's cheeks that Vanessa had hit the nail on the head.

"Without one, you have access to all he owns. Subsequently, it also gives him access to any assets in your name as well. He's trying to marry you to get control of the trust from your parents' deaths."

"Cindy," Karl rushed in. "I wouldn't have given you my ring if I didn't want to spend the rest of my life with you. Don't let Vanessa do this."

"Yeah, about *your* ring. Let's talk about that." Vanessa reached for the photo album she'd rummaged out of her father's belongings and flipped it open. "This is the miniaturized replica of our wedding album that we had made for my father."

She opened it to the first page where there was a photo of their engagement, and a zoomed-in image of their hands linked together to show off her engagement ring.

"That ring is a family heirloom my father gave to Karl to propose to me. If you read through our divorce decree, you'll see the judge awarded me the ring. The last time I saw it, it was inside my jewelry chest. Yet somehow it's now resting on your finger."

"How?" Cindy's eyes were filling with tears and it broke Vanessa's heart to be the cause of them. Unfortunately, the alternative was unthinkable.

"He came to my house after we had finalized the divorce to clear out some of his things. When I wasn't looking, he stole it. And now you're wearing it."

Karl stepped closer to Cindy, grabbing her hands and covering them with his own.

"Cindy, this is enough. I won't allow her to terrorize you like this anymore. Vanessa is poison. That's why I left her. That's why I never told you about her. I knew even to invoke her name would destroy us. Let's go, now!"

The air was quiet, except for the tension and anger crackling through the atmosphere. No one moved. Karl's eyes remained locked on Cindy, and Michael's and Vanessa's were fixed on the two of them.

One long moment passed before Cindy snatched her hands away and stepped back. When Karl stepped toward her, somehow, Michael appeared between them, acting as a blockade.

"I think that's your cue to leave, Scott."

His chest heaving and his face red with anger, Karl tried to ignore the large man standing in front of him and attempted to carry on with his pleading.

"Cindy, is that what you want? Or are you just letting your brother speak for you? Don't let my poor choice in an ex-wife destroy us."

Tears were flowing freely from Cindy's eyes now, and there was a flicker of something desperate in their depths. Vanessa prayed Karl hadn't clouded her senses so much that she couldn't accept the truth.

"Leave, Karl," the young woman whispered. "Just leave."

Vanessa could tell Cindy's response shocked Karl. His eyes narrowed and his hands were on his hips, hiking his shoulders up around his red ears.

"Cindy, please!"

"My sister told you to leave. You've got three seconds to get off my property or I'm going to arrest you for trespassing."

Karl turned toward Vanessa, his tight features seething with anger. "You did this. You've ruined my life again. Are you happy?"

Vanessa shrugged, finally seeing him as the tiny, insecure person he'd always been. She realized Karl was simply a bully who picked on people he thought were easy marks.

"Am I happy about hurting Cindy? Not in the least." She smiled, cocking her head to the side. "Am I happy about stopping a self-serving abuser from destroying another unsuspecting woman whose only crime is loving you?" She folded her arms and smiled. "You're goddamn right."

She could see his jaw tightening. He wanted to say something, probably wanted to do a lot more than toss insults at her. He was beaten, though. Everyone standing in that room knew he'd lost his advantage, him more than anyone else. In light of his defeat, he stepped away from Michael and walked backward until he was at the back door, opening it and quickly stepping through.

When he left, all three people in the room let out a collective sigh. Regrettably, as soon as Vanessa saw Cindy's face, she knew there wasn't any cause for celebration.

Her eyes were red and her face was contorting into a pained expression, and as Vanessa watched, another piece of her was torn away.

"You've ruined my life, Michael."

Michael's gaze collided with his sister's. Of all the things he'd expected her to say—"Thank you for saving me," for instance—being accused of ruining her life, that came from left field.

"Excuse me? Cindy, what are you talking about?"

"You couldn't just let me do one thing on my own. You had to take it away from me. When am I going to get a say in my own life?"

Michael was torn between compassion for her pain and anger at her ignorance and ingratitude.

"Cindy, I understand you're upset. I just need you to realize I did it to help you. That man would've destroyed you. Did you really expect me to just stand by and let that happen?"

"I expected you to let me make my own decisions. I didn't need you to go to the extreme of bringing his ex-wife here. Why can't you just trust me to know what's best for me?"

"When you're acting like an immature child, how do you expect me to trust you to know what's best for yourself?"

Cindy threw up her hands and let out a frustrated scream. "Oh, God, it's my life. Good or bad, let me make my own decisions. Stop managing my life, Michael. Leave me alone!"

Before he could respond, she blew past him, out the kitchen door, and when he attempted to follow her into the living room, Vanessa stood in his way.

"Let her go."

"Has everyone lost their goddamn minds tonight? What do you mean, let her go?"

"Michael." She called his name with a calm, even tone, as she placed a hand on his chest and moved in closer to him. "She's hurting. She's angry, and lashing out. You cannot take anything she says right now personally. Give her a minute to cool off. Let her process this on her own."

"But she's—"

"Your baby sister and you just want to fix everything for her, right?"

Her words deflated his anger, and his shoulders dropped in defeat. She had him dead to rights and even though he didn't want to admit it, out of the two of them, she was the only one thinking clearly in this room.

"You absolutely did the right thing by bringing the truth to her, but you can't ask her to be grateful for your interference right now. She's hurt, she's upset, and the only person she can lash out at is you. Let her process this however she needs to. When she's ready, she'll come around."

She wrapped her arms around his neck, drawing herself closer to him. When she was this near, he couldn't help his response. He encircled her in his arms and rested his head on her shoulder. His sister had the broken heart, yet he was the one who felt like someone had run him over with a truck. He needed this reprieve.

"I'm an asshole."

"You're a protective brother who loves his sister. I wish I'd had someone like you looking out for me back then. Maybe I wouldn't have ended up with a man like Karl if I had." She ran her fingers through his hair, her touch both soothing and exciting.

"On the other hand," she continued. "If I hadn't gone through what I had with Karl, I never would've met the two best friends a woman could have, and I certainly wouldn't have met you. And honestly, I think maybe both those things are worth going through that experience."

His heart thudded against his chest as her words penetrated his soul. He didn't know what he'd done to deserve this unexpected meeting with Vanessa. Still, he was so grateful he had the chance to know her. More important than meeting her, in this moment where she comforted him in his pain and anguish, he knew something else. He never wanted her to let him go.

"I don't deserve you."

She leaned back, bringing their gazes together. "You don't. Luckily for you, that doesn't mean I won't still extend the offer of me."

"Why would you?"

Her smile was warm and genuine, tugging both ends of her mouth into a deep crescent. "Because, silly man. I deserve you."

She was right. She deserved everything, and he wanted to be the man to give it to her. He joined their mouths in a tender kiss. It wasn't meant to titillate, even though it did. It was meant to tell her all the things he couldn't find the words for.

Like the fact that he'd never met a woman more perfect for him. Or that he'd never fallen so quickly and completely for anyone before. And most importantly, he wanted to keep her by his side always.

She must have sensed something was off because she broke their kiss and looked up at him with a questioning stare.

"Everything all right?"

He nodded. "For the first time in a long time," he began. "I think it actually is. Vanessa, this thing between us—"

She kissed him again, silencing him. "Now's not the time to talk about that. You've gotta focus on your sister. And as soon as you've sorted all of that out, we definitely need to have that conversation. Because this"—she moved a finger back and forth between them—"is worth discussing."

Michael was relieved and surprised, although he shouldn't have been. Vanessa had performed one miracle after another since she'd arrived in Monroe Hills. From helping him with the booth, to getting him out of that blasted date with Amanda, to helping him show his sister the truth, she'd saved his ass time and time again. It was like magic lived inside her. She somehow always knew exactly what he needed.

Chapter 19

~

"THANKS FOR COMING TO GET ME, LADIES."

Vanessa sat with her eyes fixed on her cup of coffee as she swirled her spoon around and around. The coffee wasn't that interesting, but if she lifted her eyes, her girls would see all the things she was trying to hide.

Things like the uncontrollable passion that had ignited between her and Michael, and the gripping disappointment that it might all come to a crashing halt before it even started.

"You all right, girl?" The hint of worry in Cree's voice put Vanessa on the defensive. Hiding things from them when they were a hundred miles or more away from her was one thing. Trying to do it while they were face-to-face was another matter entirely. It required a skill set of deviousness Vanessa knew she didn't possess.

"Everything's fine," she quipped while keeping her eyes fixed on her cup of coffee. "I just wanted to spend some time with my girls. Is that a crime?"

Janae picked up Vanessa's cup of coffee, moving it out of the way so Vanessa could no longer pretend it was where her focus needed to be.

"Spill it," Janae demanded, and when Vanessa finally pulled her eyes up to meet Janae's she could tell the woman wasn't playing. "What happened, Vanessa?"

She opened her mouth, and then her brain froze. She couldn't think up a single thing to say to divert Janae's attention.

"I slept with Michael."

Her friends stared at each other, and then slowly returned their gazes to her. "We kinda figured that was a given considering the two of you were wrapped around each other when you left the gala." Janae's response was, well . . . classic Janae. She didn't pull any punches, ever.

"Yes," Vanessa continued, "I slept with him last night, but that wasn't the first time."

Janae and Cree planted their elbows on the table and simultaneously—as if they'd practiced keeping their movements in sync—leaned in toward Vanessa.

"Was it bad?" Janae's question made her drop her jaw again.

"No!" She answered quickly, her voice turning into a high-pitched squeal that made patrons at the surrounding tables look at them. She cleared her throat and did her best to calm herself. "It was amazing. Really amazing."

Both Janae and Cree leaned in some more with their eyes wide and lecherous grins on their faces.

"Do tell, girlfriend." Cree's request may have appeared playful, although the devious spark in her eye said she was dead serious.

"I'm not getting into the specifics with you other than that man is gifted in more ways than one."

"Then . . ." Janae responded. "What's the problem? He's a good person, he's fine, gainfully employed, and he knows how to toss your salad. Why are you sitting here looking like the world is about to fall down around your head?"

Janae wasn't wrong. Michael was all the things she'd listed. Unfortunately, there was one detail she couldn't overlook.

"Cindy and Karl walked in on us last night as we were about to start round two."

They both sat up straighter with matching pinched brows and laser focused gazes on Vanessa.

"She came home earlier than expected and headed straight for Michael's house."

"What happened? How'd she take it?" Cree asked with genuine concern for Cindy in her voice.

"How did Karl?" Tinged with the slightest bit of salacious curiosity, Janae's question, laced with just enough pettiness, it was obvious she hoped things hadn't gone well for Karl.

"Cindy was shocked because she didn't know who I was. Karl was almost apoplectic. For all his smooth talking, he couldn't weasel his way out of this situation. Especially after I showed her our marriage license, our divorce decree, and our wedding album. Showing her those things accompanied with the story of how controlling and abusive he was, she could finally see him for the master manipulator that he is."

Janae regarded her carefully, nodding as she pieced things together to come to a conclusion. "So your mission was successful, then? I'm sure it wasn't easy for Cindy to accept. You have to know you did the right thing in showing her who Karl really is, though. So why the long face?"

"Because," Vanessa huffed. "She wasn't just upset with Karl, or me, for that matter. She took her anger out on Michael too. She stormed out of the house and I had to nearly restrain him to get him to agree to give her the night to handle things before he showed up at her door."

Cree shrugged before taking a sip of her own coffee. "This all sounds good, Vee. Why the worry lines in the middle of your forehead?"

"Because you didn't see how devastated Cindy was. I don't think Michael will be able to focus on us right now."

Janae slid her hand across the table until it rested on top of Vanessa's. "Vanessa, I've known Michael a long time. And if he cares about you, there's nothing he wouldn't do to keep you safe and near. Give him a chance to figure this all out. Or is this really about Michael at all?"

She felt the sting of unshed tears heating her eyes and face. This situation was so out of her depth. She had no clue how to proceed from here.

"I know he's just looking out for his sister. I know he's got this deep need to always be her hero and manage every part of her life. I know all of that comes from a good place. What I don't know is if I'm in the space where I can deal with a man who needs to manage everyone around him. Especially after everything I went through with Karl."

Trying hard to keep her composure, she picked up the coffee cup Janac had moved and took a sip. It had a pleasurable taste, it was simply worthless at helping her handle her emotions.

She blinked, and the dam broke as tears spilled onto her cheek, down her face, and into her coffee. Good thing she was drinking salted caramel, otherwise the salty tang might taste weird.

"Vanessa," Cree began. "Michael is not Karl. Yes, he's a micro-manager, he always has to be around just in case someone needs him. But like you said, it all comes from a good place. Don't confuse his need to protect the people he cares about with Karl's manipulations."

Janae gave her a sad smile. "While you know how much I hate it when Cree is right," she began as her deep brown eyes softened, "she *is* right. Michael is not Karl. Don't paint him with the same brush as your trifling ex."

She heard her friends. And she honestly wanted to hold on to everything they were saying. But deep down, there was still this growing worry that being with Michael would be like making a U-turn into her past.

Her phone rang, forcing her to wipe her face and try to get her shaky voice under control. The five-seven-zero area code made her quake even more. This was probably Michael calling her from his sister's house or the department.

"Hello." Her voice still sounding frail and raw, she cleared her throat and tried again. "Hello?"

"Ms. Jared." The unfamiliar voice put her on alert. "This is Jeb, the mechanic who towed your Jag."

"Is everything okay?" Vanessa tensed. If this man had damaged her baby, she was going to lose it. "Please don't tell me there's something wrong with my car."

Jeb's lighthearted chuckle helped loosen the ball of tension she could feel tightening at the base of her neck.

"No, ma'am, your car is fine." He chuckled again and this time she smiled, slightly tickled by his amusement. "I take it you're either tired of this town or eager to get back home."

"A little of both," she huffed, taking a moment to glance up at her friends who were watching her intently.

"Well, then, I've got good news for you. I called to tell you it's ready."

"Oh, really?" Her voiced dropped to its lower register as sadness set in. Why was she sad? Easiest answer: Michael. She didn't want to leave him behind.

"Yeah. The part came in sooner than expected, so I was able to shave a couple of days off. If you're agreeable to me using the credit card information you supplied when I towed the car, I can bill it, then deliver the car to the sheriff's house."

"Do you usually provide door-to-door service?"

"Not really," he sighed. "Seeing as I don't get to work on many Jags 'round here, driving it over will allow me to spend a little more time with her before I surrender the keys."

She couldn't blame him. It was a beautiful ride, and she treasured her. But she couldn't ignore that she wished it had taken a little longer to fix her. Then she would have been able to hold on to a little more time with Michael.

"Run the card. You can deliver it to Michael's house. I'll be there shortly."

She ended the call and lifted her gaze to the two women sitting with her.

"My car's ready. Seems fate intends for me to get out of Dodge sooner than later."

Janae shook her head, the soft curls of her hair dancing around her shoulders. "Vanessa. Cree is right. You need to talk to Michael."

Her body felt unbearably heavy in her seat. She leaned back in the chair, trying to relieve some of the pressure, even though she knew it wouldn't work. The burden sitting in the middle of her gut had nothing to do with a heavy object.

"Ladies, sorry to cut our outing short. Unfortunately I need to get . . ." She stopped herself just before she said home. The near-slip tore a shudder through her, making her sit straighter in the chair. Michael's place was not her home, yet she clearly understood that she'd be lying if she said part of her didn't wish it could be.

Chapter 20

~

MICHAEL'S SENSES WERE INSTANTLY ALIVE WHEN HE crossed the threshold of his home. The house was too quiet, and all the reasons that might be unnerved him.

"Vanessa!" He waited for a beat, dropping his keys on the small accent table in the foyer. When he didn't get an answer, he hurried to the kitchen and then directly up the back stairs to the second floor. "Vanessa!"

He knocked on the guest bedroom door, hoping she was taking a nap and didn't hear him bellowing her name through the house. She still wasn't answering him, so he slowly opened the door. A quick glance around the room revealed a made bed. His heartbeat raced as he stepped into the room. He snatched the closet door open, finding her clothes still hanging there and a pair of designer boots leaning neatly against her suitcase.

He released the breath he'd trapped in his chest out of sheer panic. In the short time he'd known her, he understood that she loved pretty footwear and would sooner part with a limb than those impossibly high heels she seemed to favor.

"Michael?"

He spun around at the sound of her voice. Too relieved to form words, in a few long steps he was in front of her, grabbing her into his embrace. Before she could speak, he plastered his mouth against hers, swallowing any words she thought to utter. He didn't need words. Not now. The only thing he craved was the feel of her skin against his.

When she threaded her hands through his hair, tugging as her lips met his, it was the only incentive he needed to take what he wanted. And right now, the only thing he ached for was the feel of her skin against his.

Last night had been perfection until his sister and Karl had interrupted them in the living room. This morning, they'd both been too busy trying to sort through the events of the previous night that neither of them had dared to seek the explosive heat they seemed to generate when they touched one another.

Today was a new day, however. His sister was safe in her own home. She was still understandably hurt, and more than a little angry. She'd taken Michael to task last night for blowing up her life. He'd worried she'd slip right back into Karl's web of lies the moment she was out of his sight. It was a relief she'd broken off the engagement. Now she just needed to take the first steps on her way to starting over without that conman in her life.

He wished he could say the same for himself. The moment he felt comfortable enough leaving Cindy, he realized Vanessa would leave soon. She'd fulfilled her end of the bargain. There was no other reason for her to stay. Except for this . . . this thing that burned between them hotter than the surface of the sun.

There was no time for finesse. This was going to be direct and fierce. The clock was running out on them and he needed to bond their bodies together for as long as he could.

He moved them back until they were in front of the foot bench. He turned her around, motioning for her to position herself on her knees. Thank God she was wearing a skirt, because his need was too intense to bother with removing clothes.

He shoved his hand into his back pocket, quickly retrieving a condom from his wallet. He pushed his jeans down enough that he could free his cock, then sheathed himself. He pulled up her skirt over her ass and nearly stumbled when he saw the thin, lacy strap of her thong peeking out at the top of her ass cheeks.

Even more determined to slide inside her, he pushed her thong aside before he slid one digit, then two at her sopping wet entrance.

She chased his fingers as he removed them. She needn't have worried. He had no intention of leaving her bereft for too long. He placed his sheathed cock at her entrance and pressed in deep on the first stroke.

He leaned over her, whispering in her ear, "Play with your pussy while I fuck you from behind."

Her answer was to squeeze his cock, demanding that he move. Determined to oblige, he pulled out and quickly dipped back in. If he were in his right mind, he'd take his time, make this last. If this were their last time together, he should want to have an endless supply of memories to hold on to. Yet he couldn't. Consumed by scorching need, his body craved satisfaction now.

His hips kept a desperate pace, driving his cock so deep on every stroke. He could hardly focus on anything except the way her pussy molded to his cock like it was made for him.

And therein lay the problem. She was made for him. He was sure of it. The ways she made him laugh, the way she called him on his bullshit, the way she gave as good as she got in every situation, it was all as if he'd found the irregularly shaped puzzle piece that would fit only him.

He changed angles slightly, drawing a loud "Fuck yes!" from her. Determined to give the lady what she wanted, what they both needed, he zeroed in on that spot, making sure his cock nudged against it every time he slid in and out. Within moments, her words were reduced to indecipherable mewling noises that rang through the air, penetrating deep into his soul.

This was supposed to be just fun. Knowing that, somehow, in a matter of days, being with her, sharing pleasure with her, Vanessa had still become as necessary as his next heartbeat.

He couldn't lose her, lose this. Unsure if she'd ever allow him to say those words to her, he poured every ounce of his heart into every stroke of his cock, every caress of her skin, every stuttered breath, all of it was an ode to this profound thing that sat in the middle of his chest, squeezing around his heart like a vise in a blacksmith's shop.

He was consumed by it, by her, and the thought of losing it all was so frightening he was rutting against her like some out-of-control beast.

Her grip on his cock tightened as her walls spasmed, signaling her climax was just within reach. His fingers dug into her hips so tightly he was certain there would be crescent-shaped marks imprinted in her skin. And if he was honest with himself, knowing proof of their lovemaking would exist long after this moment was over, put his own release just within reach.

He widened his stance, pulling her hips back against his as she succumbed to the onslaught of her orgasm. Her body locked in a powerful spasm, tightening her heat around him, pulling him along with her on this uncontrollable ride.

That first pulse was so strong he almost lost his balance. He grabbed at her shoulder to steady himself while bliss took over every nerve ending and every last bit of control he possessed. And when her tight walls had drawn the last drop of his essence from him, he collapsed unceremoniously on top of her back, whispering the only word his mouth could form: "Naekkeo." *Mine.*

When he finally found the breath and strength to stand on his own, he went into the bathroom to clean up. He returned with a damp, warm washcloth in his hand as he watched Vanessa crawl from the foot of the bed, dropping her head on the pillows at the top.

He carefully cleaned her sex, trying his best to soothe instead of stimulate. As much as he was game for another round of incredible sex, what he wanted most was to lie next to her and block the rest of the world out.

Their time was winding up. It was obvious in the desperation of their lovemaking that they both knew the end was around the corner. He wasn't normally a man to stick his head in the sand and pretend things were perfect when they weren't. Understanding that about himself didn't prevent him from crawling into bed beside her, loving how her warm body fit perfectly into his. Without regret, he would spend every minute they had left pretending the end would never come.

Michael rolled onto his back, pulling Vanessa with him, wrapping her in the safety of his arms. If he had his way, they'd remain like this, locked up, lying in bed together, carefully protecting the silence between them, keeping the rest of the world out.

Unfortunately, all good things really did come to an end, and this cocoon of bliss they'd swaddled themselves in was slowly splitting at the seams.

He could feel the thick blanket of uncertainty covering them, pushing them to face the reality of the situation they were in. He closed his eyes, hoping to hold on to the solace of their lovemaking a little while longer. One look at the somber expression on her face tore that illusion down. It was obvious they both knew if either of them attempted to unpack their emotions they'd risk losing the precious connection between them.

He tried to ignore the gaping chasm forcing them apart even though the pensive look in the depths of her deep, dark eyes made worry creep up his spine.

"I know I just had one of the best orgasms of my life, and if my memory serves, the way you wrapped your body around mine, I'd bet you had a pretty exceptional one too." He placed his finger at the point of her chin and lifted her gaze to his. "Or is that just wishful thinking on my part?"

The sad smile on her face was like something sharp slashing against his skin, leaving it inflamed and in tatters. "Vanessa?"

"The sex was great, Sheriff."

"Agreed. That still doesn't answer my question, though. Something's still bothering you. What's going on?"

"The mechanic called while I was out with Janae and Cree this morning. My car is ready."

"So, you're leaving?"

"You knew I would be at some point." She let her gaze fall to his chest, circling her fingers over his pecs. The slow rhythm was both tender and erotic. Before his body could work itself up again, he stilled her hand with his.

"That was always the plan, Michael."

He threaded his fingers between hers and held her tighter to his side.

"Yes, it was. Though I hoped that didn't mean you weren't open to changing up the plan a bit."

Her eyes narrowed into slits as her gaze locked with his. "You mean, you want me to stay?"

There was something heavy in the air between them. He could already see that whatever his answer was, it might have lasting effects on their relationship he neither intended nor wanted.

"I want you, Vanessa. For me, this hasn't just been two people jumping into bed. I honestly think there's something here. Don't you feel the same?"

He waited for her to respond and the longer the wait, the more doubt rubbed against his heart, abrading it like rough sandpaper against the delicate petals of one of the flowers in his sister's shop.

"What?" He finally found the courage to ask the question burning in his chest. "You don't want to see where this can go?"

He started to pull away from her. But she seemed to need to keep their bodies connected when she snaked her hand around the back of his neck, pulling him down into a deep, soulful kiss. "Of course I want this, Michael. Things are simply too complicated."

"At the moment, yes. That isn't the same thing as forever, Vanessa. In a couple of weeks, Cindy will be over this and we can get back to focusing on us. Two weeks is more than enough time for you to go back to Jersey and pack up and come back here."

She went to say something. What that something was, he didn't want to imagine. Michael held up his hands, stopping her. This was too important. She was too important. He couldn't let her fear make her run away.

"Monroe Hills is perfect for you. Not only are your best friends here . . ." He swallowed the lump in his throat. He needed to get this out, needed for her to understand what her leaving would do to him. ". . . I'm here too."

Her silence was sharp, like a blade to skin, tearing through him. He couldn't stop to acknowledge the pain, though. He absolutely would not let his pain make him give up.

"Not to mention, I called Mr. Montgomery this morning and he's agreed to schedule a Zoom meeting with you today so you all can talk about the value of the business and all the things you'd need to know in order to make a decision to buy it."

Her face pulled into tight lines as she narrowed her gaze. "You did what?"

"I scheduled a virtual call with Mr. Montgomery. He wants to sell you his business."

"I don't even know what to say to you right now, Michael." Her body was tense against the headboard and her jaw was clenched tight.

"Thank you, comes to mind."

She sat quietly, her intense gaze slicing right through him. "I can't do this. I've gotta go home."

She went to get out of the bed and he placed a hand on her bicep to stop her. When she gave him a sharp glance, he held up his hands. "Vanessa, why are you so upset?"

"I have asked you repeatedly not to make decisions on my behalf. I explicitly told you I wasn't interested in buying Mr. Montgomery's business. You ignored me anyway and set up a meeting with him without my knowledge or consent."

When she said it like that, with her jaw tight and her teeth clenched, it sounded like a bad thing.

"I was only trying to help, Vanessa. It was obvious to anyone looking that you were interested. I just didn't want you to regret not acting in time."

"I told you this at the auction, and it bears repeating. Whether the results are good or bad, my choices are my own. I've lived with a man who controlled everything from how I wore my hair, to what shade of lipstick I was allowed to put on. I can't do that again."

His eyes widened as understanding dawned on him. "Are you saying I'm like Karl?"

She didn't respond. She didn't need to. He could see the answer in the tight set of her lips. Her silence was like a punch to his gut, knocking all the wind out of him.

"I would never . . . I was only trying to help."

She pulled her gaze away from him, nodding slowly as she rubbed her hand up and down her arm.

"I know you mean well, Michael." She exhaled a loud breath, letting her shoulders slump when she was finished. "After everything I went through with Karl, I can't be with someone who micromanages the way you do."

Her voice was a whisper when she spoke again, yet somehow, he knew her words would be heavy.

"It's like you have this obsessive need to control everyone around you. I know you have a good heart and you'd never intentionally hurt me, but I just can't do this. I need a partner, Michael. Not a father."

He could feel the bed shift under Vanessa's weight as she pressed her back against the headboard.

"Michael, look at me, please."

He didn't want to. He feared he'd see regret in her eyes. If he thought she regretted anything about their connection . . . he didn't know if he could recover from that.

"Michael?"

He slowly turned his gaze to hers.

"I don't want this to end." That brief sentence acted like a salve on his roughed-up ego. "I never thought I'd find someone so selfless and supportive. Someone who gives everything he has to take care of the people he cares for. And even though I've only known you a short time, I'm confident enough to add myself to that number."

He grabbed her hand, lacing their fingers together, placing a gentle kiss on the back of her wrist.

"I do care for you. It's why I don't want you to leave." He kissed her hand again before whispering, "Gajima."

She might not have understood the literal translation of the word, but he could tell by the way her eyes softened with remorse that she understood the sentiment. *Don't go.*

"Trust me, I don't want to leave either." She flexed her fingers to emphasize her point. "If I stay under the current circumstances, it will only be worse."

The lump in his throat slid down his esophagus. Its jagged edges scraping against the soft skin of his digestive tract until it hit his stomach like a boulder dropping from the roof of a skyscraper.

"Vanessa, I need you."

She silenced him. Vanessa's lips trembled as she bent them into a shaky smile. "I need you too," she whispered so softly he barely heard what she said. "Even still, I need to be free to control my own life more." She cradled one cheek and placed a gentle kiss on the other.

He pulled her closer, holding her like she was something delicate, breakable, precious. He leaned in for a soft, tender kiss before responding. "I wish things were different."

She answered, "Me too." Then pulled herself out of his embrace, leaving him in bed while she made her way to the bathroom door.

He sat there for a full five minutes before he could pull himself together and find the strength to stand up. He looked toward the bathroom door and fought to keep himself from breaking it down, taking her in his arms, and telling her he would never let her go. Even though it might make him feel better momentarily, he knew she'd only perceive it as him trying to control her. Little did she know, it wasn't her he was trying to control. What he really wanted to handle was the pain he could feel swallowing him whole.

Bathed and dressed, Vanessa packed up her things. When everything was inside her weekender bag, she looked around the room. It was as if she'd never been here. She'd effectively stripped her presence from within these walls.

That should make you feel good. It's what you wanted, right, to walk away as if this had never happened?

It was. Now, as she gazed at the vacant space, all she could remember was their laughter, and the memories of the heated touches and the soul-shattering climaxes she'd experienced while sharing his home.

With her bag in hand, Vanessa headed downstairs. She dug in her purse for the spare key he'd lent her while she stayed with him. It was a standard key, no bigger than her palm. Its size somehow concealed its weight because it felt heavy in her hand, significant. She'd had access to his home as if she belonged there; giving it up twisted her stomach in knots.

Are you sure you wanna do this? She heard her conscience clanging around in her head, badgering her about things she didn't have a clear answer to. She wanted Michael. She wanted everything he offered her. She just couldn't take it at the cost of maintaining her boundaries. She'd failed to do so with Karl, giving an inch every time he asked for something until those asks turned into commands. She wouldn't give anyone else the chance to treat her like that again, not even the man her heart was aching for.

With a shaky hand, she set the key down on the small table in the foyer and saw a jewelry box with a piece of paper with her name on it tucked beneath it.

She slowly opened it with reverent caution as she read it.

It's yours, Vee. Just like my heart.

Seven words was all it took to make the stoic resolve she was holding on to for dear life crack. Feeling the hot tears slide down her cheek, she neatly folded the note and placed it in her purse. She picked up the box and opened it, finding her grandmother's ring. She could hear the comforting words she was certain the matriarch would give her if she were still here.

Just because it's the right thing to do, don't make it easy. It'll get better, though. I promise.

She'd always believed her grandmother whenever she'd told Vanessa things would improve. Now, as she walked out of Michael's home and his life, she wasn't so sure her grandmother's optimistic view of the world was correct. Because without Michael, nothing felt right.

Chapter 21

∽

MICHAEL STARED AT THE SCREEN IN FRONT OF HIM, THE blinking cursor taunting him, a reminder that he hadn't been able to focus for shit since Vanessa left.

His cellphone rang, adding to his annoyance and distraction. He pushed the keyboard away, grabbing his phone and answering it with a terse "What is it?"

"Damn, what did I do to you?"

Adam's voice came across the line with its familiar sarcasm and friendly teasing. Unfortunately, Michael wasn't in the mood for either. As a result, all it did was piss him off more.

"I'm busy, Adam. What do you want?"

Adam cleared his throat, which was always a sign things were about to get serious. "I was calling to check and see if we were still watching the game tonight at your place. I'm gonna put in our pizza order now so it'll be ready when I'm leaving my office." When Michael didn't respond, Adam continued. "What's going on with you, man?"

"I—"

"Don't try to deny it, Mike. This woman has your head all kinds of fucked-up and you're taking it out on the rest of the world. Is she really worth it if she walked out on you without a second thought?"

Adam's words scraped on his nerves, sanding down whatever patience he had left. "You know, it's not as simple as that. It's complicated. There was a lot going on and I can't blame her for not wanting so much messiness in her life."

"Bruh," Adam continued, completely brushing off Michael's vague excuse. "You're right; I don't know. I don't know how you got caught up in feelings so fast with this Vee woman. I also don't know why you won't go after her if she's important enough to fuck with your mood."

Michael took a deep breath and looked up at his office door, making sure it was closed before he started. News traveled fast in this town, and he didn't need his neighbors meddling in his business. Especially when his friend was doing a bang-up job of it now.

"Vee, or as she's formally known, Vanessa, wasn't just my date."

"Vanessa?" Adam queried. "You mean *the* Vanessa who was married to your sister's scumbag fiancé?"

"Yes," he answered. "The same."

"So you were lying when you called her your date?" As always, Adam's keen perception shone through at the worst of times.

"Yes. At that moment, it was a lie. I didn't want you talking to Derrick. You know there's only one secret he's been able to keep. I didn't want him figuring this all out or accidentally saying something to Cindy before Vanessa talked to her."

"Something changed, right? Soon it wasn't all about Cindy anymore." Again, Adam was spot on. Something had changed.

"During the time she was here, we realized we liked each other, a lot. One thing led to another, and before you know it, I was making love to her on my couch when Cindy and Karl walked in."

The long groan coming through the phone relieved some of Michael's tension. At least his friend was beginning to understand how problematic things were.

"Damn, man, that couldn't have gone well."

Michael shook his head as the memory floated across his brain.

"It didn't. After we dressed, Vanessa confronted Cindy and Karl with the truth. Cindy was devastated."

"And probably furious to boot," Adam added.

"Yeah. That too." He mustered a wry chuckle as the memory played out in his mind.

"I could see how that might make things weird between you. It's just . . . to leave and not call for two weeks, man, that seems extreme. Or was there something else going?"

Michael wanted to let Adam believe the lie. It would make things so much easier if he did.

"Michael?" Adam was using his principal's voice now, and like always, Michael was susceptible to it.

"All right," he snapped, annoyed that his friend could read him so well, even over the phone. "There was something else." The line was silent as his friend waited for him to speak. "Things were so good between us, I didn't want to let her go. So, I encouraged her to buy Mr. Montgomery's accounting business. When she didn't bite the first time, I went behind her back and tried to set up a virtual meeting with Mr. Montgomery so she could buy the shop."

Adam was silent again, and Michael knew whatever he was about to say was probably going to be something he didn't want to hear. "I take it Vanessa didn't care for this surprise meeting, did she?"

"I was only trying to help, man."

"No, you were trying to manage her. The same way you attempt to manage everyone you care about."

Michael wanted to deny it. In fact, he was gearing up a strong argument to the contrary. "Because you couldn't manage what happened to them?"

Michael remained quiet. Not sure he could talk even if he wanted to. To verbalize it still hurt too much.

"Don't, Adam."

"Mike, it wasn't your fault. Your father made a decision. The fact that he made that choice means the outcome wasn't your fault or your responsibility. You keep holding on to everyone so tightly, and you're gonna lose the ones you love."

"I didn't want her to leave." His voice was clipped and his chest was tight as the pulsing knot in the center of his rib cage compressed his airway. The last time he'd felt like this was when his parents had died and he was left to pick up the pieces. Gratefully, Vanessa was alive. She simply wasn't here and yet her absence was pushing him to the edge.

"I know you didn't, man. I can tell from the way this is affecting you that she meant a lot. But you can't keep everyone you love in a box. Life doesn't work like that."

"I know that . . . now." It was a moot point at this time, still, he'd learned his lesson well. "She doesn't want anything to do with me. She said I'm too controlling and she won't put up with it."

"Did you tell her why?"

Silence filled the line again as that damn emotional knot seemed to press harder against his lungs.

"Michael. Tell her. If you do, she might understand that you're not a manipulative asshole like her ex. If you care about this woman, and I think you do since you seem so tore up by her leaving, you've got to let her know why."

He could not do this right now, if ever. He could not think about everything one bad decision had cost him.

"Adam, I can't deal with this right now. Cindy needs me, and as shaky as things are for her right now, I don't want to push Vanessa in her face."

"Cindy needs you?" Adam's voice went up a note, a tell-tale sign he was about to enlighten the less intelligent people around him. "Why is Cindy a factor in your happiness?"

"Because I ruined hers. How can I flaunt my happiness when I destroyed hers?"

"My G," Adam said pointedly. If he were here in person, this would be the part where he'd open his hand and start ticking off his points with his fingers. "First of all, Cindy is a grown-ass woman. You are not responsible for her happiness. She's hurt right now, and I applaud you trying to give her the space she needs to get herself together, but she's smart enough to know you and Vanessa saved her life. And if she's not, that just proves she was too immature to commit herself to someone, anyway."

Again with the rationalism when all Michael wanted to do was cling to his illusions that he was doing this for his sister's sake and not for the scared little boy inside him that crumpled whenever he lost someone. Of course, Adam had a point, he still couldn't openly agree with him even if he was right.

"Second," Adam continued, "sacrificing your happiness for someone else is stupid. If you care so deeply about Vanessa, you wouldn't let anything get in your way. I'm not saying you have to rub Cindy's nose in it. But damn, man. It's been two weeks. How much longer are you going to be without the woman you care about to keep your sister happy?"

"Adam, can we please drop this subject?"

"Third, stop being a goddamn martyr."

"Wait," Michael interjected. "I've never claimed to be any kind of saint."

"Bullshit, Mike." Adam's frankness was getting on his nerves, except for some reason, he couldn't make himself end the call.

Maybe because he's telling you something deep down, you know you need to hear.

"The sacrifices you made when Cindy was still a kid made sense. She's grown now. She's entitled to find her own path to happiness, and so are you. Come down off that goddamn cross already and let yourself live a little."

"Adam—" The phone went silent when he spoke his friend's name. Probably because Adam could hear how pathetic he was even over the phone. "You're right. Cindy is grown and I should let her live her life. The problem is, even if I wanted Vanessa back, she left me. She doesn't want me."

"Nah, man." His friend's soothing voice calmed the noise that had been cluttering his mind for the past two weeks. "This ain't about Cindy and you know it. You're caught up. Do you realize you've referred to Vanessa as someone you care about twice? Don't let your own fear of losing someone else rob you of someone meaningful in your life. Mr. and Mrs. Park wanted you to find happiness too. Not just Cindy."

Of that, Michael had no doubt. His parents definitely would've given him their blessing to love Vanessa as strongly as he wanted. That didn't mean he could shake the feeling that he was somehow unworthy of her love, though.

"Adam, I feel like I'm being pulled in different directions. I don't know what the hell the right thing to do is anymore."

"You'll figure it out." Adam's support lightened the load on his chest enough that he could take a deep breath. "Just don't give up on someone who means so much to you without trying to find a solution to the problem. Don't let this crack in your foundation become a gaping sinkhole."

Michael's tired chuckle crossed his lips as a weary smile planted itself on his face. "I didn't know that fancy PhD you have was in relationship counseling."

"I'm multitalented like that. I can teach high school calculus and fix your life all at the same time. Iyanla Vanzant ain't got shit on me."

Michael couldn't argue with that. In this instance, his friend was much smarter than him. "Thanks for trying to get me out of my own head, Adam. I appreciate it."

"No worries," his friend responded. "Buy me breakfast after our pickup game on Saturday and we'll call it even."

"You got it, man." Michael hung up the phone feeling much lighter than when it rang. He still wasn't sure what he was going to do. The only thing he knew was that he couldn't let this continue any longer. He had to make things right.

A few hours later, Michael stepped through his back door and the aroma of Napoli's Pizza welcomed him home from a long day. Knowing Adam must be in the living room, he headed in that direction, but came to an abrupt stop when he heard his sister's voice.

"Adam, I don't see how any of this is your business."

"Young'un, your brother was my business long before you came along. So, sit down, because you and me need to have a conversation." The large living room which carried sound all throughout the house was eerily silent and Michael contemplated making his presence known until Adam spoke again.

"Your brother's hurting. You know that, don't you, Cindy?"

Cindy let out what sounded like an exhausted breath, and all of Michael's brotherly instincts wanted to run in there and shield her from Adam's probing. With Adam's earlier advice about letting Cindy find her own path still rattling around in his head, his muscles locked in place. Their stiffness rooted him to the floor like the trees in his backyard.

"I know he's not happy, Adam." Cindy finally spoke, and the worry tightening the center of his chest loosened a bit. "I know it's about Vanessa, but he won't talk to me. Has he said anything to you?"

"We had a brief conversation earlier today. He's worried about you. You're always his first priority. Yet this time, I feel like he's using his devotion to you as an excuse not to reach for more with Vanessa. I know things might be uncomfortable at first; the situation is definitely awkward. You just have to ask yourself, would you really be that upset by the two of them getting together?" There was a softness to Adam's voice that Michael heard only when Adam was talking to someone he cared for. Be it his friends, family, or students, when he needed to explain some uncomfortable truths, the man had a talent for meeting you where you were to get you to open up.

Michael didn't know if that would work with Cindy. Especially since he'd seen stronger people fall under Adam's spell. What was worse, Michael didn't know if he wanted to hear her answer. If she didn't mind, he'd have no excuse not to go after Vanessa other than the fact that he was afraid.

"You think he's really that into her?"

"Cindy," Adam responded, "your brother has sacrificed everything to make sure you never needed or wanted for a thing." Adam held up his palm and started ticking his fingers. "The job he loved, the woman he was seeing, the friends he'd made in Philly, all of it gone because he wanted you to be okay."

Michael heard Cindy take a breath to speak again. Adam didn't let that stop him, however. He just continued on as if he hadn't heard Cindy's pause.

"And he's never asked for a thing in return, nothing except your happiness. Even if it's with Vanessa, please tell me you wouldn't begrudge him the only thing he's wanted for himself in all this time."

Another beat of silence passed before Cindy spoke. "You're right. It would be weird. You're also right that I wouldn't want him to hold back on my account. If anyone deserves some good karma, it's Michael."

"Yes, he does. And since we both care about him, I think we need to tell him to get out of his own way. I already started that conversation earlier today. I'm handing it off to you to bring that message home."

Michael's heart tightened at Adam's words. He was sitting there treating his sister like an adult and wondering why he'd never bothered to do the same. Was it just because of what happened with their parents? Or was it because he was just too afraid to live his own life?

Michael heard heavy footsteps move toward the front door.

"Tell Michael I'll reschedule. I think you two need to talk without me being here. Have him call me later."

The front door closed with a loud click. Michael waited a moment before silently opening the kitchen door and walking into the living room.

"How much of that did you hear?"

"All of it," Michael answered while taking cautious steps toward the sofa where his sister sat hugging her knees to her chest. She looked so delicate and breakable, tugging at his protective instincts until he had to shove his hands in his pants to keep from wrapping her up in his embrace like he'd done since she was born.

"Do you think I'm breakable, Michael?"

Michael took a deep breath and blew it out slowly. He knew the answer was hanging on the tip of his tongue. Cindy was spoiled and used to getting her way.

"No. I just didn't want to give Karl a chance to hurt you. I had to step in."

She shook her head. "No, telling me what Karl was doing would've been sufficient. You needed to make sure I didn't have a choice except to kick him to the curb, that's why you arranged all of this with Vanessa. I was angry because it was obvious you didn't trust me to make the right decision. And if things are weird between you and Vanessa, I can't help but think you didn't trust her on some very personal matters either."

Damn, that one hit hard. That helping of truth was piping hot and he didn't know if he wanted to swallow it.

"Cindy, I've overindulged you and treated you like a fragile flower who couldn't survive without my guidance and direction."

He sat down next to her and turned his gaze to hers. "I was wrong to set up this intervention with Vanessa. I should've sat you down and told you the truth instead of trying to make the truth so shocking you couldn't deny it. I owed you more respect than that and I'm sorry I didn't treat you like the adult you are."

Her rigid shoulders relaxed as she dropped her hands from her knees and twisted her slight body around to look him directly in the eye.

"It wasn't all your fault. Maybe if I didn't always act like such a brat, you wouldn't think I needed to be handled." Her lip quaked and the tears she'd been holding back cascaded down her cheeks. "I really loved him, Michael. I won't let my broken heart destroy me, though. Will you?"

The crack in her voice tore at his heart. His first instinct was to jump in and save her. Unexpectedly, something had changed between them, or rather in her. She was hurting. That was clear. And even in the midst of her pain, she found a way to show concern for him.

"I want you to be happy, Oppa. If Vanessa makes you happy, please don't use me as an excuse not to fix whatever's wrong between the two of you."

"When did you get so wise, yeodongsaeng?" His quiet voice sounded strange to his own ears when he used the Korean term for little sister. It wasn't that he'd never called Cindy that before, but he was so proud of her in this moment, he said it with such reverence it surprised even him.

"My oppa, who's usually smart, was a great example to follow. Although, right now, he's got his head stuck up his ass where the woman he cares for is concerned."

He chuckled. She wasn't wrong. He'd handled this thing with both Cindy and Vanessa terribly wrong.

"Would you mind if I hugged you? Not that I think you need babying, simply because you've been through something really terrible and I just want to comfort you."

Her eyes scaled his face, as if she were trying to figure out the trick he was obviously playing on her. When she was apparently satisfied that he wasn't gonna yell "gotcha," she nodded and he pulled her into his arms.

"I know all of this hurts. I also know you're stronger than either of us believed."

"You know what, Michael?" she asked with her face pressed into his shoulder. "So are you."

He slumped down onto the couch, resting his head against the cushions. "Don't worry about me."

"I am worried," she hedged. "When I walked in on you and Vanessa, among other things"—she shared a nervous laugh—"you were laughing, playful . . . happy. And it didn't seem like it was just because you were buck-ass naked with my fiancé's ex-wife either."

He held up his hand. He didn't really want to think about the fact that his baby sister had caught him ass in the air in his living room.

"Can we never speak of that moment again?"

"Fine by me," she responded. "I just was trying to say that aside from the awkwardness of the moment, you were genuinely happy. I want more of that for you."

He shook his head. "Cindy, you don't have to say this just because Adam was busting your chops."

"I'm not. This isn't about Adam. This is about wanting my brother to be happy and Vanessa makes you happy."

He couldn't argue that point. Vanessa did make him happy and living without her for the last two weeks had been absolute torture.

"Don't let me be the reason you don't reach for what you want. I'm not saying things won't be slightly weird with you dating my ex's ex. If she treats you right, I guess I can forgive her for her previously poor taste in men."

Something warm filled him from the inside out, spreading through his being so quickly he barely had time to notice what it was. It wasn't until his sister smiled at him that he could finally put a name to it. It was pride. He was proud of the young woman sitting next to him. Proud to be her brother, proud to have had a hand in raising her, and proud she was stepping into her power as the master of her own destiny.

He'd probably always worry about her well-being. She was his little sister, after all. Only in that moment, he realized he didn't need to be a helicopter parent anymore. Cindy was truly ready to live her own life. It was time for him to let go and find his own path. And he knew exactly where that path would lead.

Vanessa.

"She might not want me after all my antics."

Cindy shrugged, giving him a lopsided grin. "Oh, don't worry about that. I'm going to give you the perfect thing to help you tell her how much you care about her. Because I know if I leave it up to you"—she pointed an accusatory finger at him—"you'll fumble it up."

He looked up to the ceiling, shaking his head as he took stock of his current situation. "God help me," he lamented. "I'm actually desperate enough to take advice on my love life from my baby sister."

She clapped her hands together, rubbing them as a sinister smile blossomed on her lips. "You'll thank me later."

Chapter 22

~

"ARE YOU SURE ABOUT LEAVING ALL THIS STUFF?"

Vanessa looked up from the box she was tossing her toiletries in to see Cree waving her hand to span from one side of her bedroom to the next.

"Cree, this house was never a home. I have no attachment to anything in it except my clothes, shoes, toiletries, and a few family heirlooms in the kitchen and dining room. Everything else can stay. Fortunately, the buyer wants the place as is, furniture included."

Janae sat down on the empty end of the supple leather ottoman sitting at the foot of the four-poster bed.

"Girl"—she sat back against the footboard, folding her arms as she gave Vanessa a loving smile—"when you told us you were doing this, I gotta say, I didn't believe it. You've always seemed so attached to the life you had with Karl, I was actually worried you were having some sort of mental breakdown."

Vanessa could certainly understand why. Two years was a long time to swim in your pain.

"I promise you, my mind has never been clearer. This really is the best thing for me."

Janae tapped her foot against Vanessa's, sharing a mischievous smile with her. "Is this because of the sheriff? You and Michael patch things up yet?"

Vanessa's heart pounded hard inside her chest like a big drum, its vibrations reverberating throughout the walls of her body. Two weeks and the sound of his name still lit a fire inside her.

"Not yet. I need to close this place up first. Once I do, talking to him is the next thing on my agenda." Her answer was intentionally vague. She loved her girls and could share anything with them. Save this thing between her and Michael . . . they needed to figure it out before they let other people in.

"Vanessa," Cree moaned as she moved closer to the bed. "I still don't understand why you walked away in the first place. He asked you to stay."

Vanessa sealed the box and placed it on the floor before taking a seat next to Janae and scooting over and patting the remaining space for Cree. "Karl was so subtle that I barely recognized his control issues. For a long time after it ended, I wondered what was wrong with me that I didn't see what he was doing to me until it was too late. I don't think Michael is like Karl. I just couldn't put myself in a situation where I was losing my agency again. It wasn't until I came back home that I realized the fact that I was able to walk away meant that I was a very different woman from the one who married Karl. As much as it hurt, I needed to know I was different the second time around too."

"Does that mean you're gonna try to work things out with Michael?" Janae might have asked the question, but a brief glance at Cree showed Vanessa that Janae wasn't the only person waiting anxiously for her answer.

She raised her arms, wrapping one around each woman's shoulder and tugging them into a tight hug. "Again, Michael and I need to talk and figure some things out. In the meantime, I'm finally coming to terms with my old life and getting ready for the next phase of my new one. And with my Savvy, Sexy, and Single ladies by my side, I'll get through this just fine."

She stood up, picking up the box and giving them one last look before she headed to the door. "Come on, ladies. Let's get the last of these boxes downstairs so the movers can get in and out and not charge me any overtime when they finish up tomorrow."

"Aren't you loaded?" Cree reminded her. "What do you care about overtime for movers?"

"True." The smirk on Vanessa's face was met with an equally sassy smile from her friends. "I am loaded. That doesn't mean I want to pay overages. How do you think rich folks stay rich? We never pay more than what we have to for anything."

"Ms. Jared, which room did you want us to empty next?"

Vanessa looked down from the top of her spiral staircase to see Johnny, the supervisor for the moving crew currently packing up her home.

"You can start in the dining room next." Johnny tipped his baseball cap to her, then directed his men to the room. "If you need me, I'll be in the first bedroom on the right."

Vanessa stepped inside of her bedroom and looked around. She'd moved into this room once she'd discovered Karl's infidelity. She'd seen it as a safe place back then. Now, it felt more like a prison, locking her away from the future she knew was waiting for her.

Not after today.

Today marked the first step into the rest of her happy life. All she had to do was put the relics of her misery away for good.

She hugged herself as excitement spread through her. Selling this house, and everything in it, had been a scary first step into her future. She quickly realized, however, as the movers picked up all the boxes in each room, that she was effectively closing a door to the pain she'd carried for so long.

She picked up one of the empty boxes scattered on the floor and began packing up her vanity. Reaching for a bottle of perfume, a knock on the door startled her.

"Johnny, you nearly scared me to death."

She turned around to find Johnny standing at the bedroom door with a huge bouquet. Its red and white roses were somehow oddly familiar. "Where'd you get those from, Johnny?"

When he didn't answer, she walked to the door, taking the flowers out of his hand and nearly dropping them when she saw who'd been holding them.

"Michael?" She hoped the unspoken—*What are you doing here?*—went without saying because her tongue was too busy falling out of her mouth for her to actually articulate her thoughts.

He tilted his head and gave her a playful half smile that didn't help the fuzziness in her brain that was keeping her from forming words.

"Would you believe I was in your neighborhood with what probably amounts to a ton of red and white roses?"

His humor disarmed her, giving her just enough time to stop worrying about the why of his appearance and focus on the spark of excitement that zipped through her once he smiled at her.

She pulled herself together as best she could, offering him a small smile in return. She had no clue why he was here yet. It was probably best if she tempered her expectations.

Too bad her palpitating heart didn't get the memo about keeping things chill. Because if it beat any faster, she'd need CPR. Which might not be so bad if it got Michael's mouth on hers.

"The flowers are lovely." She looked around for a flat surface for him to set them on and pointed toward a nearby windowsill. "Sorry, every surface is covered with a box. I've been packing like crazy for the past few days."

He walked over to the window, setting the flowers down before turning back to her.

"Thank you so much for the flowers, Michael. I just wish you hadn't traveled all this way to deliver them to me."

He smiled in her direction, and that inexplicable feeling of burning from the inside out took hold.

"Oh, I didn't bring these for you. These are the flowers you had sent to me. The card you sent with it said, 'Follow your happy.' It sounded like great advice, so I came in person to thank you for the flowers and the wisdom."

When she'd placed that order at his sister's shop during the festival, she'd never thought she'd have a chance to see how he reacted to her gift. And now that she knew, her heart ached a little more thinking of the two weeks they'd lost.

"So." He swept his hand around the room. "Are you giving away things to Goodwill?"

"Not exactly?" She lifted her eyes to his and the ache she'd been nursing since she'd left his house felt fresh, like she'd popped a stitch on her sutured wound. "I've sold the house."

Something akin to sadness flashed across his eyes. It called to her, that was the only reason she could come up with that would explain why she found her legs moving her closer to him.

"You're leaving?"

It took her a while to focus on what he was saying because she was still trying to figure out what she'd seen in his eyes. "It was time for a change. Staying in this house only makes me relive my pain repeatedly. I wanted a fresh start. If you'd come later this evening, you'd have missed me."

He lifted his hand as if he were going to touch her, then he stopped midway between them.

"What the hell am I doing?" He let his hands fall to his waist and shoved them inside his jeans pockets.

"Michael, what's going on? Is something wrong with Janae or Cree? Is Cindy okay?"

He waved his hand in the air before hooking it into his belt loop.

"Everyone's fine. I . . ." He closed his eyes, taking a long breath before he locked gazes with her again. This time, instead of sadness, she saw determination and her heart went right back to its erratic rhythm.

This man is really going to be the death of me.

"Vanessa, I didn't need to wait until later today to miss you." He reached out slowly for her hands, taking both of them in his, stroking his thumbs slowly back and forth over her knuckles. "I've missed you every moment since you left. I'm just glad I got my shit together to get up here before you moved."

"Meaning?" She laced her fingers through his and searched his face for some clue as to what he was attempting to say.

He tightened his fingers, holding on to her as if he needed to make sure she didn't somehow float away from him.

"Vanessa, every moment you've been gone has been torture for me. It doesn't make any sense. We knew each less than a week and yet, it's like nothing works right in my life since you've walked away."

She opened her mouth to speak, but he shook his head. "Please," he begged. "Let me say what I came to say. If you want to throw me out afterward and never speak to me again, fine. I simply need you to hear me out."

She nodded, and he took a few more deep breaths to fortify himself before he began again.

"I was wrong. Dead wrong for contacting Mr. Montgomery without your permission. My only excuse is since my parents died, it's been really difficult not taking care of everything for everyone.

"The day before my parents died, my dad called and asked me to drive him up to an impromptu get-together happening with some of his friends. My dad had gotten to the point where driving at night was hard for him, so anytime they had a long-distance trip planned, I'd take time off work and we'd make it a family trip. Unfortunately, because this happened so quickly, there was no way I could get the time off from work. I begged them both to decline the invite and promised that on my next weekend off, I'd do the drive. My father wouldn't hear any of it. We argued, and he drove anyway."

He took a deep breath and smoothed his hand down the front of his chest, as if he was reminding himself he was here in the present with Vanessa and not back in that terrible nightmare ten years ago.

"Because of his declining sight, it was hard for him to read road signs. He'd take a million wrong turns before he could find his way back to his route, even with GPS. That's what happened that night. He'd taken a wrong turn and ended up on a highway he wasn't supposed to be on. And that put them in the path of the semi-truck driving the wrong way. After it happened, I felt like it was my fault. Like if I'd been better at controlling my father's stubbornness, I would've been able to get him to see reason. And I think in that moment, I decided that the only way I could protect the people I love was to keep them from harming themselves. No matter what it took."

Out of all the things she thought would've come out of his mouth, that wasn't it. She lifted her hand slowly to his cheek, cupping it, trying to soothe the pain that filled his eyes.

"I was wrong for what I did to you. I promise you it wasn't about controlling you, not in the way you think. I just wanted to keep you near me so I wouldn't lose you. And that fear of losing you made me do something so out of line that pushed you away."

He was right. His actions were completely out of line. That didn't mean she didn't understand why he was driven to act as he had. Fear had locked her frozen in place for two years. "I know I was wrong. Just please, baby, give me a second chance. If you want to date long distance, we'll do that, I'm begging you not to pack us away in one of these boxes those movers will carry out of here today. Grant me this one request and I'll never give you a reason to doubt me again."

Once he spoke those words, the tense lines in his face seemed to relax a little.

"I've spent the last decade of my life disconnected from everything that made me happy because I needed to pour everything I had into making sure my sister was all right. At least I thought that was the reason. After you left, I realized what I was doing was managing her life so I wouldn't have to worry about losing her or facing my own pain. After meeting you, after knowing how your body feels pressed against mine, after knowing what if feels like to be in your arms and live and breathe again, I can't just pretend it never happened. I can't walk away.

"And I know you're gonna ask how we're supposed to make it work with Cindy. Cindy isn't an issue. The truth is, she never was. I was the issue. So, if you could give me just half a chance to prove that I'm the man for you, that I was made to love you, I promise you'll never regret it."

She stared at him and the longer she did, the deeper his brow furrowed.

"You're not going to say anything?"

Those tight lines were even deeper now, pulling at his face, yet somehow still displaying how devastatingly good-looking this man was. His jet-black hair was tousled, as if he'd been so busy rushing out of the house to get to her, he hadn't taken the time to do anything more than run his fingers through it. His jaw, usually bare, had just enough stubble to cast a slight, but sexy shadow on his features.

"Vanessa?"

The worry lines he wore were so cute she couldn't keep her amusement off her face.

"You want me to speak now?"

He gave an enthusiastic nod that made her tug her bottom lip between her teeth to keep from laughing at him.

"I'm glad you told me about your parents, Michael. It explains so much." She stepped closer before she continued. "I'm very flattered by this . . ." She waved her hand as she searched for an appropriate description of his tortured, yet adorable proclamation. ". . . outpouring of affection, only I have to tell you, it's wasted. You didn't need to come all the way here to tell me this."

His eyes widened, and his hands slipped from hers. Before he could speak, she closed the tiny bit of space between them and cupped his cheek, loving the prickle of his facial hair against her skin.

"You didn't have to come all the way here because I was on my way to you."

He scanned her face as if to confirm she'd actually spoken the words he'd heard. He opened his mouth to speak and she ran her thumb across his bottom lip, delighted as the confused fog clouding his eyes gave way to something much sharper and fiercer.

"You were wrong for overstepping the boundaries I'd set. But I was wrong for not explaining how trapped you made me feel. Instead, at the first hint of a problem, I ran. When I came back here, I realized I ran not because I was actually afraid of you. I was afraid I was turning into that woman again who stayed with Karl way too long. Once I realized that, I knew we had to sit down and talk. I just needed to close the door on this life I had here before I did so. I wanted to come to you as a free woman."

"You could've told me that," he interjected and when she raised a pointed finger at him, he held up his hands in surrender and asked her to continue.

"If I had told you that, you'd have tried your best to help me. That's who you are, Michael. You help people. It's your nature. This, however, was something I needed to do alone. I had to be sure I was ready because what we have is too important."

She smiled as she recalled the time she'd spent putting all her energy into finalizing everything. "The moment I came back, I knew I couldn't stay here anymore. I knew I couldn't stay away from Monroe Hills. All the people I love are there. It just made sense that I should be there too. So, I put the house up for sale and made arrangements to come back to where I left my heart."

He narrowed his gaze as his hands circled her waist, resting firmly on her hips.

"What arrangements?"

"I contacted Mr. Montgomery, and after a good talk, I made him an offer on his shop. And I booked a room at the inn. I didn't want to assume you or Cindy would be okay with me staying with you. I didn't want to overstep."

"Overstep?" He spoke those words as if put together they were a crime against nature. "I'm here begging you to come back to me because my life isn't right without you in it."

She lifted her brow, playfully tilting her head to the side. "You know, all the dating books I've been reading since my divorce say it's pretty much a law that you can't be so open about your feelings. You're supposed to play hard to get."

"I'm too old and too wrapped up in you to care about dating rules. All I want is to be with you."

She buried her fingers in his hair, pulling him down to her and locking her lips to his. It had been too long since she'd experienced his touch, his taste, and she needed both those things like a thirsty woman surrounded by nothing but dry sand.

She licked inside his mouth, coaxing him to deepen the kiss. It was all the encouragement he needed. He moaned as he slipped one hand into her hair, cupping an ample handful of her ass with the other, pressing her against the growing bulge behind his zipper.

This was heaven. Any doubts she'd had about picking up her life and going after Michael—despite their complicated situation— were put to bed. And that's exactly where she wanted this moment to lead. In bed, with him buried so deep in her she'd lose all sense of time and space.

A hard rap against the door pulled them apart, leaving them both panting for much-needed air. Vanessa wiped her hand over her mouth. Thank goodness she had forgone makeup today, otherwise they'd both have it smeared all over their faces.

"Ms. Jared." Johnny stepped into the bedroom. "I'm sorry to interrupt. We're finished downstairs, the only thing left is this room." He pointed to the boxes spread all over the room. "You ready to pack all of this up and move on?"

She turned to Michael, joy seeping down into every cell she possessed, and said, "For the first time in a long time, I am."

Epilogue

"A LITTLE TO THE LEFT." VANESSA STOOD BACK AND watched as Michael hung an OPEN FOR BUSINESS sign in the display window. "Now a little to the right."

She smiled as he leaned in the opposite direction, the muscles in that rounded ass of his on display in his jeans.

"Is it right now?"

"Oh, it's very right."

He turned around, narrowing his gaze as he stared at her. "Are you scoping out my ass?"

She smiled, not even sorry he busted her. "Can you blame me? It's a really nice ass."

He nodded, leaving the sign, and reached for her hand. When she gave it, he pulled her into his arms and tightened them until she pressed against his hard wall of chest.

"It is a really nice ass, isn't it?"

"I certainly think so," she replied, wrapping her arms around his neck, running fingers through his dark strands.

"Yours ain't bad either."

She tended to agree with him. The way he always had a handful of it whenever he could, was proof of that.

"Since you're the boss of this here establishment, how about we play hooky and spend the day comparing who likes whose ass better?"

She held up a finger just before she spoke. "First, that sounds weird. Second, this is my first day and you've already put up the sign telling everyone I'm here for their business. I can't make people think I'm unreliable from the start."

He leaned down, placing gentle kisses on her mouth, trailing down to the sensitive bit of skin at the curve of her neck.

"Please," he begged. "I promise it won't take long."

She moaned, partly from how good his lips felt against her skin. Hot blood rushing to the site he was paying such loving attention to.

"No, the last time you said it wouldn't take long, I almost missed my office furniture delivery."

He nibbled on the area a little longer before raising his head. His eyes shone with playful desire, tempting her to say, "To hell with it," and shut down for the day.

She was about to say as much when the chime over the front door rang.

"Saved by the bell," she said with a chuckle as she stepped out of his embrace.

"Literally," he responded.

"Excuse me." Vanessa shook her head at Janae's distinct and confident voice. "I thought this was a reputable place of business."

Cree stepped through the door behind her, the delight at catching them hugged up written all over the knowing look on her face. "Looks like the only business going on 'round here is funny business. Maybe we should leave you two alone so you can pick up where you left off."

"That's a perfect idea," Michael replied. "We'd see you out, but we're busy."

Vanessa laughed, sidestepping his attempts to pull her back into his arms.

"Pay him no attention. What do you two need?"

Janae waved a dismissive hand at Michael before turning to Vanessa. "Nothing, we just wanted to wish you good luck before you got swamped with work."

Vanessa opened her arms wide, bringing them in for one of their joint hugs. "Aww, the two of you are so sweet. What would I do without you?"

"Me," Michael mumbled. "You'd do me."

Vanessa laughed because she knew he was only half joking.

"We love you, girl. Of course we'd be here." Janae's proclamation warmed her heart, reaffirming she'd made the right choice in coming back to Monroe Hills to start her life over.

"Well, since it seems we're leaving you in good hands"—Cree looked over her shoulder to glance at Michael—"we'll let you get to it. Whatever *it* is."

They turned toward the door when Janae stopped abruptly. The door opened slowly, revealing a familiar tall man with a butterscotch complexion and locs hanging free around his broad shoulders.

Adam's distinctive good looks meant it was hard to not notice how fine he was. If Vanessa wasn't already sprung over Michael, she might ogle him the way Janae seemed to be doing.

Vanessa watched the two carefully as they seemed to instantly lock on to one another's presence, forgetting the rest of the people in the room.

"Adam." Michael interrupted whatever was going on between their mutual besties, pulling Adam's attention away from Janae. "What'cha need, man?"

"Morning, everyone." Adam may have included the rest of them in that greeting, though it was obvious the only person he truly noticed in that room was Janae.

"You need something?" Michael asked again, and Adam blinked, finally bringing his attention to Michael.

"Oh, I just picked up those two tickets for the reunion you asked me to get when I was near the school?"

Michael went to pull out his wallet to reimburse his friend. Adam shrugged him off. "Don't insult me like that. You're my boy, we look out for each other."

Michael accepted the tickets Adam held out to him and pushed them quickly into his pocket.

"Did you get one for yourself?" Michael asked.

"Sure did," Adam affirmed.

"You're coming all the way from New York for our high school reunion?" Janae's question seemed louder in the silent room, making her the subject of everyone's attention.

Vanessa was still trying to figure out the dynamic between the people standing in the middle of her reception area. They all knew each other and seemed to have some sort of friendly connection between them. There was something unspoken going on between Janae and Adam, however, that Vanessa was determined someone was going to fill her in on soon.

"I don't live in New York anymore, Janae," Adam answered. "I moved back to Monroe Hills at the end of the summer."

Janae turned to Michael, her eyes in narrowed slits. If dirty looks could kill, Michael would've been in trouble.

"And you didn't see fit to tell anyone, Michael?"

Michael shrugged. "Excuse me, kinda been dealing with family drama over here. I didn't have time to run down the movements of a grown man for you, Janae."

"Derrick is going," Cree added. "You know those three are joined at the hip. If Derrick and Michael are going, it's a safe bet Adam would be there too."

"Don't blame Mike." Adam directed his response to Janae as if no one else were in the room. "I've been so busy getting settled, I haven't had time to do much more than get in on a couple of pickup games with Mike and Derrick. I'm glad I got the chance to run into you." His eyes scanned Janae's form up, down, and then up again. That was all it took to let her know there was *definitely* something going on between her bestie and Michael's. "You look good, real good."

That's when something happened that Vanessa never thought she'd live to see. Janae didn't open her mouth. Not even a quick comeback. Vanessa tore her eyes from the picture Adam and Janae were making and turned to Cree mouthing, *What the hell?*

Cree smiled and shrugged as if she didn't know what was going on. It was an obvious lie and the spark of amusement in her eyes exposed it.

"Well." Adam tore his gaze away from Janae to face Michael and Vanessa. "I still have a lot left to do today. Take care, everyone." He walked toward the door and looked over his shoulder one last time. "Janae, we should talk sometime. Mike's got my contact info. Get it from him."

Adam gave Janae one last look before he opened the door and stepped out of the shop.

All eyes focused on Janae again as she stood completely still, staring at the door Adam had since exited. She blinked as if trying to clear her vision before she turned to the rest of them in the room and said, "What the hell are y'all staring at?"

Seeing the real Janae, the one who wouldn't hesitate to cut a bitch with her words, show up made Vanessa, Cree, and Michael all shake their heads in unison. They all might've noticed what transpired. None of them, not even Michael, the man who walked with a sidearm and badge on his hip, would dare test her friend.

"Cree, let's get outta here," Janae groused as she walked toward the door. "I've got a bunch of errands to run before I'm due for my shift tonight."

Cree, forever the bubbly whiff of fresh air, winked a conspiratorial eye at Vanessa and Michael, leaving them the task of trying to stifle their laughter in Janae's presence.

"See y'all later." Cree fell into step behind Janae and waved to them as she stepped out of the store.

Michael crossed his arms over his chest and huffed, "Thank God they left just as quickly as they arrived." Before she could respond, he slipped his hands around her waist, pulling her against him as he placed a sweet kiss on her jaw.

"As much as I tease them about being cockblockers, I don't think I'll ever be able to thank them enough for bringing you to me."

She glanced up, confused by his statement. "They didn't bring me here, you did."

He shook his head. "No, I brought you here to help my sister. But that had nothing to do with the reason you came back. You moved because your friendship with those two taught you that you were strong enough to take the next step in your life."

He was right. She couldn't have done this without the support of the Savvy, Sexy, and Single Club. Her fellow members were the force that had pushed her into taking control of her heart and her life.

"They may have been the reason I could decide to come back to Monroe Hills, but you are the reason I stayed. I love you, Michael."

He tilted her chin, pressing his lips to hers as he held on so tightly, she was sure she might shatter into tiny pieces.

"I love you too, Vanessa."

The deep rumble of his voice was like warm scotch over ice, smooth and soothing, pouring heat into the very vessels that carried life-giving blood throughout her body.

She kissed him once again, then stepped out of his embrace. She walked to the window, turning the OPEN sign over to CLOSED and pulling the blinds shut over the display window, and then the door. A quick flip of the lock, and she was walking back to him.

"Aren't you about to start your workday? Why are you closing everything up?"

"Because I'm the boss. And if I want to spend my workday

christening every room in this office with you, then that's exactly what I'll do. You got a problem with that, Sheriff?"

He cocked his head to the side, his lips spreading wide into a conspiratorial grin.

"No, ma'am." He reached for her, quickly pulling her into his arms as he tugged her blouse out of the waist of her slacks. "No problem at all."

"Good." She looked around the empty waiting area before returning her attention to him. "Let's start with this one."

Acknowledgments

To God, from whom all blessings flow, thank you for the gift, the desire, the support, and the opportunity. To Damon, this does not happen without you. You literally poured life into my dreams and made them—and forced me to make them—come true. Love you forever. To Sterling, Semaj, Mason, Mackenzie, and Myles, my heartbeats, the best parts of me. To my family and friends, thank you for putting up with my craziness. To Monique, thank you for your belief in me, and all the support you give me. To Latoya, thank you for the continued support and partnership. Thank you for understanding my dream and helping me carve a path to achieve it. To Christie Caldwell, Kenya Goree-Bell, and Naima Simone, thank you for your support during this project. The three of you are the best accountability partners/beta readers ever. To Lexie Craig, thank you for supplying me with my motto, "Hustle until you don't have to introduce yourself" (source unknown). To all of my JMC, LIJ, and York people, your love strengthens me. To my readers, you hold me down and keep me going. Thank you so much for the loyalty and encouragement. You will never know how much I appreciate your support. Thank you for taking this journey with me.

Keep it sexy,
LaQuette ❧

Newsletter Signup

Hello,

If you're interested in staying current with all of the happenings with my writing, previews, and giveaways, sign up for my monthly newsletter at LaQuette.com.

Keep it sexy,
LaQuette 👄

LaQuette

2021 Vivian Award finalist and DEIA activist in the romance industry, **LaQuette** writes sexy, stylish, and sensational romance. She crafts dramatic, emotionally epic tales that are deeply pigmented by reality's paintbrush.

This Brooklyn native's novels are a unique mix of savvy, sarcastic, brazen, and unapologetically sexy characters who are confident in their right to appear on the page.